Smith's
MONTHLY

Every Month Original Novels, Stories, and Articles

USA Today Bestselling Writer
Dean Wesley Smith

I0554019

TABLE OF CONTENTS

SHORT STORIES

Dead Even
    A Poker Boy Story   6

The Wages of the Moment
    A Thunder Mountain/Jukebox Story   16

The Keeper of the Morals   38

Iron Eyebrows   54

Mom's Paradox   62

FULL NOVEL

The Life and Times of Buffalo Jimmy
    Headed West   70

SERIAL NOVEL

An Easy Shot
    A Thriller
                    Part 3 of 8   24

NONFICTION

Introduction:
    A Serial Novel Returns   3

Smith's Monthly Issue #20

All Contents copyright © 2015 Dean Wesley Smith
Published by WMG Publishing
Cover and interior design copyright © 2015 WMG Publishing
Cover art copyright © by Philcold/Dreamstime.com

Dean Wesley Smith

Introduction
A SERIAL NOVEL RETURNS

Way back twenty issues ago, I talked about starting up serial novels in this magazine. So far I've serialized two novels, one short novel, a nonfiction golf book, and in this issue is the ongoing serial novel *An Easy Shot* that will be going for five more months.

I promised that once a serialized novel was completed, I would put it together and publish it here as a full novel for those who either started late into this magazine, or who don't like reading three chapters of a book every month.

So this month includes the full *The Life and Times of Buffalo Jimmy* novel that appeared three chapters at a time for thirteen months in this magazine.

Interestingly enough, I didn't make that many changes in the book when I put it together. And I will be continuing on at some point with the next Buffalo Jimmy novel. He and his friends just seem to be asking me for more adventures, as if getting to Nevada wasn't adventure enough.

I hope to continue serializing novels and other books off into the future of this magazine.

On a different topic, a couple readers mentioned that I had dropped the poetry. It will be back at times as well along with more nonfiction books. One thing about this magazine is that I don't have a boss looking over my shoulder. Of course, that could have both good and bad elements.

At some point in the future, I have planned a short fiction issue as well. That might be fun, since I will be writing most of the stories for the issue out so people coming to my blog can watch me write them.

Some needed housekeeping will be done shortly on the web site for this magazine, www.smithsmonthly.com, which will get a facelift and a new theme and look. And the full contents of each issue

Thanks for the Support

Dean Wesley Smith

will be there, including links to all the novels that were in each issue and lists of all the stories in each issue.

Also, every week there I will be doing a free short story to read there on the site. Watch for the announcement for that, or you might want to check when you read this because the time lag of me writing this introduction and you getting the issue might be enough to start the new free story of the week.

The web site will be better. It should have been updated before now, but I think a lot of people weren't sure I was going to get this magazine to Issue #20.

Well, here we are and this magazine is doing great and I'm having fun. So looks like it's here to stay for many issues to come into the future.

I'm just very glad that so many readers have been following this adventure, and coming on board as more issues go past. The reader support is very much appreciated and I will do my best to keep each issue at least entertaining in some way or another.

Onward toward the end of year two. And beyond.

—Dean Wesley Smith
May 6th, 2015
Lincoln City, Oregon

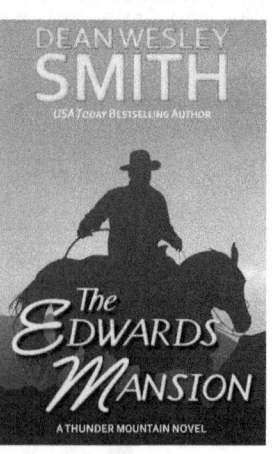

The First Six Thunder Mountain Novels
Available at your favorite booksellers.

Coming Next Issue in Smith's Monthly
The Full Thunder Mountain Novel
that is the Origin Story for all the Jukebox Stories
MELODY RIDGE

Dean Wesley Smith

USA *Today* Bestselling Writer

A POKER BOY STORY

Dead Even

Superheroes in the gambling universe sometimes find themselves helping people who normally don't need help.

Poker Boy met Bob on Christmas Eve and proceeded to take his money at the table because Bob played horrid poker and did so while being a real jerk.

But Bob needed that money for a very special and personal reason. A reason Poker Boy found worthwhile.

DEAD EVEN
A Poker Boy Story

BOB SHOWED UP in the poker room at Spirit Winds Casino on Christmas Eve. Bob, like his name, was a very short man. I guessed he came up to my shoulder at best, even with heels on his boots. It's always interesting to me how names fit people. Bob fit Bob perfectly.

His black hair was short, the nails on his fingers were trimmed short, and even his nose was short. He wore a golf shirt that seemed a size too small, and brown slacks that covered brown dress shoes. He did not have the appearance of having money, but over the years I have come to not trust appearances very much, since I look like a slob most of the time, yet I have money and am a super hero.

In looks, I am, for lack of a better way of putting it, the cliché white male. I'm six feet tall, have brown hair that's graying slightly at the temples, and green eyes. Bob was the cliché short man who walked quick, talked quick, and had a flaring temper that might go off with just a wrong remark, or more likely, a bad beat at the table.

Cliché meet cliché.

Bob took every turn of the cards as if it was more than just a bad beat. He seemed to take it as an affront to his height. A ten would hit the table to give someone else a pair of tens to beat his pocket nines, and he acted if someone had just called him a runt.

It was a guaranteed way to lose money at a poker table.

Bad beats at poker tables are when a person thinks they should win, but the cards at the end of the hand say otherwise. Every poker player I know tells bad beat stories about how his pocket aces were beaten by jack/ten suited. Bad beats are the nature of poker, and I put them on people as often as people put them on me, so I pay no attention. Someone starts into a bad beat story and I just nod and think about what I'm planning on having for dinner.

All night long Bob kept complaining, and then continuing to play. He wasn't a bad player, but he wasn't a good one either. He knew just enough to think he was the best, and just enough to think he knew what he was doing, and just enough to think he could beat me and the rest of the group at the table. Of course he was wrong on all three counts. And he complained about it bitterly.

Clearly short Bob was not a happy man, either in poker or in life.

The turning point of the evening came when Bob had aces beat twenty minutes before midnight on Christmas Eve. He stared at the aces, then at the winning flush a guy named Carl had drawn into, then at the dealer, and for a moment I thought he was going to punch the dealer.

Now understand, during the evening so far, he had lost upwards of three grand in just under five hours, with about half of it sitting safely in the stack of chips in front of me. However, it was not my flush that had just put the bad beat on his aces.

I'm Poker Boy, and Christmas Eve or not, I played fair, and if someone wanted to give me their money across a poker table, I took it. There is no Santa in a poker game, but good old short Bob sure wanted to give me his money, so I was thinking kindly of him at that moment, even with him yelling at the dealer and complaining all the time.

I'm not sure yelling describes what Bob was actually doing. He was ranting, screaming, shouting, and even foaming at the mouth a little. He had stood up and was even leaning over the table. For a tall man, this might have been threatening. For Bob, it made no difference.

The rake, a guy named Henry, watches over the dealers in a poker room. Henry came over and asked Bob to calm down. All the while the dealer named Scooter just sat there, staring ahead, ignoring Bob's ranting and shouting and carrying on.

"I'm not going to calm down!" Bob shouted.

At this point, Krissy, the room manager on duty showed up at the table. She was about Bob's height, with long blonde hair and a smile that could fill a room.

Scooter kept ignoring Bob, shuffled up, and got ready to deal the next hand.

"What's the problem?" Krissy asked Bob, as if she didn't know exactly what the problem was.

"Your dealer's cheatin' me!" Bob turned and shouted right into her face. Then he stepped toward her.

I just sat there watching. These situations were not the things that Poker Boy got involved with. My job was to save helpless people and dogs, not stop idiots from making fools of themselves.

Besides, Krissy was one tough broad who had many different colored belts from different martial arts disciplines. If Bob was stupid enough to take a swing at Krissy, he would be lucky to see it turn Christmas day.

"Our dealers do not cheat, sir," Krissy said, her voice low and level as she spoke right into Bob's face. "And we have cameras to make sure they don't."

"I don't care about no damned cameras!" Bob shouted. "For all I know, the dealer and the camera man are in this together."

I glanced around at the other seven players on the table. All of us had some of this idiot's money. Did he think we were all in on his great conspiracy as well? Of course, I didn't say that. Instead the rest of us just sat there as if nothing was happening, staring at either our hands, the felt tabletop, or the wall beyond the table. The number one rule when there's a problem at a poker table was to stay out of it.

"I think maybe a little walk might calm you down," Krissy said, moving to take Bob's elbow and turn him from the table.

"I don't need a walk!" Bob shouted, his face really red.

The next chain of events happened quickly.

Bob went to shove Krissy aside.

Krissy grabbed Bob's arm.

Bob tried to push Krissy.

Krissy moved a step out of the way, grabbing Bob in such a way that the man sort of lifted off the ground using his own forward motion, flew through the air with Krissy still holding on, and then came down flat, face first, on the empty table beside the one we were playing on.

Krissy now held Bob's arm behind his back with one hand and the back of his neck with the other, acting as if she had to do this every day.

Bob kicked for a moment trying to break free, but it looked like with each kick, he hurt himself, so he stopped.

Man, I was going to have to get to know Krissy better. She might come in handy as a sidekick on some of my

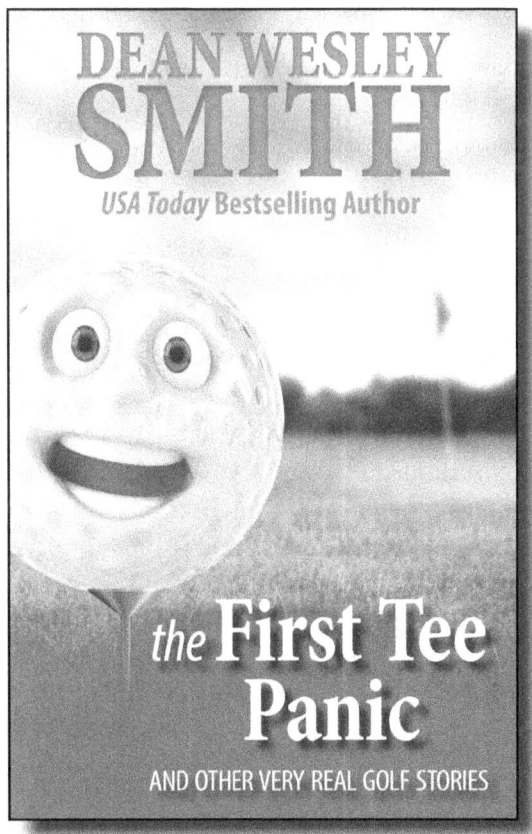

Former PGA Golf Professional and USA Today *bestselling writer Dean Wesley Smith walks you step-by-step, club-by-club from your car to the first tee and beyond in a laugh-out-loud style that not only teaches, but entertains.*

A perfect gift for the golfer in your family.

Now Available
from all your favorite booksellers
in trade paper
and electronic editions.

adventures. Sure, I had super powers and all that, but sometimes a good hand-to-hand fighting master could beat a super power in the clinch.

"Deal this man out," Krissy said. She didn't seem excited or even winded. "And cash in his chips and give him his money."

Henry, the rake, moved to take what was left of Bob's chips. More than likely his anger had just saved him the last of his money.

A moment later, two large security men came in the poker room door, handcuffed Bob, and started to lead him away, with Henry carrying Bob's money right behind.

"Wait!" Bob shouted. "I have to stay. I have to win enough!"

Suddenly my Poker Boy alarm went off. I sometimes call this alarm my Ultra-Intuition Power. And right now that power was telling me in no uncertain terms that Bob needed my help, and not to escape the security guards.

I got up, leaving my chips on the table, and followed Bob, the guards, and Henry the rake. It felt as if we were having a little parade as the crowds parted to let us through.

The two large security men, with Bob walking between them like a small child being escorted to the principal's office, headed for the front door of the casino. When they had him safely out on the sidewalk and the handcuffs off, Henry gave Bob the remaining money and went back inside.

"Please don't return to this casino, sir," one big guard said.

"You're lucky Krissy's not going to press charges against you," the other said.

Bob just nodded, standing there in the cold evening air, the last of his money in his hand. He looked to be completely in shock and beaten, as if his world had just ended. Clearly he must have been playing poker with scared money, and the worst way to ever play poker is with scared money.

Scared money means the money you are using is not money you can afford to lose. You never gamble with rent or food or car payment money. Never. Ever. Only gamblers with problems do that.

"Where's your car, Bob?" I asked, stepping up between him and the guards and taking his arm. I turned him gently toward the closest parking lot.

"Around on the other side of the building," Bob said.

"I'll walk you," I said, glad I always wore my black leather coat and Fedora-like hat when playing, since we were going to have to go around the building and it was a cold Christmas Eve. It wasn't snowing or anything, but it felt cold enough to.

We walked in silence for a hundred yards or so, then finally Bob said softly, "I knew better."

"I know you did," I said. "How much did you need to win?"

"Six over the top of the four I had," he said, without looking at me.

We kept walking in silence, our breathing making frost waves ahead of us in the parking lot lights.

Now a couple times a year I have nights in live games where I win far over six thousand. And I've won numbers of tournaments with payouts a great distance over six thousand. But I doubted Bob had ever won that much in a casino, so whatever had made him try this stupidity on Christmas Eve had to be very important to him.

I clicked on my special Empathy Power.

To be honest, I just don't know what else to call the power. It makes people believe they can tell me anything, trust me with their very lives. And sometimes they do. But Empathy is the wrong name for it, but Trust Me Power just doesn't sound right. And neither does Make Them Talk Power. I'd figure it out some day.

With my Empathy Super Power on, I asked the next question. "Bob, what did you need the money for?"

Bob glanced at me. "What do you care?"

I notched up my Empathy Power. Little Bob needed a big dose. "Trust me, I care," I said, staring right at him to focus the strength.

He shrugged. "You wouldn't believe me if I told you."

I turned up the Empathy Power to the top of my capabilities and focused it at him like I was staring at a fly. Bob stood no chance. He was going to tell me.

"You would be surprised what I would *believe*," I said.

He shrugged. "I wanted to die even."

Now, of all the reasons he could have told me why he wanted ten thousand dollars, that was not one I expected. I wouldn't have been surprised at his daughter needing an operation, or his needing to replace money he took from his wife to bet on the horses, or maybe even he needed to buy a girlfriend a new sports car.

I really didn't want to spend Christmas Eve babysitting a short guy who wanted to kill himself because his life sucked and he was a bad poker player.

"You're going to have to explain that one," I said, keeping my Empathy Power cranked up.

"Christmas morning at six-ten," Bob said, his voice level and matter-of-fact. "Not long from now, actually, I'm going to die."

"And how do you know that?" I asked, even more stunned.

"I told you that you wouldn't believe me."

"Oh, I believe you," I said. "I'm just wondering how you know, or are you planning this exit from the here-and-now."

I really didn't want to spend Christmas Eve babysitting a short guy who wanted to kill himself because his life sucked and he was a bad poker player. I would do it to save his life, but I didn't want to.

He laughed, the sound echoing over the frost-covered cars as we headed down a row, clearly getting closer to his car.

"Not planning a thing," he said. "In fact, I wish I could stay around long enough to learn how to play poker like you do."

"But, you're not?" I said, ignoring his compliment.

"Nope." He glanced at his watch. "About six hours from now I'll be as dead as they come. I just know it, like I know the sun is going to come up tomorrow, and the tide is going to change. Call it a special power of mine. Most people never understand that I get these feelings about things, so a long time ago I quit telling people."

I knew that feeling. I dropped my Empathy Power and focused another of my super powers on him to see if he was telling me the truth.

After a moment I realized he seemed to be.

"All right," I said, "I buy that you think you're going to die in about six hours. And you need the ten grand to pay off one last debt?"

"Naw," he said. "Actually I got a bunch of money in stocks, good equity in my house, and both cars paid off. But when I add up the worth of everything, now that the market is down, the balance owed on my house is ten thousand over what I got in assets. I wanted to leave this life even, just like I came in. It seems that's too much to ask, isn't it?"

Again he laughed and stopped beside a late model SUV. For such a little guy, he sure drove a big, expensive car.

"You got a wife and kids?" I asked, still not completely clear on why this guy wanted ten thousand.

"Sure do," Bob said, smiling. "She's back in Minnesota visiting family, and both my kids are grown and married. They are both with their spouse's families this year."

"They left you alone?"

"I wanted them to," he said. "I sort of set it up, and let me tell you, it took some convincing. But I figured why have them hanging around when this heart of mine lets go? It's going to be hard enough on them as it is."

I nodded, not knowing exactly what to say. Either they watched him die, or they got a phone call saying that he was dead. I honestly didn't know which was worse either. But Bob clearly knew for him and his family, and I gave him that.

"Well, it was good playing cards with you," Bob said. "A real pleasure to get beaten by one of the best."

He beeped his SUV unlocked and opened the big door, getting ready to climb inside. I couldn't just let him go off like this, especially since I knew he was telling the truth.

"Bob, wait," I said. "I'm a gambling man, I'll make you a wager. How much do you have left?"

He reached into his pocket and pulled out the bills Henry had given him, made a quick count. "About a grand."

"All right, I'll give you ten to one odds you don't die this morning. If you do, you have ten thousand from me and go out even, if you don't, I get your thousand."

He stared at me for the longest time. Then he asked, "Why would you do that?"

I shrugged. "I'm a gambler. It sounds like a safe way to get that last thousand of yours, since you won't give it to me at the table."

An aside. Actually, I'm not a gambler. In fact, I never play if I don't have what's called "the-best-of-it." I never bet slots, or any other house game where the odds are in favor of the house. I am a poker player, and in poker, skill is everything. And since I'm one of the best in the country, I usually get the best of other people.

But tonight, I placed a bet to help someone.

Again he sort of stared at me for a moment. Then he said, "You're not kidding, are you?"

"Nope," I said. I dug into my pocket and brought out a roll of bills and counted off ten big ones.

I usually carry about twenty thousand in cash on me when I'm headed into a poker room. Then, no matter the size of the game I find, I can handle the buy-in. It never occurs to me that most people would be scared to death walking around with that much cash. I'm a super hero, so I don't have a lot of worries about getting mugged.

"Give me your card," I said.

I figured him for a businessman, and every businessman I knew had a card, and he was no exception.

He dug it out of his wallet and handed it to me.

"Robert Day," I said. "Portland, Oregon. That's you and a current phone number?"

"It is," he said, nodding.

"And this is your car?" I asked.

"It is," he said.

I went around back and recorded the license plate number of the big SUV, then moved back to where he stood.

"Here's the deal," I said, talking quick so he didn't have a chance to say anything. "I give you the ten thousand right now. You go home, do what you had planned on doing tonight, and if you're dead in the morning, the money is yours. If your fear is wrong, and you live through the morning, you come back here tomorrow night at eight and give me my ten grand back, plus one thousand of your own money."

He sort of stood there, his mouth open.

I knew I was just giving him the money. This was the biggest sham bet ever come up with, and I was doing my best to sell it to him. But I knew I had lost the ten big ones if he took this, and I didn't care.

An aside. Bob was a real jerk, of that I had no doubt, but he was a jerk who needed my help, and just because someone was a jerk, that didn't mean I shouldn't help that jerk.

I held up the card and smiled. "I know where you live. And I figure I can trust you. Just don't go offing yourself to win this."

At that he laughed. "Are you kidding? I'd love to come back here tomorrow,

give you your money and a thousand, and buy you a drink. If they let me back in the casino, that is."

"I'll set it up so they will," I said. "But I doubt they're going to let you play poker for a while."

"Not a problem there," he said, laughing. "I needed my head examined to go up against the likes of you and the others at that table."

"So do we have a bet?" I asked, still shoving my sham bet, which was the only way I knew how to help him.

He again looked at me for the longest time. I had long ago turned off my Empathy Power, and I can't read minds, so I had no idea why he just sort of stared at me.

Then he stuck out his hand. "We have a bet."

His handshake was firm and quick, as you would expect from someone who moved and acted like Bob.

I handed him the ten thousand.

He handed me back one thousand of it. "Nine-to-one odds," he said. "I only need ten thousand total to be even in life, and I have one thousand already."

"Even better," I said.

Did I mention I wasn't a gambler? I could figure the math of a poker hand to exact figures, but a sham bet like this one, I had no clue.

"Thanks," he said, staring at the money. "I don't know why this is so important to me. Seems silly, actually, now that I think about it. No one's going to care that I went out even except me, and I'll be dead."

"Just make sure you're back here tomorrow night with my money. My nine and your grand. I'm going to collect on that drink as well."

"If I'm alive, I'll be here," he said. "Thank you."

With that he got into his big SUV and started it up. He backed out, and with a blink of his lights, drove off.

I went back inside, got myself a large mug of hot chocolate to cut the chill, and went back to the table. I had just given a guy nine thousand dollars to make him

feel better during the last few hours of his life. I had no doubt he was going to die, just as he said he would. I had the same power he had, only I called my power Precog-Power.

He was going to die at the exact moment he told me he was, from a massive heart attack. Not even being in a hospital would change the result, that much I was sure of. Otherwise I would have been working to get him to one.

No, the only thing I could do for him was help him make his goal of going out the same way he came into the world: Dead even.

It cost me nine thousand, but what the hell, it was Christmas.

I waited around the next night at eight, just in case we were both wrong. He didn't show, and by midnight, in a very good game, I had won most of my money back.

His death was reported in the paper the next day, exactly as we had both known it would be.

Two weeks later, a very short man came into the casino poker room asking for me. He looked like a younger and shorter version of Bob. He handed me an envelope with nine thousand in it.

The guy looked puzzled, then said simply, "My father willed this to you. Said it had to be cash and left instructions that I was to buy you a drink after I gave it to you. And never play poker with you."

I laughed and steered Bob Junior out of the poker room and toward the bar. On the way he asked, "How well did you know my father?"

"Not that well," I said. "Played some cards with him is all, but I liked him. An honest man."

"That he was," his son said, smiling. "That he was."

Some Classic Dean Wesley Smith Stories
Available at your favorite booksellers.

Dean
Wesley Smith

USA Today Bestselling Writer

A Jukebox
Story

The Wages
of the Moment

When Stout watches himself appear and disappear a bunch of times right in front of his own jukebox, he knows his time machine needs some repairs.

And in doing so, he finally gets to meet the inventors of the jukebox.

But first he must deal with himself, in more ways than one.

THE WAGES OF THE MOMENT
A Thunder Mountain/Jukebox Story

ONE

YOU KNOW your time machine is screwed up when a person just starts appearing and disappearing at random times. And that person is you.

Jenny and I were back in town from San Francisco for the Christmas holidays, actually the first Christmas back since we had gotten married.

And I was back in the Garden. I still hadn't gotten used to not owning the place and being on the other side of the bar, but since I had sold the Garden Lounge to Richard Cone ten months before, I had made myself stay on the customer side unless Richard asked me to do otherwise.

The Garden Lounge is a very special bar that I had owned for over a decade. An old-fashioned neighborhood place with vinyl booths, a few tables, some artificial plants and a long, polished wooden bar with nine bar stools. Richard, to his credit, had changed nothing, even keeping the lights low all the time as I had done.

To the right side of the bar was an old Wurlitzer jukebox that was never turned on or plugged in except for very special occasions, usually Christmas Eve. That jukebox was a time travel machine of sorts. It could actually take a person back to the memory of a song for the length of the song.

And that person could change their future while in their past and maybe not end up back at the Garden Lounge, which was why the jukebox was so dangerous. And why it was almost never plugged in. It created new timelines if anything was changed.

But every Christmas Eve we plugged it in and let friends take rides back into their own pasts with instructions to change nothing. It had become a special evening for all of us and the reason why Jenny and I were back in town for the holiday.

But at one point there was a dark side to the Christmas Eve ceremony. I had lost a number of friends, friends that I could remember when the timeline changed because I had been touching the jukebox when they didn't return.

It was two in the afternoon, two days before Christmas. Richard had just opened and was sipping on an orange juice as he leaned against the back bar, just as I used to do when I owned the place.

I was sipping on my normal Christmas eggnog without alcohol, sitting on the bar stool closest to the jukebox that Richard used to sit on. We had just switched places. It felt weird, but somehow right.

Jenny was off shopping and wouldn't be here for a good hour. She liked to give me time with my old friends without her hanging around, even though all the regulars thought of her as just another member of the gang.

Dave, my best friend, a retired airline pilot, sat beside me at the bar and Big Carl, a contractor who had been a regular since I opened the place sat next to Dave. If I remember right, we were talking about a football game I had attended a month before in San Francisco when

suddenly Richard's eyes got huge and he said softly, "Stout?"

I said, "Yeah."

And from the direction of the jukebox someone else said, "Hi, Richard."

I spun toward the voice.

That someone else was me, looking very dirty and a decade or more older.

If my mug of eggnog hadn't been sitting on the bar, I would have dropped it.

My older self looked at me, nodded and then said, "Good, got this one right. Glad you are here. I remember this now."

And with that he vanished.

TWO

THE SILENCE in the bar seemed like a big thick weight.

I glanced at Richard whose eyes were huge, then back at where the old me had appeared beside the unplugged jukebox.

Dave cleared his throat. "Looks like you're going to have a rough time at some point in the future."

It did look that way, I had to admit. I had gotten dirty helping Jenny in her garden down in San Francisco last year, but even at my worst I hadn't looked as bad as I had looked a moment before.

Suddenly the air near the jukebox shimmered and the older me appeared again, just as dirty and dust-covered.

The older me smiled at me, then said, "Good, got this one right. Glad you are here. I remember this now."

The exact same thing he had said the first time.

Then he also vanished.

'Oh, oh,' Richard said right before more versions of older me, or copies three-through-nine appeared in quick order, all saying exactly the same thing before vanishing.

We all just sat stunned. I mean, when nine copies of yourself suddenly appear, it takes a moment to get used to the idea. Actually, I doubt I would ever get used to the idea, but by the time number nine disappeared, I knew I had to do something to stop this and stop it quick before the numbers of me got really, really big.

When version number ten appeared and started to speak, I held up my hand. "You've said that and a bunch of you have already been here."

The older, dirtier me stopped, thought for a second, then said, "Damn, I remember that now."

And then he vanished.

The silence again filled the Garden Lounge as we all sat staring at the jukebox, waiting for another version of me to appear.

Nothing.

Finally, from down the bar Carl said, "You think he kept leaving because we didn't offer him a drink?"

Richard just shook his head and Dave chuckled.

"Got any idea what might be going on?" Dave asked as I sat staring at the jukebox.

"Not a clue," I said. "I've never opened up the real interior of that thing. Richard?"

Richard just shook his head. "I haven't touched it at all since you left, Stout. Wouldn't even begin to know what I was looking at."

"You looked older," Carl said. "Got any sense of how far into the future they are coming from?"

I shook my head. "Never tried to guess what I was going to look like. At this point I'm just happy getting out of bed every morning. But now I'm going to have nightmares for years."

I turned back to face Richard behind the bar and took a sip of my eggnog. I could see the jukebox out of the corner of my eye and if there was movement I would know it. I had a hunch this was far, far from over, whatever was going on.

"Might not be that far in the future," Richard said. "The gray hair and extra wrinkles on his face just might be dirt and dust."

'Possible," Carl said. "I got caught in some cement dust and looked like that once."

"But why now, why at this moment?" Richard asked.

I knew the answer instantly on that. "Listen."

"Silence," Carl said after a moment of all of us pausing.

"Exactly," Dave said, nodding, understanding what I was thinking.

Richard had not turned on the background music, so there was no music on to trigger the jukebox or to plant memories of this moment in any of our minds.

"I wonder why your statement stopped the appearances," Carl said.

I glanced past David at the big contractor. He clearly looked rattled and his drink was empty. I had a hunch Richard knew that and was pacing the big guy's consumption.

"You locked him into this timeline," David said.

All of us stared at him as if he had lost a bolt.

He just shrugged. "We all know that if we go back and change something in the past, we create a new timeline. When Stout here let me go back and save my wife, I created a timeline different from the one I left. One where she lived and I never had come into the Garden. Right?"

We all nodded.

"But there are many timelines, more than likely millions, where I didn't go back, where Stout didn't open this bar, and so on and so on. Those versions of Stout were just from different timelines,

all close, but yet different, where you are trying the same thing, whatever that may be, at some point in the future."

I could see where he was going. "So by talking and telling him what he was doing, I locked him and me together in this timeline, blocking out the others."

"At least the first nine," David said. "But this could be going on in millions of timelines in different ways right now. You just stopped the timelines from crossing into the same event."

"Richard, you don't have enough eggnog for that many Stouts," Carl said.

"This makes my head hurt," Richard said. "Have I ever said how much that machine worries me?"

"Me too," I said. "But if I know all of this in the future, what am I trying to do? And how am I getting back here without a song?"

"Seems to me you figured out how the jukebox works," Richard said and Dave nodded.

"But why would I do that?"

"Because the jukebox was full," my voice said from beside the jukebox. "It needed to be fixed."

THREE

WE ALL TURNED to see the dust-covered me standing beside the dark jukebox. I watched as my future self patted the jukebox and said, "In fact, it's full now. I'll fix it so you all can have Christmas Eve like normal."

"Sounds like we didn't have a normal one in your original timeline," I said to my older self.

"You got that right. The jukebox didn't work. It took me three years to track this actual jukebox to where it was made originally as a regular jukebox. Then I followed through old sales records what happened to it to make it into this special jukebox."

I nodded. I had thought of doing just that a few times, but had never really had a reason.

"Where are you coming from?" Dave asked.

"An old abandoned gold mine called the Trade Dollar above the old ghost town of Silver City, Idaho," the older me said. "That's why the dust. It's hard to get a crystal off a wall without doing damage to it."

I watched as the older me spread out his arms and sent dust flying in the air. With that he turned and with a key opened the jukebox, lifting the lid and showing the metal box inside that I had never had the courage to open.

As we watched, the older me clicked open the metal box with another key, showing a vast array of long crystals with wires running from the crystals out of the back of the box.

They looked like a mass of growing quartz crystals, only they had a slight rose color about them. And an odd light seemed to come from them, like they were almost alive.

Numbers of the larger crystals were a good half-foot long and thousands of small ones seemed to grow around the big ones, most the size of the tip of a pen.

I just stared, unable to speak.

"Wow," Richard said.

The older me pointed at the mass of crystals. "Each one is a different timeline created by the jukebox travelers. The machine was never meant to last this long and let this many timelines grow in it."

"How do you know that?" I asked my older self.

"I have talked to the guy and his wife who built all this. He's a twenty-something who lives a few miles from here, actually. His name is Duster Kendal and

USA Today *bestselling writer Dean Wesley Smith returns with a second novel to the world of* Dust and Kisses *from the first issue of* Smith's Monthly.

Together, Callie and Fisher work to discover the secrets of a galaxy that have been hidden in plain sight, even from the powerful humans who had rescued millions.

And in the process, they just might change everything.

Now Available
**from all your favorite booksellers
in trade paper and electronic editions.**

his wife's name is Bonnie. Wonderful people. His family owns the mine. He built the jukebox on one of his trips into the past, thought it might be kind of fun to attach songs to time travel. You ought to hear some of their stories. They have both actually lived hundreds and hundreds of years. Not kidding."

"Does he know the jukebox is here?" Dave asked over my shoulder.

"He has always known where it was," my older self said, smiling like a ghost, the white dust covering his face making me look just weird. "He likes how we've been treating it and being careful using it, so he's helping me fix it. He didn't realize it had broke."

My older self pulled out a smaller crystal from his pocket and placed it carefully beside the jukebox, then as we watched, my older self unhooked the large mass of crystals and pulled the entire thing from the jukebox, placing it gently on the floor.

I stared at the mass of crystals, knowing that somehow in there was my entire life, and everyone who had known about the jukebox at the Garden, and all the lives we had changed.

My older self carefully installed the small crystal, then closed the interior box and locked it, then closed the jukebox.

Then he patted it and said, "Now you can have a normal Christmas Eve celebration."

"Wait!" I said as the older me started to pick up the mass of crystals. "We're not going to remember any of this, are we? Since you are changing this timeline."

"Not a bit of it," the older me said, smiling. "You know, by me doing this I am creating a different timeline for you, one where the jukebox will work on Christmas Eve."

"And you'll still have your memories of the jukebox not working?" Dave asked.

"Exactly," the older me said. "That's my timeline. Have a great time, so to speak."

I had to remember this.

I had to.

I wanted to see that gold mine, I wanted to talk to the man who built the jukebox. I couldn't let these memories vanish.

I just couldn't.

My older self picked up the mass of crystals from the floor as I jumped toward the jukebox.

I got my hands on the edge of the jukebox as he stood upright. He smiled at me and shrugged. "Just might work."

Then he vanished.

FOUR

A WAVE of energy, like a heat mirage, seemed to shift over the Garden Lounge. I knew that feeling well. It happened any time someone went back through the jukebox and changed the past and changed the timeline.

I stood there, both hands pressed as hard as I could against the glass of the old jukebox, letting the wave pass.

And when it did I could still remember everything that happened.

I knew where the mine was and everything.

Looks like Jenny and I had a trip to make up to an old Idaho ghost town next summer.

"What are you doing, Stout?" Richard asked from his position behind the bar.

Dave and Carl were also looking at me with puzzled looks.

Then Dave said, "You're touching the jukebox. Something happened, didn't it? That we don't remember."

"I hate it when that happens," Carl said.

I carefully took my hands off the unplugged machine, then smiled. "Yeah, we just had a visit from a jukebox mechanic. The old baby had to be tuned up for the Christmas Eve celebration."

All three men just stared at me like I had lost a bolt.

"So who was this imaginary mechanic," Richard asked. "And how much do I owe him?"

I sat back down on the stool and smiled up at my friend. "It was me," I said. "A future me. You owe me another eggnog and we'll call it even. And I promise I'll tell you all what just happened as soon as Jenny gets here."

"Sometimes that machine just scares hell out of me," Richard said, going for the eggnog.

"You met yourself?" Carl asked, shaking his head. "Now that would creep me out."

"Actually," I said, "he was a nice guy."

All three of my friends just groaned.

Behind us the front door to the Garden Lounge opened and I turned around to see a young couple enter. The man was wearing a long leather coat that swirled around his cowboy boots. A brown cowboy hat was tucked over his eyes, but he quickly pulled the hat off. The woman had on a long coat that looked like it was from the turn of the 19th century in fashion and high black boots. Both had long brown hair and both were very, very attractive people.

"We have new friends," I said, smiling at Richard, who looked puzzled.

"Who are they?" Dave asked.

"The inventors of the jukebox," I said.

Then I stood and headed toward them, sticking out my hand. "Duster and Bonnie Kendal I presume."

The young guy shook my hand, a huge smile filling his face.

"You look a lot younger not covered in dust," he said.

Bonnie also smiled as she shook my hand. "You are just amazing, you know that? I hope Jenny's on the way."

"Any time now," I said.

Duster shook his head. "I'll be damned, you told me it might have worked and you would remember yourself being here and I didn't believe you. Only reason we know as well was because we were touching our machine on our side. The one that doesn't require music."

I laughed. "I would love to see it. But that's an amazing jukebox you built here."

Then I turned and indicated that they should join us at the bar. "We've got some stories to tell you about your wonderful invention and how it has saved lives."

"And since you teased us with a few of those stories three years from now," Bonnie said, "we're dying to hear them."

Richard, Dave, and Carl all sat staring and listening.

Finally Richard said simply, "Does this stuff give anyone else a headache?"

Everyone laughed and I knew this first Christmas not owning the Garden Lounge was going to be as wonderful as any in the past.

~

USA TODAY BESTSELLING AUTHOR

DEAN WESLEY SMITH

AN EASY SHOT

A GOLF THRILLER

In the first installment, Seattle Police Detectives Bonnie and Craig, while taking a late night walk on a Scottsdale Arizona golf course, happen to overhear a conversation between two men plotting to kill a United States Senator.

At the same time, a young golf professional's wife is kidnapped. Scheduled to play with the Senator, he must do what they ask or his wife will die.

Bonnie and Craig get the FBI and local police involved. Everything is set for the next day, including the fact that they will play with the Senator to help protect him.

AN EASY SHOT

Part 3 of 8

CHAPTER SEVEN

Saturday, April 8th
8:04 a.m.

AT SLIGHTLY AFTER eight in the morning, the desert sun was still a good hour from completely taking the chill off the morning air. Craig hadn't bothered to grab a jacket when he left the room for breakfast, but after walking from the clubhouse to the cart area, he wished he had. He was only wearing golf slacks and a short-sleeved shirt. He knew that by noon he was going to be too warm, but right now he was darned cold.

No doubt Bonnie was as well. She had on a pair of tight white shorts and a thin, see-through blouse with a white halter-top underneath. It was an outfit that was sure to drive the Senator to distraction by the time the round was over. Watching that wonderful body in those tight shorts wasn't going to exactly help keep Craig's mind on the game either.

Right now, because of the cold, Bonnie's nipples were clearly visible as sharp bumps standing out against the halter-top and blouse. She had her arms crossed under her breasts for warmth, not covering anything.

About a hundred identical golf carts were all lined two abreast along a wide area of concrete to one side of the club-house, ready to go for the tournament. Each pair of carts had white pieces of paper with different tee-times on the steering wheels.

Craig and Bonnie moved down the line until they found their 8:46 time that Hagar had arranged last night with the tournament staff. Their golf clubs were already loaded into two carts, Bonnie's in the cart with Senator Knight's bag and Craig's beside a large black bag that had the word Titleist covering one side. Clearly Craig was riding with the pro and Bonnie was riding with the Senator.

Craig wasn't too sure if he liked the idea of Bonnie being that close to the possible target of an assassin, but he couldn't think of any logical reason to change the pairing.

There were a lot of people coming and going from around the carts and bags, but there was no sign of the Senator or Maxwell or Hagar.

"Damn, it's cold out here," Bonnie said, grabbing her visor from the front pocket of her bag.

"Wait an hour and that will change," Craig said.

"I may be frozen stiff in an hour," Bonnie said.

"Parts of you already are stiff," Craig said, glancing down at where her nipples were trying to break free from her blouse.

She smacked his arm in mock anger, but he could tell she was enjoying the attention.

"Excuse me, Detective Craig and Officer Stanley," a man said, moving up beside them.

Craig glanced up as a guy in blue slacks and white jacket approached. He was either FBI, one of Hagar's men, or one of the golf pros. Craig would bet a month's salary on FBI.

"I'm Agent Howard," the man said. "The Senator is on the driving range. He told me to tell you to bring both the carts."

"Thanks," Craig said.

"One more thing," Agent Howard said, moving in so his voice could only be heard by Craig and Bonnie. "In the outside pocket of both your bags are loaded weapons. Detective Hagar wanted me to make sure you knew where they were."

Craig nodded and turned to his bag. He unzipped the outside pocket just enough to see the handle of the police special stuffed down in his rain gear. It was the exact same model as his gun back in Seattle.

"Got it," he said, zipping up the pocket and turning back to the agent.

Bonnie looked up from her bag, a grim look on her face. "Should work fine if I have to use it."

"Let's hope we don't," Agent Howard said.

"Couldn't agree more," Craig said. "Thanks."

Agent Howard turned and moved away from them, walking down the row of carts as if he belonged here.

"I wonder how many other FBI and Scottsdale police are around," Bonnie said.

"More than we're going to spot," Craig said, "if they are doing their job."

Now Available
from all your favorite booksellers
in trade paper and electronic editions.

Craig moved over and sat down on the cold cart seat. "Follow me."

Bonnie dropped down behind the wheel of the other cart, then said, "Holy shit, that's cold."

Craig laughed.

"What's so funny?" Bonnie asked, glaring at him. "I didn't come to Arizona to freeze my ass off."

"Trust me," Craig said, turning the cart out of line and starting toward the driving range. "You'll be wishing for a cold seat in two hours."

He couldn't hear Bonnie's answer.

The path to the driving range was at least four hundred yards of winding pavement that led up over the top of a rock bluff and down into a steep valley hidden from the clubhouse. The wind in his face was biting-cold, and he drove with only one hand, keeping the other under his leg for some warmth.

As he cleared the top of the ridge, he was colder than he could remember being in a long, long time.

The driving range spread out below him, filling a massive open area of green that sloped down the floor of the rock-sided valley. Colored flags were placed at different distances from the teeing area.

Twenty or so people were scattered over the teeing area that looked like it could hold at least fifty people hitting balls at the same time. Each player had his or her own area marked by a metal stand to lean clubs against, a small rock, and a shining pile of red-striped golf balls. Craig loved the free driving-range balls when coming to the desert. Back in the Northwest, driving-range balls were normally sold by the bucket. Down here they just piled them up for every player to use as many as they wanted.

Maxwell was sitting in a cart just off the path on the far side of the range and Hagar and two others were talking off to the right side.

Craig waved at them and then looked around for the Senator. He was at the far left side of the range, his back to the hill and Maxwell. It was the easiest spot to guard in the entire area.

Craig took the cart down the path, parking it directly behind the Senator. Bonnie pulled up behind him, clearly even colder than she had been back at the clubhouse. Her fingers looked white as she blew on them, and Craig could swear her teeth were chattering.

"Are we having fun yet?" he asked, smiling at her.

She only glared at him and moved around to get some clubs out of her bag.

"Not yet, huh?" he said, laughing as he grabbed a few clubs and headed to a pile of balls. The Senator glanced up and said, "Good morning."

"Morning, sir," Craig said.

The Senator was wearing green Bermuda shorts and a Hawaiian shirt that would clash with anything. He had on white socks and black golf shoes. Anyone trying to take a shot at this guy would be laughing too hard to shoot straight.

"Good morning, Senator," Bonnie said, walking up and standing behind him. "You look colorful this morning."

The Senator laughed. "A natural politician. I knew I liked you for more than your fantastic looks."

Bonnie blushed.

Craig could very seldom get that kind of reaction out of her, yet the Senator seemed to be able to do it at will.

The Senator pointed to a man two spots over hitting balls with a fluid golf swing. "Craig, Bonnie, that is Danny Baines. From Sedona."

Danny turned and stepped toward them, his hand outstretched, a smile filling his face. Danny had to be all of twenty, if that. He had the kind of face that Craig figured women loved. Sort of a cross between Paul McCartney and Paul Newman. But there was something about him that bothered Craig almost instantly. And he wasn't sure what it was.

"Nice to meet you both," the kid-pro said. "Looking forward to our round."

"Yeah," Bonnie said. "Me too."

After she had shaken the kid's hand, she turned and gave Craig the eye-brows-up, wide-eyed look. He wasn't sure if that meant she thought the kid was hot, or if it meant she was feeling the same way he was. He'd ask her when he got a chance.

Thirty minutes later, Craig rolled his drive off the first tee, the Senator hit his drive into a large pile of rocks to the left of the fairway, and Bonnie and the pro hit the fairway. It was a good indication of how the day would go.

CHAPTER EIGHT

Saturday, April 8th
12:44 p.m.

BONNIE FIGURED she had gotten the best deal, riding with the Senator. He was charming, laughed easily, and was determined to have fun, no matter how bad his golf game was. And it was bad, plain and simple.

The first hole he had managed a nine from the rocks, and except for a bogey four on a short par three, that was his best

score. The good thing was that he didn't take much time over any single shot. He just walked up to it, took his stance and hit it, often sideways and never very far.

The young pro was another matter. He was the silent type who had had it two under par by the end of the first nine, and took lots of time over each shot. However, he had taken so many fewer shots than the rest of them, it didn't really slow them down at all.

Also the kid hadn't said much more than "Nice shot!" or "Your turn," the entire morning. Bonnie hadn't been able to figure out what bothered her about the kid, but one thing for sure, he had a beautiful golf swing.

The Senator had Bonnie so relaxed with his jokes and friendly patter that by the second hole, even with the distraction of always looking around, always being aware of any danger, she had played well.

Far better than Craig had, that was for sure.

The temperature had finally warmed up enough to be comfortable by the third hole, and by the time they had reached the tenth hole it was warm. By the scenic sixteenth hole tee box on the back nine, it was just plain hot.

The sixteenth was a fairly long par three, with the tee boxes for the hole carved out of the side of a large hill, and the green a good hundred feet below them across a deep rock canyon. The group in front of them was still on the green, so Bonnie climbed up the dirt and wood steps to get on the highest tee box. Maxwell and another FBI agent were already up there, off to one side, scanning the surrounding area.

The light wind blew at her blouse and hair, cooling her as she looked around. The view was just spectacular. Where she stood was by far the highest place on the golf course, and from there she could see out over Scottsdale and Phoenix.

"Wow," Senator Knight said, moving up to stand beside her. "This is a sight."

"I didn't know Senators were prone to understatement," Bonnie said.

The Senator laughed. "The spectacular view took my words away."

"That's better," Bonnie said, smiling at him.

Below them the cart path wound back and forth, switchback after switchback, down the almost cliff-steep side of the mountain between the tee box and the green.

And there were dirt footpaths in the rocks and scrub brush leading down into the canyon where golfers had climbed down to search for balls. If she hit one down in there, she wasn't going down looking for it, that was for sure. Too many snake-warning signs around this course for her tastes. Since she saw the first sign back on the fifth hole, she hadn't gotten off the cart path or fairway without a club in her hand.

Two of Hagar's men stood on the hill on the far side of the hole, waiting. She could imagine how boring the day had been for them. Climbing around in the rocks and desert, watching four people play golf.

Thank heavens that was all that had happened so far.

Craig moved up beside her and whispered in her ear. "What do you say we come back up here tonight?"

"And do what?" she whispered back, teasing him.

"An encore performance," he said, just loud enough for her to hear.

"Sex on the top of a mountain," she whispered. "I like that idea. As long as you carry me up here."

Craig laughed and said loud enough for the Senator to hear. "It might just be worth it."

The Senator gave her a raised-eyebrow look and Bonnie could feel herself blush again.

Then he said, smiling at her, "Green's open."

What seemed like an outrageous distance below her the foursome in front of them cleared the green and Danny moved to the tee.

His shot sailed into the air and then seemed to drop forever. At first she thought it was going to be so far over the green that it might land on one of Hagar's men on the far hillside. But finally the ball dropped about twenty paces short of the pin, bounced once and stopped. In all the years she had played golf, she had never been on a hole like this.

She hit two balls into the canyon before she declared she was done and was going to drop a ball up by the green. This might be the most spectacular vista in the desert, but it was also one impossible golf hole.

Craig managed to hit one over the canyon, landing it on the right of the green and they all cheered him like he'd just hit a home run. As far as Bonnie was concerned, that was his best shot of the day.

Even Maxwell applauded.

The Senator rolled a shot off the end of the tee box. They all watched as the ball bounced, clattered, and fell like a pinball gone crazy down the rocky slope. It bounced twice on the cart path, once about twenty feet below the tee box, and a second time somewhere even with the green about three switchbacks down. The ball finally disappeared into the canyon in front of the green.

The Senator glanced over at Danny. "I think that ball went four hundred yards at least, if you count every bounce."

Danny nodded. "Thank your lucky stars it didn't get stuck somewhere on that cliff. You would have had to try to hit it."

"Not in this lifetime," the Senator said, glancing down the steep, rocky slope.

The Senator tried one more shot—this time flying his ball into the canyon—and decided Bonnie's idea of dropping one on the other side was the best policy. Everyone agreed.

Bonnie climbed into the cart beside the Senator and stared at the sign twenty feet in front of them.

WARNING!
STEEP DOWNGRADE.
SLOW!
USE BRAKES!

Thank heavens the Senator took the warning to heart. The hole was no more than one hundred and seventy yards as the crow flies, but the cart path down that cliff face had to be five times that long. And very, very narrow and steep. She was sweating more from the fear than the heat by the time they reached the flat bridge over the canyon in front of the green.

The Senator's knuckles were white on the steering wheel.

It was a golf hole, and a golf cart ride she would never forget.

They made it the rest of the way through the round without problems, and the Senator agreed to meet them in the bar for drinks after a shower and change of clothes.

"You don't mind, do you Senator," Craig asked, "if we play with you again tomorrow?"

Hagar and Maxwell were both standing close by and both nodded their agreement with the idea.

"Sounds fine with me," the Senator said. "As long as Bonnie wears those white shorts again."

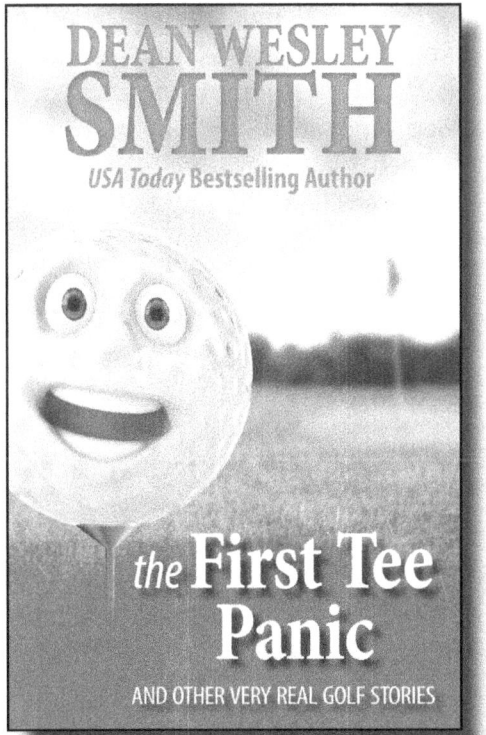

For the fifth or sixth time, Bonnie blushed. Why he could do that to her, she didn't know.

"She has another pair that is even tighter," Craig said, winking at the Senator.

Bonnie punched him in the arm as the Senator laughed. She did have a tighter pair, and now she planned on wearing them for sure.

"Then I look forward to the round," the Senator said. "I'll meet you in the bar in an hour."

Bonnie glanced at her watch. It was a little after two in the afternoon. A shower sounded perfect to help cool down and rinse off a layer of suntan lotion.

"Sounds great," Craig said.

"Drinks and dinner are on me," the Senator said. "For all of you. No arguments." He glanced at Maxwell and Hagar, who both nodded, then at Bonnie.

"It sounds like a wonderful time," she said.

"Good. An hour then." He turned and headed up into the hotel.

Maxwell moved with him and Bonnie had no doubt there were other FBI agents working ahead of the Senator. She really liked the guy, even though he made her blush with the slightest look. She was glad they were doing everything in their power to make sure nothing happened to him.

So far all was well. But there was still the rest of the afternoon and tonight.

And all of tomorrow.

CHAPTER NINE

Saturday, April 8th
9:07 p.m.

AFTER A QUICK shower in the strange waterfall tub, Craig had ended up having two rum and cokes in the bar. Those drinks, combined with a lot of laugher and jokes, had stretched over two hours. It had been almost six by the time they finally went into the restaurant for dinner, and Craig had been famished.

Bonnie had only had one drink and a lot of water and she whispered to him as they walked into the restaurant that she was so hungry, she was about to eat the bar napkins.

Parsons, Hagar and Maxwell had joined them in the bar. Parsons said he didn't drink and Hagar and Maxwell had both stuck to Diet Cokes since they were on duty. Craig could see a few other detectives and agents stationed around the bar and restaurant.

The food had turned out to be even better than Craig would have expected, and his expectations were high in this beautiful resort. He had had a perfectly cooked New York steak, while Bonnie had lamb.

The food was so good, Craig just didn't want to stop eating.

Finally, at nine the Senator excused himself, saying it was time to get back to his room, do a little work, and get some sleep, since their tee time in the morning was 8:15.

Maxwell and Hagar left the table with the Senator and Parsons, leaving only Craig and Bonnie. As she pushed away the last few bites of her raspberry-covered cheesecake she moaned.

"Full?"

"Stuffed like a turkey at Thanksgiving," she said, sipping on her coffee.

"Before or after roasting?"

She touched her suntanned arm. "After, clearly."

"So what do you say we go for a walk?" Craig asked. "It's getting dark."

"To walk off the dinner, or did you have something else in mind?'

"Maybe both," he said.

"Perfect."

Hand in hand they strolled out of the restaurant and through the lobby. Not only was the restaurant and bar still busy, but so was the central area of the massive hotel. Craig figured at least a hundred people milled around in the vast wood and stone space, talking and laughing and generally enjoying the party atmosphere of the charity golf tournament. Even with the fear for the Senator, he was enjoying himself as well.

And, it seemed, Bonnie was too.

"Let's go out this way," Craig said, pulling Bonnie through the lobby away from the front door and down a wide hallway that led to the pro shop area. He knew there was another door there that went out toward the back nine.

Last night they had gone out the front and ended up on the second hole. When they went past the spot this morning Bonnie had pointed out to the Senator where they were sitting when they overheard the men. The Senator's only comment was, "It looks like a nice private spot to me."

Bonnie had blushed.

Craig was enjoying the fact that the Senator could make her blush with a simple comment.

The Pro Shop was closed, so Craig led Bonnie down the wide staircase to an outside door between the entrances to the locker rooms. Where the carts had been lined up early that morning was an empty expanse of concrete. To the left Craig could see a large, open door behind a massive boulder. It looked as if it led down into what was clearly a cart storage area under the hotel.

There was no one around. Compared to the massive number of people just a short distance away in the lobby and restaurant area, it felt odd to be alone.

Bonnie ambled toward the open door. "I wonder how many carts a place like this has?"

"They have two courses here," he said. "It has to be a lot. A couple hundred at least." He followed her down the ramp around the rock and into a massive, low-ceilinged garage area.

"Try four or five hundred," Bonnie said.

Craig stood in the door beside her, amazed at the expanse of lined up carts that seemed to almost vanish into the distance in the dim light. They were in perfect rows, with cords draping from the ceiling. Each cord was plugged into a cart in the center under the seat.

To Craig it looked like each was hooked into an umbilical cord.

The carts were all empty and cleaned, waiting, the clubs clearly off in a locked storage area somewhere.

Bonnie walked slowly down one aisle. Each cart was numbered, and that number matched a number painted on the concrete. It looked like something he'd seen in a bad science fiction movie: aliens waiting to be activated. And the dim light didn't help the image.

"I wonder what their power bill is like for all this," Bonnie said, pointing up at all the chargers on shelves along one ceiling beam.

Craig followed, not sure that they should be in there, but not stopping either.

Bonnie glanced over at Craig. "You remember what our cart numbers were today?"

"You and the Senator had 167 and Danny and I had 168," he said, surprised at himself for remembering. But since he and Danny had been following the Senator's cart all day, and the number to their cart was on the back right bumper, it had pretty much stuck in his mind.

They were walking along the carts with low eighties for numbers. Bonnie kept going, deeper into the dimly-lit room. He had no idea what she had in mind, but he followed anyway.

She led him between cart 104 and 105 over to the next row. Cart 167 was backed against the concrete wall five or six carts from the back of the room. Bonnie climbed in and patted the seat beside her.

"Just what are we doing?" Craig asked, sliding into the passenger seat.

"Shhh," she said softly. "Just listen."

The silence seemed to suddenly get louder than his own heartbeat as they sat there in the darkness. The light from the door they had come in was the only bright area. The rest of the massive garage was illuminated by dim nightlights scattered on support pillars. There was a faint hum that filled the air, more than likely coming from the chargers above each cart.

Nothing else.

Bonnie moved her hand to his lap and squeezed. Then she whispered, "Every time you climbed in the cart today I wanted to do that."

"Don't stop now," he whispered back.

Her hand worked over his crotch, rubbing him through his slacks, making him grow quickly hard.

"Nice," he whispered. "Very nice." He leaned into her and they kissed, long and hard, the taste of the cheesecake desert covering her breath like a sweet mint.

He moved his hands up to her breasts, rubbing them through her blouse and bra. He felt like a high school kid again, out parking on a date, touching a girl's

breasts through her blouse. Those nights were exciting and frustrating at the same time. He had loved the feeling and had always wished he could recapture it.

Now he was and it was great.

Excitement of being in a different place combined with sexual touching, all wrapped into the fear of getting caught. This weekend was going to be memorable for a number of things.

Bonnie seemed to be enjoying it just like his dates had back then. Actually, he was enjoying it more than he had in high school, since none of his dates had ever put her hand on his crotch like Bonnie was doing now.

They kissed again, long and hard and passionately. It seemed it had been years since the two of them had felt so passionate with each other. Craig knew right then they were going to have to take vacations much more often.

Bonnie started fumbling to unzip his pants and open his belt. He broke the kiss to help, but before he could get his belt undone the sound of something metal dropping echoed through the massive empty room.

Both Bonnie and Craig jerked away from each other to stare out through the carts. Craig thought his heart was going to jump right out of his chest from the shock. Across the massive garage, at least six rows over, Craig could see two men moving toward the door.

He couldn't see their faces, since their backs were mostly turned toward them, but one had short hair, the other wore a golf cap. Both looked to be about six foot, one had wider shoulders than the other.

As the two neared the door, one spoke, clearly loud enough for Bonnie and Craig to hear. "Man, you two need to get a room."

Then the two men were gone out the door and up the ramp.

Craig glanced at the shocked look on Bonnie's face. Instantly he knew she thought the same thing he did. That voice was one of the voices from last night.

"Come on," he said, jumping out of the cart and running down the aisle toward the door, making sure his zipper was up as he ran.

"We don't have our guns," Bonnie said from behind him.

Craig knew that. "I don't plan on stopping them. Just following."

At the large door he stopped and quickly peered around the corner. As he had expected, they were not in sight up the ramp. With Bonnie right behind him he ran up to the door into the clubhouse. There were two couples walking out near one of the putting greens, and a maintenance man working in the ground near a planter, but no sign of the two men.

"They must have gone inside," Bonnie said, pointing to the double doors that led past the pro shop and up the stairs.

Craig agreed. It was the only place they could have gone that quickly.

At a run they went back up the stairs, down the hall, and into the main lobby. There seemed to be even more people up here than there had when they left a half hour before.

He and Bonnie moved to one side and stood, scanning the people. Not a sign of the two men.

They had vanished.

"Damn," Bonnie said.

Craig couldn't agree more. "We need to inform Maxwell and Hagar. Let's head up to the Senator's floor."

"Just don't tell the Senator what we were doing," Bonnie said. "I get embarrassed enough around that man."

"Agreed," Craig said, smiling. "But we have to tell the others what the guy said."

"Damn, damn, damn," Bonnie said. "Caught parking in a golf cart inside a garage. How bad is that?"

"And with a married man as well," Craig said. "What's your husband going to say?"

"I hope he says rain check."

"Rain check."

Ten minutes later, with Hagar and Maxwell and two other FBI agents with

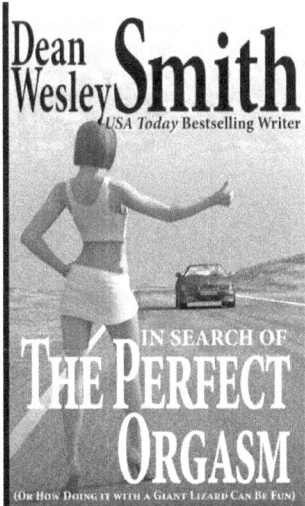

them, they did a sweep through the hotel lobby, bar, and restaurant, looking for two men who matched the vague description of what Bonnie and Craig had seen. No luck at all, which just made Craig even that much more frustrated.

They all then went back down to the cart storage area. With Bonnie's help, they managed to figure out which row the two men had seemed to suddenly appear in. Hagar got one of the hotel security staff to turn up the lights and they searched the entire area without finding anything.

Maxwell pointed at a regular-sized door in the back wall near the end of the cart aisle they were searching. "Maybe they came out of there." Maxwell glanced at one of the hotel security guards. "Where's that lead?"

"Service area," the security guard said.

"We didn't hear a door open or close," Craig said. He glanced at Bonnie to make sure and she nodded her agreement.

"They might have already come through it when we came in," Bonnie said.

Maxwell nodded and moved to the door. It was locked, but the security guard quickly had it open. The door was the kind that could be opened from the inside even if locked so the two men could have easily come through it from the inside. Behind the door was a staircase leading upwards into a main floor service area of the hotel. And right across from where the staircase came out were three service elevators.

"It seems the two we are looking for know their way around this place," Bonnie said.

"I hope you have those guarded," Craig said, pointing at the service elevators.

"On the Senator's floor we do," Maxwell said. "But I'm beginning to think we may need to cover the floor below as well."

Craig could only agree.

To be continued...

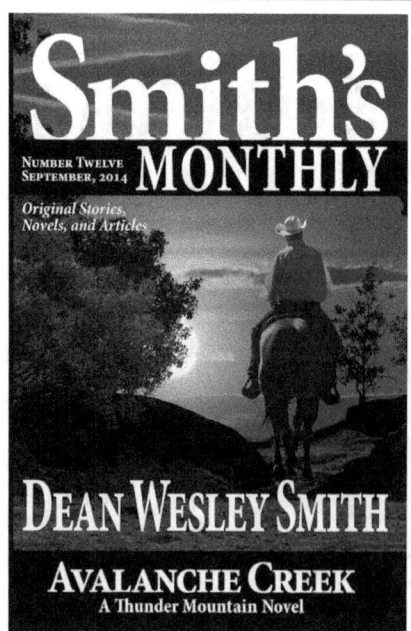

Now Available
from all your favorite booksellers in trade paper and electronic editions.

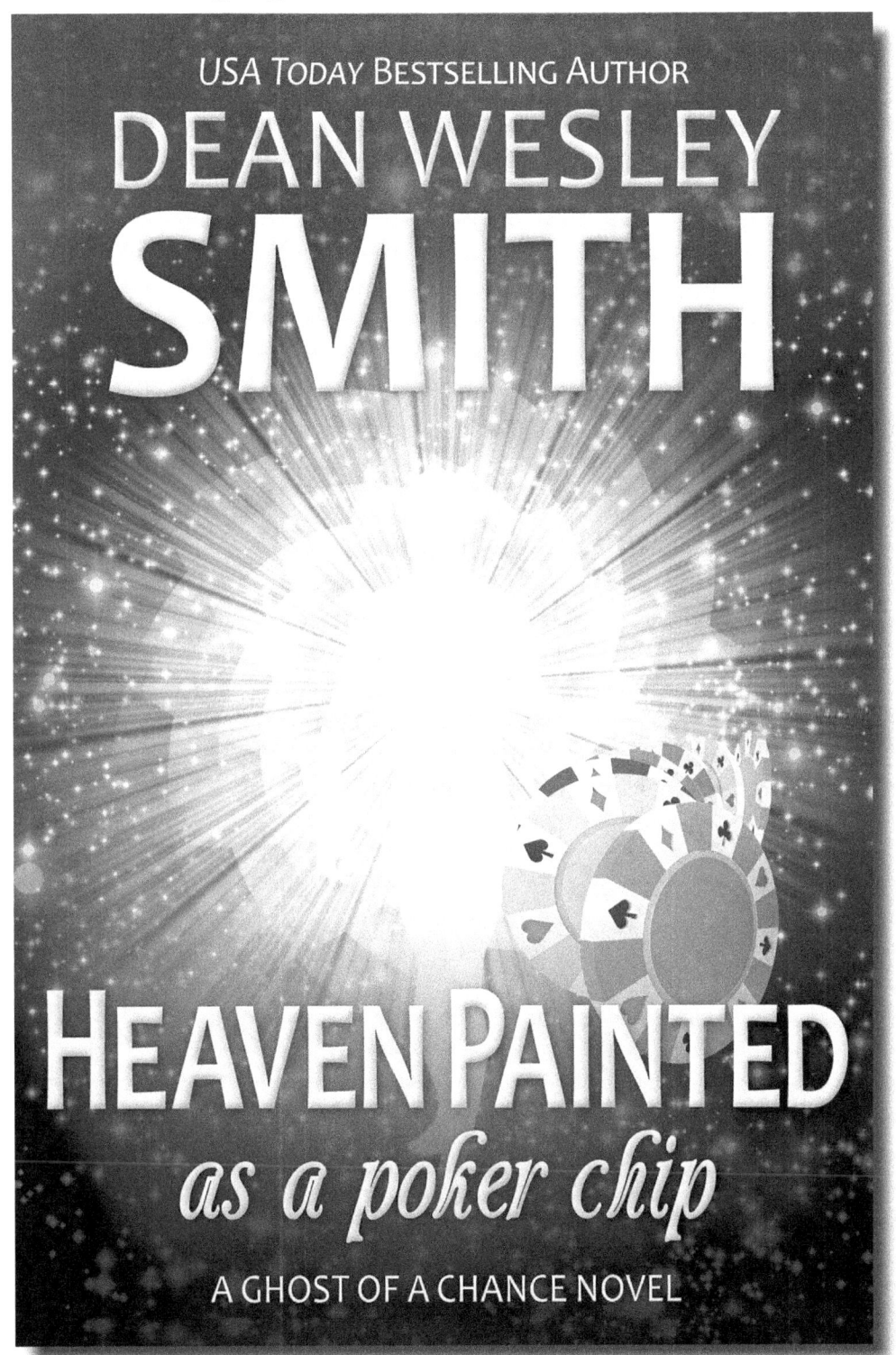

USA TODAY BESTSELLING AUTHOR

DEAN WESLEY
SMITH

HEAVEN PAINTED
as a poker chip

A GHOST OF A CHANCE NOVEL

Dean Wesley Smith

USA Today Bestselling Writer

What happens if the morals
you used to cherish get taken
by the women you love?

The Keeper
of the Morals

Do you really need a lack of morals to climb the corporate ladder?

What happens if the morals you used to cherish get taken by the women you love?

A story of love, greed, corporate ladders, and blondes.

Lots of blondes.

"The Keeper of the Morals" was first published in the anthology Wizards, Inc. *from Daw Books, edited by Martin H. Greenberg and Loren L. Coleman.*

THE KEEPER OF THE MORALS

CHAPTER ONE

I NURSED the scotch-rocks like it was the last drink I was ever going to have instead of just the first for the night, twirling the glass and the golden liquid on its paper napkin like a kid's toy. More than likely, it was going to be the drink I remembered most in a long line of drinks, followed by picking up some blonde—they were always blondes—and taking her back to my big house in my Porsche for some fast, sloppy sex and then uncomfortable good-byes.

Around me, the party atmosphere of the "Danny's Crib Lounge," combined with the music from too many speakers, kept the noise level just under that of a jet taking off. I had been lucky tonight to find a place at the bar. Usually I ended up standing, drink in hand, pretending to actually talk to someone I mostly couldn't hear.

But tonight was special. That's what my six co-workers from the legal department had told me. I had closed negotiations on one of the company's biggest deals today, opening up a wildlife refuge for my company's oil rigs to go in and drill. Tomorrow, when the news got out, our stock would shoot up, the left-wing environmentalists would cry, I would get a bonus, and then I would go back to work on the next big deal.

But tonight I got to celebrate.

But I didn't feel like celebrating anything.

Thirty-six years old and I had no idea how I had gotten here.

In this bar.

Doing the job I did.

None. Not a clue.

I used to be one of those liberals who would think of the now-me as the devil. I started off using my legal degree to fight to keep wildlife refuges closed up to companies like the one I now worked for. I took the job with my current employer thinking I could stop some of the company practices from within.

Yeah, right.

What the hell had happened to me?

That wasn't a question I asked myself that often these days. I usually just thought about the money, the stock options, and buying a bigger house, even though alone, I rattled around in the one I had like a kid lost in a big, new school.

I had enough money, but I kept thinking I needed more.

Why?

A soft touch on my shoulder made me turn to my right and into the gaze of a beautiful woman with golden hair and large brown eyes.

My stomach twisted as she smiled a perfect smile showing off perfect teeth. I had barely sipped my first drink and this woman looked fantastic.

My type. She fit it perfectly. In looks as well as everything else. Side-by-side, walking down the street, we would look like Ken and Barbie. The perfect American couple. Her features were almost as chiseled as mine.

Could I get any more superficial? There was more to women than just blonde hair and a beautiful face. I used to look past all that surface stuff, looking for a soul mate, but now it seemed, I never did.

Just like I never really looked at what I did at work.

I felt like I knew her, then shook *that* thought away. I always felt like I knew every blonde I ended up with, but never did. Someday I'd have to get some counseling on that, figure out where in my past the blonde search started.

She leaned in real close and indicated she wanted to say something in my ear over the music and noise.

I turned my head just slightly

"James, Bob sent me," she said, her breath on my ear like what I imagined a whisper from an angel might feel like. "He thought you might need a little boost."

I turned to stare at her directly, then shouted into the music. "Bob? My boss?"

She nodded.

Bob, the short, fat bastard, had sent me a hooker. How crude was that? No matter how good-looking this woman was, I just wasn't interested. Even if she was bought and paid for already.

"Tell him thanks, but no thanks," I said into her perfectly formed ear. "I like to find my own dates."

She laughed, and the laugh seemed to cut through the noise like sharp scissors through tissue paper. "Not *that* kind of boost," she said, leaning in close again.

Her breath smelled of faint cloves mixed with vanilla.

"This kind of boost."

She touched me on the shoulder and I closed my eyes as her hand stroked my arm, filling me with the warmest sensation. Man, she could "boost" me any time she wanted.

Suddenly, all my doubts about what I had done were gone, my drive to get the bigger house was back, and my need to get laid by a beautiful blonde hit me like a sledgehammer.

I opened my eyes to thank her and suggest we go somewhere a little less noisy, but she was gone, vanished into the crowd like so much smoke.

"Well, not sure what old Bob was thinking," I said. "That was lame."

I downed the drink, ordered another, and turned on the bar stool to study the crowd, the memory of her already forgotten. I was looking for a companion for the night. After all, I had some celebrating to do.

CHAPTER TWO

I AWOKE to my alarm the next morning, my head fuzzy from all the scotch and my tongue feeling like I had ran it through sawdust. The sheets on my massive bed still smelled of last night's conquest, a blonde with a chest twice the size of her IQ. She wore a perfume that, after six drinks, had driven me nuts. But this morning, the remains of it smelled like an air-freshener in a men's room urinal.

I vaguely remembered she had left at some point in the middle of the night, calling a cab and taking enough money from me to buy her own cab. I didn't care, it was only money, and after yesterday's closing of the big drilling deal, I was going to be making a lot more of it.

By the time I was through my morning routine and powering toward work in my Porsche, the remains of the scotch hangover were gone and I was looking forward to all the praise I was going to

get at work, not counting the bonus. There had better be a damn big bonus.

Then, like a cloud lifting, I remembered the encounter with the woman Bob had sent. My bonus better be a lot bigger than some strange blonde in a bar, making promises and then not even hanging around to follow through. If Bob paid her more than a few bucks, he was going to have to get his money back, that was for sure.

It took me a few more blocks to really put her face back in my mind. It was as if the scotch had erased it. I prided myself on never forgetting a name or a face. Then what she had said came back. She had promised a "boost." She had touched me and my attitude had changed. Often just the touch of a woman did that to me. Or at least took my focus temporarily away from a problem.

But this time it had felt different, and there was just something about her I couldn't shake. That feeling that I knew her, that same feeling I had with every damn blonde-haired woman I met. That was part of it, sure. But there was more. Bob was going to do some explaining on this one.

As I expected, when I arrived in my office, on the seventh floor of the ten-story corporate headquarters, there was a message waiting with my secretary to join Bob in his office. I usually beat him into work, sometimes by hours, but on days after closing big deals, I gave myself the freedom to just get there when I wanted to. After all, I deserved that luxury for one day.

Tomorrow, I would be back working harder than anyone in the place, coming in earlier, staying later, working weekends. It was the only way to get ahead in this business, and I planned on getting very, very far ahead by the time I was done.

Bob was sitting in his big chair, feet up on his desk as I knocked and then entered his office. He was almost as wide as he was tall, and had a face like a troll stuck in the mud. I tried hard to never stand beside him in any function or picture. It would just make him look bad, and making a boss look bad was never a good career move, even though I was after his job. He was number one in the corporation's legal department; I was number two.

"Nice job on closing that deal yesterday," he said. "Stock is going through the roof, and the guys upstairs are taking hundreds of phone calls from every media outlet there is."

"Great," I said, smiling and sitting down across his desk from him. But it didn't feel that great. It was done, I had managed to pull it off; now it was time to move on, get to the next big deal. The fun was in the chase, not in the having.

It was that way with women as well.

And with my cars and houses. What I owned or had at the moment didn't mean anything. All that mattered was what I was trying to get.

"Bonus check coming your way this afternoon, approved from upstairs," Bob said, smiling a smile that turned his wrinkled face into a mass of sneers. I knew that smile. It was sincere, even though it didn't look it.

"Thanks," I said. "And if you paid that blonde you sent my way last night more than ten bucks, you got taken. She vanished without so much as a kiss goodbye."

He actually jerked, glanced at me, then looked away, as if I had surprised him by remembering her.

"No big deal," Bob said, shifting his gaze to something in an open drawer beside his desk as he sat up.

I'd hit a very sensitive topic for some reason. I knew Bob after the last two years, and I had made it my job to know his moods and actions. I had surprised him.

"Who was she?" I asked, pushing the topic. "She was sure a looker."

He shrugged, which I knew meant he was going to flat out lie to me, or give me a half-truth.

"Just someone I know from personnel," he said. "I just suggested she stop by and see how the celebrating was doing."

"This someone have a name?" I asked.

He laughed and wagged a fat finger at me. "You know the rules on dating someone in the company."

I smiled. "You were the one that sent her, remember?"

"Not to screw your eyes out," Bob said, shaking his head and pretending to laugh. "Now, can we get to work and leave your personal life outside these walls? What little I already know about it scares hell out of me."

I dropped the subject and Bob and I started in on the next project, working to get right-of-ways through some old family farms for a pipeline. But I had no idea of letting the chase for the blonde from personnel go that easily. When I got my teeth into something like this, I never let go until it was finished.

While Bob was off with the higher-ups having a two-drink, two-hour lunch, I told my secretary I was not to be disturbed, then used my company security clearance to access employee records on a secure screen on my computer.

Sometimes certain legal work required me to do just that, so no one would think what I was doing odd if they noticed at all. It didn't take much of a scan of the people who worked in personnel to tell me that part of Bob's story had been a flat out lie. But I didn't doubt she worked for the company. The question was in what department, and why hadn't I seen her before?

I used the fact that I hadn't seen her to eliminate a dozen different departments I worked in and around regularly, depending on the project. But that still left over five hundred personnel photos to go through.

It took me until two in the afternoon.

She wasn't there.

So who was she, and why had Bob been surprised I had remembered her? She was clearly doing a favor of some sort for him. And the way he had acted, knowledge of her was not something Bob was willing to share.

I sat back, put my feet up on my desk, and covered my eyes, trying to sort out all the details like a giant legal puzzle.

I still believed she worked somewhere in the company. That was the way

Bob lied, with half-truths, or truths that left out real basic information.

And I believed now that she had been sent to give me something she called a "boost." More than likely some sort of drug or something on her hands. The fog about last night had now completely cleared and I had a very real memory of what her touch had done to me. If it was a drug, I didn't much like that idea at all. I took my share of alcohol, but drugs were not something I did, or ever wanted to do. Too damn scary, and too much chance of messing with my mind. I made my money with my mind. I ruin that and it would be all over.

She had to work here somewhere, but where?

I looked up the official number of employees in the company from the records I had just gone through, then went into the payroll records and asked how many people were drawing official compensation.

Bingo.

The number was different by one.

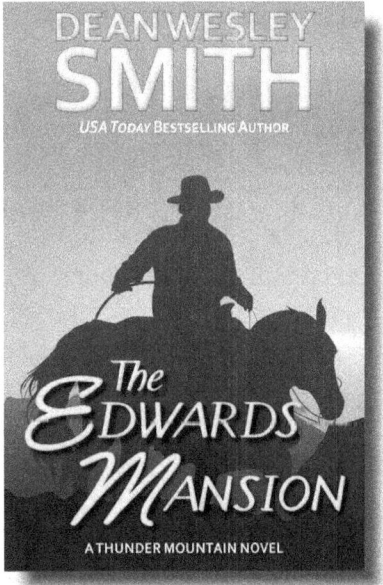

Two Thunder Mountain Novels
Available at your favorite booksellers.

So somewhere, this company had a secret employee, and I had no doubt that when I found that employee, it would be a beautiful blonde with wonderful brown eyes and a very scary touch.

CHAPTER THREE

I HAD very little time over the next three days to continue the search for my elusive Blonde Booster, as I was starting to call her. But then, on Saturday, Bob didn't come in, and I was pretty much alone in the building. When I worked a Saturday or a Sunday, I was often one of the only few people in the big, ten-story building. I always got a lot done and liked the quiet. Besides, except for drinking at night and searching for blondes to take home, I didn't have a hell of a lot more to my life than work. Kind of sad when I thought about it, but I didn't much think about it that often.

This Saturday I liked the quiet for another reason. I had a quest.

Instead of going out last night, I had actually stayed at home with take-out Chinese food and studied floor plans and office layouts of the entire company building. There were only a few offices not clearly marked, and those would be my first targets.

I arrived at my office around ten, carrying a large mocha coffee and wearing jeans and a sweater. The old suit and tie were just not needed on a Saturday.

I took the floor plans out of my briefcase and spread them over my desk, studying them once again while I sipped the wonderful flavor of my coffee. Somewhere in this building the Blonde Booster might have an office. If she did,

I was going to find it. If she worked from home, then I'd go into personnel records next, working through the payroll until I found out where her checks went. Having high-level security clearance sure came in handy sometimes.

I was staring at the map when a soft voice said from the door, "Looking for me?"

I somehow managed to remain fairly contained, and didn't snort any coffee out of my nose, which, considering the surprise I felt, was a miracle.

"Actually, I was," I said.

She was more beautiful than I remembered. Long, blonde hair flowed down over her shoulders, and her eyes were round, her smile real. She wore a baggy sweater and jeans with tennis shoes, but even that dressed down, nothing about her amazing body was really hidden.

She moved over to my desk, glanced down at the floor plans of the big structure, and then pointed with a fantastically perfect finger and short fingernail to one office that wasn't marked. "That's my office."

"That was going to be my second stop," I said. "Do you have a name?"

"Glenda," she said. "For now, just call me Glenda."

I pointed to a chair on the other side of my desk and then sat down as she did, keeping the desk between me and her. No way I wanted to get near that booster touch of hers again. Or at least not right away. I needed some answers first.

"I'm guessing from Bob's reaction that it's a surprise that I remembered you."

"Not really," she said, shrugging. "I can only do so much on the memory fogging aspects. But it really doesn't matter anymore, since I got the last of what you had at the bar the other night."

I didn't much like the sounds of *that*, but she went on before I could ask what exactly I was now missing completely.

"Since I did," she said, holding my gaze, "you're going to be promoted upstairs next week, over Bob and into a VP position in management, and then you would have been told about my presence here anyway."

I had so many questions about all that she had said, I couldn't think of which one to ask first, so instead I just sipped my coffee and stared at her beautiful face. My goal was to be a vice president, then maybe even higher, but I sure hadn't expected it this soon, and not over the top of Bob.

I did a quick run-through of all the questions, then settled on starting with the most basic. "So, what's your official title here?"

"Keeper of the Morals," she said with as straight a face as I had ever seen.

"And your job description?" I asked, trying not to laugh at her.

She looked me right in the eye. "I extract and contain employee personal morals, mostly in the legal and management departments, so that they can work with the full interest of the corporation at heart."

"And just how do you do that?" I asked, remembering what I had been thinking about at the bar, how I had changed, how I had no idea how I had become the person I had become. That memory scared hell out of me suddenly.

And made me angry at the same time. I didn't much like the idea of something being taken from me without my knowledge, especially under orders from Bob.

"Magic," she said. "Every major corporation has someone like me, a person

of magic who can, for a fee, do as asked. And I have to admit, my fee is *very* high."

She smiled at that. She clearly enjoyed money as much as I did.

"I'll bet," I said, trying but failing to push all the memories of what I used to think, how I used to feel about the job I now did.

"Remembering your morals, aren't you?" she asked, smiling at me.

"I have to admit I am. And you're starting to scare me, to be honest with you."

She laughed. "Take a deep breath and look at those memories, at how you used to be. You're going to be a vice president of this company, with a big office two more floors up. Do you really care about how you used to feel when you drove that Volkswagen and camped out at music concerts?"

I started to say that I did, then realized she was right. I didn't care. But I didn't care because she had taken that caring from me. She and Bob.

"What did you do to me?" I asked.

"The first day you were here at work, we met. Remember?"

I started to shake my head, then suddenly the memory of her shaking my hand and holding onto it that first day came flooding back. We had spent a wonderful lunch and afternoon together, talking, laughing, touching.

The memory of that fantastic day flooded back over me like a wet dream. "We went back to my place that night, didn't we?"

She nodded.

I remembered now that I felt like I had fallen in love with her in that one short day. How could I have forgotten that? It still felt like I was in love with her now that I remembered. No wonder I kept going home with blondes. I had been looking for Glenda all this time.

I shook my head. I hadn't felt this far off balance in years. I looked into those wonderful eyes and managed to get out my question again. "What *exactly* did you do to me?"

She shrugged. "I used my magic to take your morals, so you could be a better attorney for the company. That's all. Got the last of a vast supply the other night in the bar."

I wanted to shout at her, call her a common thief, but my legal mind just wasn't believing what she was saying. My memories of my actions, of how I used to feel and think, were clear. I used to care about something more than money and a bigger house.

But now that was all I cared about.

That thought hit me like a hammer to the skull, and I knew, without a doubt, she had done just what she said she had done. She had taken all my caring away.

And the moment I accepted that, my mind snapped back to clear thinking and I knew what I had to do.

"I seem to remember that afternoon and evening as being very special, at least to me. You do that with all the lawyers?"

She actually had the decency to blush. "No, only you. You were my first, and the only since. I've been just waiting until this day came, so I could show myself to you again."

I stood and moved around my desk, kneeling at the side of her chair and touching her wonderful soft skin. "You could still care about a man who has had his morals destroyed?"

"I'm pretty sure that not having morals doesn't mean you can't still love," she said, putting her other hand on mine and holding me to her. "And I didn't destroy

them. They're just stored, just like all the others."

"You're not kidding, are you?"

"Not kidding," she said softly.

"And you can put them back into people?"

She nodded and said nothing.

I laughed and stood, moving away from her, pacing, thinking. I often did some of my best thinking while pacing. I was angry, in love, and scared to death about what had been done to me. I needed to get those thoughts sorted out so that my next action wouldn't be completely stupid.

All the time I paced she sat silently, watching me.

Finally, I needed a little more information before I went any farther. I turned to her frowning and worried face. "How easy are these morals moved around and put into people?"

She held up what looked like a small fountain pen. "I have yours right in here. I promised myself I would give them back to you if you asked. That's how much I care about you."

That thought suddenly set me back.

"All my morals fit into a pen?" I asked, stunned. "Guess I didn't have that many, huh?"

"Highly compacted," she said. "You had an overabundance of them, to be honest."

"Yeah, I remember that," I said, laughing. "But for the time being, put that away. I don't want to accidentally get them back just yet."

She now looked puzzled, then the pen vanished back into her baggy sweater somehow. Maybe later, if things went the way I was hoping, I'd get to inspect those pockets a little closer.

"One more question," I said. "Who ordered you to take those from me?"

"Bob," she said. "With approval of the president of the company."

I nodded. That was all I needed.

"I think I owe you a long, early lunch, don't you?" I said, smiling at Glenda. "You saved me a lot of searching around the building."

She still looked worried, but I had a hunch if this woman could really do what she said she had done, and liked money as much as I did, then we were going to be very, very happy for a time in the very near future.

I took her by the arm, and like a modern version of Ken and Barbie, dressed down, we headed to lunch.

CHAPTER FOUR

I ESCORTED Glenda to this fantastic, small restaurant where I knew we could talk for hours and not be disturbed. Over chicken slices and strong cups of mocha, we discovered we really liked each other. And that we both had the same goals, to be fantastically wealthy and powerful.

And I came to remember that even with my morals, I had wanted that same goal. Only I had planned on doing really good things with all the money once I got it.

I asked her why she just couldn't magic-up money and she said it didn't work that way. Her talents were more personal based, either giving someone good feelings or taking feelings from them. That's why the company had hired her to help them with the attorneys and management teams.

"Better than what a lot of my type do for money," she said, looking very alluringly at me.

"What's that?"

"Call girls, dating services," she said. "We can *really* make a man feel good."

"I've noticed that."

"I'm not doing anything," she said, laughing.

"I'm kind of wondering why not?"

"Yeah, me too," she said, smiling a smile at me that I would never forget.

With that, we moved to my house, with me breaking far too many speed limits along the way. We barely managed to get inside and to the bed before working as much magic on each other as we could do.

In the euphemistic sense of course.

More directly, we had great sex. Better than great, actually. But I won't go there.

Finally, after who knows how long, we both lay there exhausted. And for the first time, I didn't want this blonde to leave. I wanted her to stay right beside me.

"So, what exactly can you do with my morals?"

Naked, laying there with her golden body facing me, she suddenly become very worried again. No doubt she thought I might ask for them back, and to be honest, I had thought about getting them back into me as quickly as possible. Not much thought, but the idea did sound right. They had been taken, I wanted them back, just like anything else I owned that was taken.

"You said you can put them back, right?"

She nodded.

"Can you put mine, or Bob's, or the president's, or someone in general from the corporate supply into someone else?"

She now looked puzzled, then nodded. "I don't see why not."

"And even though what you give

them is not their own morals, they would still work?"

"Sure. I'm sure it would be as if they got their own back."

I kissed her, then said, "How about we use that vast supply you have in storage to sabotage our company's rivals? Think we could do that?"

She blinked once, then twice, as if not really hearing me.

"You and me," I said, stroking the soft skin on her arm. "Working together. You get the morals into some of those decision-makers in other companies, cripple them with good intentions and feelings for the underdogs, and I'll take advantage of the situation. Together, we can make a fortune and just keep on moving up in the company."

Again she blinked, then she moved into me with her full body and kissed me like I had never been kissed before. Clearly, she liked my idea. I had no doubt that a woman who could steal other's morals for corporate and personal gain would like it.

The rest of that afternoon and evening we did things sexually I had never done before, or thought possible. Amazing how the promise of a lot of money and a little lack of morals can motivate a person. And I'm sure there was some magic involved as well.

CHAPTER FIVE

SIX MONTHS LATER, I moved into my new corner office on the tenth floor, right next to Glenda's and two doors down from the president's office. Given a little time, that office could be mine as well if I wanted it. I didn't want it.

The view out my window was stunning, looking out over the city. I had gone through two levels of vice presidents since my move out of the legal department. My official title was now Executive Vice President in Charge of Corporate Acquisitions. And I had bought enough of the company stock that, if I wanted to, I could have a seat on the Board of Directors.

I didn't want that any more than I wanted to be president. And besides, most of my stock was in special holding corporations very hard to trace back to me.

I just wanted to be rich. Fantastically rich. And I was almost there.

In my top drawer was the pen that held my morals, locked away safely. Glenda had told me how the pen inserter worked and let me keep it just to make sure it didn't get mixed up with all the other morals we were taking from the corporate 'morals pool.'

Over the past six months, Glenda and I spent every night together in my big new mansion. Next month we had decided I was buying a yacht. All of it was in my name, of course.

I had taken care of dear old Bob quickly after moving upstairs. A little planted evidence and a double dose of morals from Glenda sent him scampering. The little bastard was working as a legal aide down in a shelter and living in a studio apartment after his wife had kicked him out. Served the bastard right for stealing from me.

Now, it was time to put the rest of my plan in motion. With one last look at the fantastic view from the office I had worked so hard to get to, I unlocked my drawer and took out the magic pen holding my morals, then tucked it safely in my pocket.

Then I quickly went over my resignation letter. It said what I needed it to say. I had moved nothing into my office that I wanted to keep. There was nothing about this job that I cared about. Nothing to pack. Having no morals could make you feel that way.

All I ever wanted was the chase, the hunt, the excitement of the search, keeping score with the money. I had been that way even before having my morals stolen.

Now, things were going to get really exciting.

After six months, I had convinced myself that I didn't much care about Glenda either. After all, she was the one who took from me what was mine. There would be other blondes I was sure. Granted, Glenda was damn fun in bed, but as she had told me that first afternoon, many witches were good in bed. It came with the magic.

Sally was almost as good as Glenda. I had met Sally two weeks ago, when she joined Glenda and me for a little three-way afternoon fling. And with a little training from me on some of Glenda's special moves, Sally would be almost as good.

I dropped off my resignation letter with the president's secretary. Then dropped off my good-bye letter in Glenda's office. I told her that her things had already been moved out of my house and which storage unit she could find them in. Granted, it was a cold way to end a relationship, but what did she expect from someone who didn't care? She knew what she had gotten into with me. After all, she was the one who took all my caring and stored it in a magic pen.

On the way down to the main entrance, I stopped off in the basement and slipped a tiny, but very powerful device

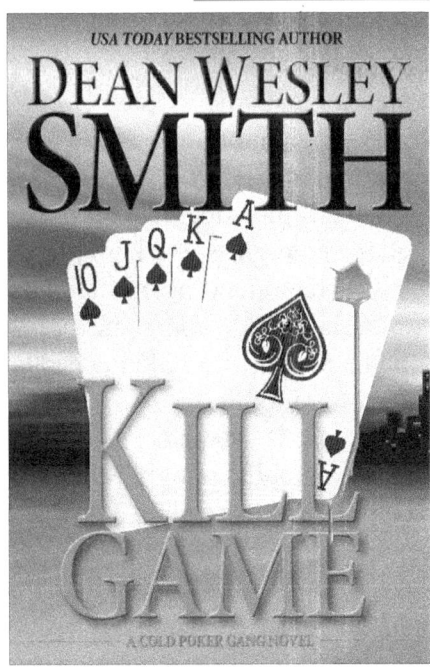

into the main air flow duct. Glenda and I had come up with the device to use on other corporations, and it had worked wonderfully, spreading morals throughout a building in high doses; so high that often before I could schedule a corporate takeover, the company was dissolving into chaos.

This company, in a short time, would be experiencing the same thing. Glenda would be able to stop some of it if she wanted to, but not enough, and I doubted she would even try.

I had six more of the tiny morals bombs in my briefcase.

I made sure I was outside the building before the thing triggered and started giving back all the corporate executives and lawyers their morals. In very high doses.

The next morning I called my six different stock brokers and put in orders to short a large chunk of my corporate stock, buying options on some more and running puts. I had no doubt the stock was going down, and I was going to make a ton of money on the way down.

Six weeks later, I was richer than I had ever imagined as my former company stock hit bottom and was bought up by yet another rival. During those weeks, Glenda had tried to call me twice, but both times Sally answered the phone.

Sally said Glenda was crying, which meant that she too had been dosed. All I could do was shrug. What did Glenda expect, anyway? The sex had been good, she should let it go.

I didn't tell Sally that I dreamed of Glenda every night, and imagined having sex with her when I was with Sally. I figured that given enough time, that would change. But so far it hadn't.

CHAPTER SIX

TEN MONTHS LATER, I had bought massive amounts of stock in six other companies, morals-bombed them, and then got even richer as they crashed and I shorted the stock all the way down. I had become a morals terrorist, destroying companies by making them do the right things. I was sure my bleeding-heart liberal self would be proud of me.

By this time, Sally was also a distant memory, just like I had hoped Glenda would become. Now I spent every night back at Danny's Crib, getting drunk and searching for that perfect woman. Blonde, of course.

None of them measured up to Glenda, but I still searched.

Tonight seemed to be no different than any of the others, yet it was. I knew I was done for the moment, the big plan finished, the last stock sold. I was so rich, it seemed almost silly to keep going. But I knew I wanted more.

I swirled my scotch, letting the ice clink against the side. I could feel it through the cold glass, but I couldn't hear the ice over the pounding of the loud music. I was sitting on the same bar stool that I had been on when Glenda had taken the last of my morals.

My world, it seemed, had come full circle. Now, finally tonight, over a year after that night, was as good a time as any to get who I really was back.

I took out the magic pen I had been carrying for the past month. It was time to retrieve what had been taken from me, to become a whole person again.

I was fantastically rich, I could use that money for some of the causes I supported before I took the corporate job. And the old me would be proud of the fact that I had brought seven greedy corporate giants to their knees. I was sure of that.

I took a quick drink of the scotch, set the glass on the napkin, then without another thought, placed the pen against my skin on my palm and triggered it.

It was as if I had a bad cold that suddenly had cleared up. Everything I had done over the past years in my corporate job came flashing back to me like a movie in fast forward.

And then I suddenly realized how many people I had hurt along the way.

I could almost feel their pain.

Bob, Glenda, Sally, a hundred different blondes, and thousands of employees with families and jobs.

I had hurt them all.

And suddenly I knew that. And suddenly I cared.

"Oh, no, what have I done?" I shouted into the loud music.

And with that I broke down right there on the bar.

And I couldn't stop sobbing into my arm. The bartender finally had me escorted outside and I sat in my new Porsche in the parking lot, banging my hands on the steering wheel and shouting at nothing while I sobbed.

I just couldn't stop.

I had hurt so many people. I could almost feel all their pain, understand everything I had put them through. It was like waves washing over me. Every memory, every deed suddenly was real, had real people attached, had real consequences.

I had nothing to live for any more.

I was the lowest of scum.

I had guns, lots of guns, back in my house. Just one with one bullet would end

this, take these thoughts, these memories away, these feelings away.

As I reached to start the car, Glenda climbed into the passenger seat. It took me a moment to realize who it was.

"I was wondering how long it would be before you took back your morals."

All I could do was sob that I was sorry. So sorry.

I had never felt so sorry for anything in my entire life. I had loved Glenda, had hurt her.

I didn't deserve to live.

"I know you are sorry," she said, her voice cutting through the massive waves of self-pity and sadness for what I had done.

Her hand touched me, that wonderful hand, and I suddenly started feeling calmer.

"I'll take about half," she said. "Then we can talk. Is that all right with you?"

All I could do was nod. At this point, I needed anything to make this pain go away.

She kept stroking my arm and I calmed down, got a part of my brain back, got some basic control of myself.

Finally, she stopped. I could feel all the remorse and sadness for my actions, but only as background thoughts. My brain was back.

I turned to stare at her. "You knew I would take my morals back?"

"Of course," she said. "From that first moment in your office. I had money in dummy corporations and shorted our company's stock just like you did as it went down. I got almost as rich as you did."

I sat there for a moment, my mouth opening and closing, realizing just how smart Glenda was, how she had played me just as I had played her.

"And the other corporations?" I asked. "You were following me, weren't you?"

"Of course," she said. "I love you, remember? But that didn't stop me from making even more money while you were doing what you were doing."

I could feel the guilt starting to come up again from what morals she had left in me. She could clearly see it as well.

"You need another little bit drained off?"

I nodded, and she touched me again, and like climbing a long staircase, I got closer to thinking even clearer, like coming out of a dark basement into the light of day.

"Thanks," I said. "I would have killed myself if you hadn't come along."

"I know," she said, her voice sad. "No person with as many morals as you had to start with could live with what you've done over the last few years."

"So, after what I did to you, why did you save me?"

"Love," she said. And then she smiled that smile I had come to know so well. "And greed. We make a really great team."

"Yeah, but you'll never trust me again."

She laughed. "I didn't trust you the first time. Any more than you trusted me. But the sex was great. That's good enough to base a pretty good relationship on, don't you think?"

With that, she actually managed to make me laugh a little, which came out like a hiccup.

I turned in the car seat to face her. "Yeah, it was. I must admit, I've missed that. And I've missed you, every day. I was just so damn angry with you for taking something of mine."

"I know," she said. "But this time you wanted me to take them. And you can have them back any time you want."

I held up my hand. "No, let's just leave it at this level for the moment. Small enough to not control my thoughts, but not completely gone."

"That was the level I settled on for myself as well," she said.

I realized, right at that moment, staring into those golden eyes and smiling face, that I never wanted to hurt her in any way again.

"I really do love you," I said.

"I know," she said. "I love you as well."

"So how come I didn't feel that when I had no morals?"

She shrugged. "I have a hunch that without morals, you don't care about anyone else but yourself. And love requires that caring to work for any length of time."

I nodded, deciding I'd just accept that for the moment and think about it later, when all the swirling emotions were a little more under control.

"So what next?" I asked.

She laughed. "Well, I'm blonde."

"Right on that," I said.

"And I have it on good authority you like picking up blondes in this bar here." She pointed to the front door of Danny's Crib.

"Right again," I said, smiling at her.

"So how about you take me back to that obscenely large mansion of yours and show me what tricks you've learned in bed over the last ten months."

"I'd love to," I said. "And you can show me what you've learned."

"Not a thing," she said. "I've just been waiting for you."

Again, I just sat there, my mouth opening and closing like a damn fish out of water. I stared at her, into those wonderful golden eyes, taking in that fantastic smile. And I let myself feel the love for her, the emotions of sadness at what I had done to her, and the fantastic feeling of happiness that she actually wanted me back, and had waited.

It seems we had a lot of real feelings to talk about.

But that could wait. Sex came first.

Lots and lots of sex.

She was a blonde, I had picked her up at Danny's Crib, just like all the others. But I had a feeling, an honest feeling, that this time, she would be the last blonde I ever picked up there.

And it was a feeling I liked.

Some Classic Dean Wesley Smith Stories
Available at your favorite booksellers.

Dee W. Schofield

Can a nude and
very magical guy
with a lot of hair
change everything?

Iron Eyebrows

A Romance With Too Much Hair

Maria Webb hated men with too much body hair.

But then a magical guy with a lot of hair came striding nude toward her on the beach and everything changed.

This time she fell in love with a man with very bushy eyebrows and some special talents that no one would have expected to find with a nude man on a nude beach.

Published under the pen name Dee W. Schofield.

IRON EYEBROWS
A Romance with Too Much Hair

MARIA WEBB watched with growing disgust as the brown-haired, naked man strolled down the beach along the water line toward her and Cindie. He seemed like he didn't have a care in the world, the white towel over his shoulder, his private parts swinging back and forth like a clapper in a church bell. The long brown hair that covered most of his body blew in the faint breeze and seemed to ripple over his body like waves on a glistening lake.

She hated hairy men. Her counselor said her hatred came from her short-lived first marriage to Ben. Seven months, actually, but they had only been together for two of those seven months. Ben had a lot of hair, and when they first met as freshmen in college, she had loved running her fingers through the long hair on his chest and back. Now, after he had gone and slept with five other women by the second month and then left her, the idea of running her fingers through any man's hair just made her shudder.

The guy walking toward them down the beach was certainly hairy. More than she had ever seen before, but she had to admit he was built better than Ben had been, not only in both muscles, but in other ways. She could tell that even from a hundred paces.

He had very broad shoulders and a walk that just sang of confidence. Maybe too much confidence. Arrogance was more like it.

Of course, he was completely naked, so he had to have confidence, even though they were on a nudist beach.

She went back to reading her Kindle, trying to lose herself in the newest J.D. Robb book, a blue towel over her naked butt, her breasts pressed enough into the towel and the sand below that she wasn't exposing anything.

Cindie, on the other hand sat upright, her knees up to her chin, exposing things that never should be seen on a public beach as she painted her toenails like she was sitting alone in their apartment back off the Oregon State University campus.

Maria couldn't believe she had ever let Cindie talk her into getting an "overall tan" on a nudist beach while they were on spring break in California. Cindie might be tanning parts that shouldn't ever see the sun, but no way was Maria going to tan anything but her back. Just the idea of getting a sunburn on her butt scared her enough to keep that part covered.

As the guy got closer, Maria again glanced up and then flat stared. The guy's hair seemed to be vanishing. And with each step that he got closer, more of his hair disappeared. Including the brown hair on his head. Only his pubic hair seemed to be staying.

And his thick eyebrows.

He was going to walk along the water line about ten paces in front of them.

Cindie, focused on her nails, hadn't even seen him.

Maria just stared. By the time he was almost even with them he was essentially hairless except for the two places. And his body was a stunner, his muscles rippling in the warm spring air.

Suddenly he looked over and smiled.

It felt like the old cliché electric shock had hit her. He was the most attractive man she had ever seen.

Ever.

But she was sure he had been covered with hair at first. But no one got rid of body hair like that. It must have been the sun and her overactive focus on ex-husband Ben playing tricks with her mind.

Her counselor back in Oregon next week was going to have a field day with this.

"Is there something wrong?" the man asked as he stopped right in front of them and stared at Maria. He had the decency to bring his towel down and around his waist as she looked up.

Cindie also glanced up, then immediately put her legs down and together as she sucked in a breath.

"Excuse me?" Maria asked.

"You seemed to be frowning," the man said, his voice deep and almost hypnotic. "I noticed you watching me as I came up the beach; I hope I didn't do something wrong."

Cindie glanced at Maria, clearly shocked, then back at the man. Of the two of them, it was always Cindie who did the flirting while Maria held back and stayed out of the way.

"No, nothing," Maria said, shaking her head. "The light was such that I thought you were covered with a lot of hair is all."

"And you don't like men with a lot of hair?" he asked, smiling at her, and making her sweat even more in the warm afternoon sun. This guy was a real charmer.

"I don't," Maria said.

The man ran his hand over his bald head. "Not a problem then."

Maria laughed, a kind of high-school giggle. "No problem at all."

"I love your laugh," the man said, holding Maria's gaze.

Maria was sure she was blushing, but hoped her sun-red face didn't show it.

"My name is Jason," the man said.

"Maria and Cindie," Maria said before Cindie could say anything.

"Very nice to meet you both," he said, bowing slightly.

Maria could feel her mind spinning as she just couldn't look away from his eyes and that wonderful chiseled face and bald head. What she really wanted was to rub her hands over his head. Maybe he needed some suntan lotion on some of that exposed skin.

She shook her head, trying to clear the thoughts.

He continued to smile at Maria, then with that voice that seemed to just fill the warm air, he asked, "I assume you are not from around here."

"Oregon," Maria said, smiling back. "Not used to this sun, so we have to be careful. How do you manage to not burn?"

He laughed. "I'm from San Diego so I'm used to it, but it still takes lots of lotion. In fact, I've been walking for a ways. If you wouldn't mind, could I borrow a little of your lotion?"

"No problem," Maria said.

She reached over beside Cindie and grabbed the bottle, catching Cindie's puzzled expression. Cindie hadn't even said a word, which was very, very strange for her. In fact, Cindie started to open her mouth to say something, then just shook her head and closed it again.

Jason sat down on the sand next to Maria, keeping the white towel around his waist in perfect position to not show anything.

Maria actually felt both relief and disappointment. Again she shook the thought away

She started to hand the bottle to him, but he shifted slightly so his back was toward her with the shining skin and rippling muscles.

"Would you mind putting some on my back?"

Beside her Cindie coughed lightly, but still said nothing.

"Sure. Would love to," Maria said.

She sat up, leaving the towel on the sand. Her breasts were now exposed to the California sun and the man sitting next to her.

As she started to rub the lotion over Jason's back, part of her mind was just enjoying the wonderful feeling of once again touching a man while another part of her mind kept asking, *What are you doing?*

It was spring break, she was enjoying herself, that's what she was doing.

"Would you get the back of my neck as well?" Jason asked.

"Glad to," she said, letting her hands roam all over his large, smooth back and up to his neck.

It must have been the sun and her overactive focus on ex-husband Ben playing tricks with her mind.

After a moment he broke the wonderful feeling and said, "Okay, my turn to get your back."

He turned around and took the bottle as Maria turned to face Cindie, who was sitting there staring, her mouth open. They had been roommates since Maria and Ben had broken up. Cindie knew more about Maria than anyone else, and Maria knew for a fact her actions were surprising her roommate right at this moment.

She was surprising herself, actually.

Then Jason's hands started rubbing in the lotion, working his strong fingers all over her back, and she wanted to just melt. It wasn't as if the afternoon sun wasn't hot enough, in a moment she was sweating like she was in a sauna just from his touch.

Twice he brushed near the sides of her breasts, both times her breath caught. And she damn near choked when his hands went down near the crack of her butt.

His fingers worked the lotion into her skin in a way that felt heavenly.

After what seemed like the shortest eternity she had ever lived through, he patted her shoulder and said, "That part is all protected for a while. Has anyone ever told you that you have wonderful skin?"

"You have fantastic hands," she said, turning as he poured more lotion on his hands and started to rub it on his chest.

"It's my job," he said. "I'm a massage therapist."

She took the bottle of lotion from him and sprayed some on both of her breasts and started to rub it around, hoping he would notice, which he seemed to a couple of times. But both times he quickly averted his gaze out over the calm ocean.

A real gentleman.

With very, very thick eyebrows. Now that she was sort of facing him up close, she couldn't believe the bushiness of his eyebrows. And they really stood out because of his bald head.

And then she remembered how she had thought he looked at first, covered in hair almost completely. But now he didn't even have any hair on his arms or legs.

And some voice in the back of her head warned her that something wasn't right. She just kept staring at his eyebrows, and with each passing second they seemed to get thicker and even bushier, if that was possible.

He smiled. "Some people think they are my best feature. Others have called me *Iron Eyebrows.*"

She jerked and looked into his eyes. They were brown, deep brown, and his gaze was something she wanted to lose herself in. And in his wonderful body.

But the voice in the back of her mind kept bothering her. So she thought clearly at him. *Can you read my mind?*

He turned away, then his voice came back into her mind clearly. *Yes, but only surface thoughts. But I find you so attractive I just wanted to please you.*

Now that was enough to make her jump a little and glance at Cindie, who still just sat silently watching.

"I'll prove it to you," he said out loud. "Look at my eyes and let me open up to you."

She didn't want to. The chance that someone could really read her mind and all her secrets scared her to death.

But still she looked into his eyes and suddenly she was inside his head, knowing everything about him. He actually did work as a massage therapist in San Diego, and liked sunbathing and walking in the nude.

He had had an awful childhood, treated like a freak by everyone around him until he moved away from his Montana home to Southern California where he didn't let anyone know his secret.

He used his talents to read surface thoughts of customers' minds to give them perfect massages, exactly what they wanted.

He had suggested that Cindie not talk and implanted the thought in her head, so Cindie kept forgetting what she wanted to say when she opened her mouth.

He was single and had the ability to slightly change his appearance to please someone, something that he had only told three people. Two had run away. She was the third.

He hoped she wouldn't run as well.

And he was really, really attracted to her. He didn't understand why but he was.

Just as she was really, really attracted to him.

And he couldn't change his eyebrows.

"I could trim them, maybe," he said out loud. "But they grow back quickly, sometimes overnight."

She laughed. Then she asked, "Are you controlling my thoughts?"

"No," he said, shaking his head and looking worried. She liked that look on him almost as much as she liked his smile.

She could tell, since he left his mind open to her, that he really was concerned. Concerned he would scare her. That they were moving far, far too fast. That he had trusted someone he didn't know.

And suddenly she could tell that he had told the truth, he really hadn't looked into her mind past the surface thoughts.

He really didn't know her and hadn't pried.

"How do I open my mind to you?" she asked.

"Just give me permission," he said.

"That's damn scary," she said.

He nodded. "I know."

She took a deep breath and decided to go for it. "You've shown me around your place, you should see mine before we go any farther."

He nodded and suddenly she could feel another person in her mind, gently looking around. It felt very, very strange as thoughts and memories came up she hadn't thought of for a very long time. He could see everything about her short marriage, about graduate school, about what she liked about sex.

Within a few seconds he knew more about her than anyone ever had. He knew her favorite foods, her inability to ride a bike, even her deepest secret of lusting after a teacher when she was eighteen.

Then he was gone.

And his mind was closed to her as well.

For the first time in a long time she felt very alone.

And that surprised her. She was an independent woman who didn't mind being alone.

She had *loved* having him in her mind. She had loved seeing into his mind as well. It was like a speed date only really, *really* getting to know everything about someone in just seconds instead of years.

She knew so many things about him, she didn't want to be turned away now.

"Did you see something you didn't like?" she asked, very worried

He smiled and opened his mind to her again. What he was thinking was about how much more he liked her now, more than ever after seeing her true self. And how he wanted to get her into bed.

And spend time with her.

Lots of time.

That's why he had closed off his mind. He was embarrassed by those thoughts.

"I like that idea as well," she said out loud, smiling. "How about we go for a walk and get to know each other even better?"

"I would like that very much," he said, his smile beaming.

And she could tell he really, *really* meant that as well from his thoughts.

Maria stood, taking the towel that had been over her butt and tossing it over her shoulder.

"I'll be back in a half hour," she said to Cindie. "We're just going to take a walk."

Cindie, looking completely stunned at the sudden change in her roommate, nodded and didn't say anything.

I really love that you can silence my wonderful roommate. Normally she can really talk your ear off. Can you teach me that trick?

He smiled. *You never know.*

Jason took his towel and put it over his shoulder as well.

Then Maria took his hand and through his touch could feel his mind again, open and happy.

And with a thought she invited him back into her mind.

It felt right. Perfect, actually.

"I thought you didn't like being nude out in public," he said, smiling as they started off.

"After what you've seen in my head, there's no reason in covering up anything is there?"

"You have a point," he said, laughing. *Besides you have a wonderful body. You don't want to cover it up.*

"Thank you," she said. "Am I blushing?"

"Too much sun to tell."

She could tell from his mind that he was fibbing. She was blushing and he liked it.

"Do me a favor," Maria said. "Let the hair grow on your back as we walk away. Might as well really give Cindie something to talk about, when she can remember again what she wants to say."

He laughed and Maria knew, without looking, that the hair was long and thick on his back again. And maybe, just maybe some day, she would enjoy running her fingers through it.

"I hope so," he said. "I would enjoy that."

"I'm starting to think I would as well. Given time."

"We've got the time," he said.

Hand-in-hand and thought-to-thought, they walked down the beach together, naked, in more ways than one.

~

Now Available
from all your favorite booksellers
in trade paper and electronic editions.

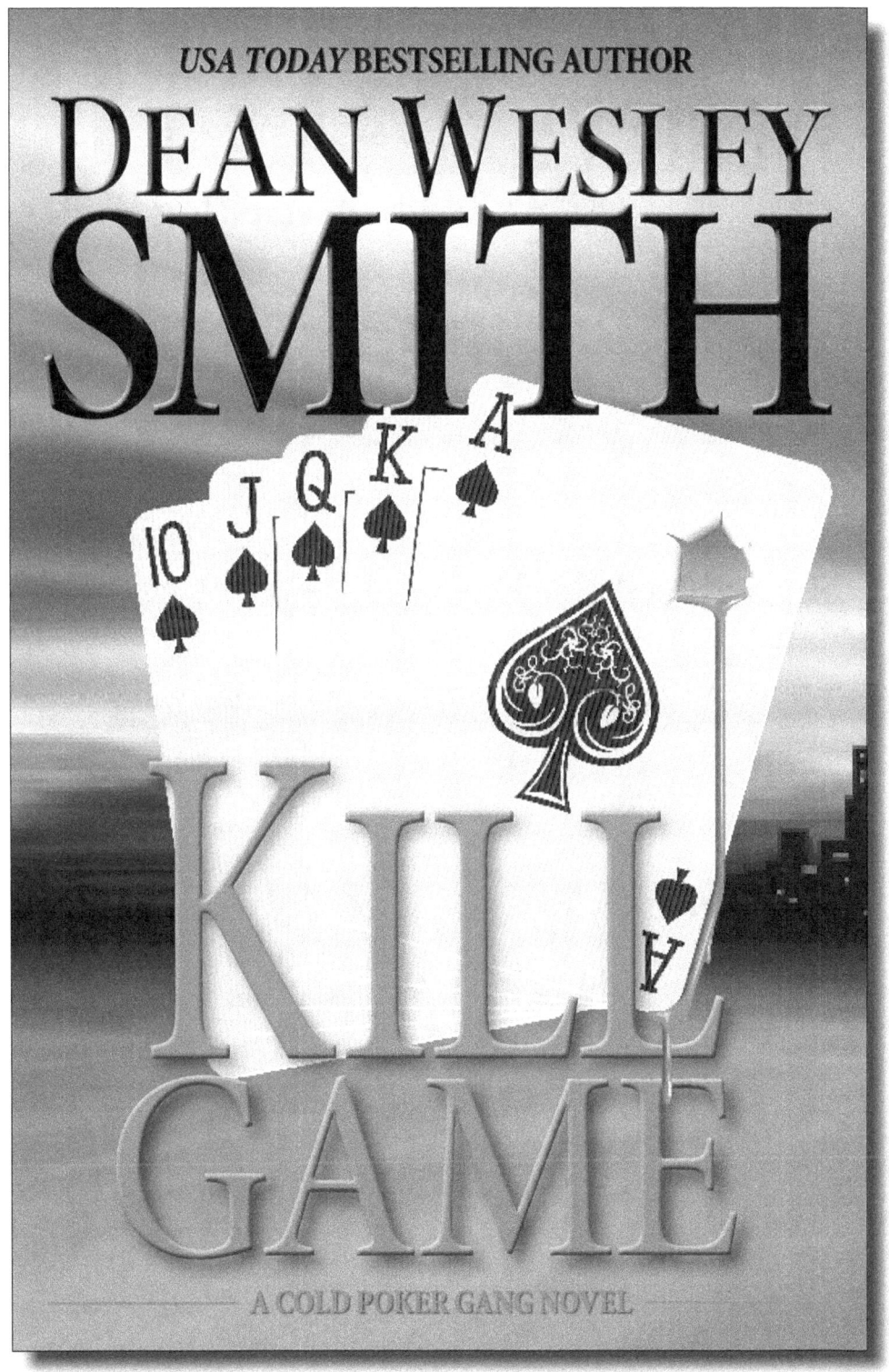

Dean Wesley Smith

USA Today **Bestselling Writer**

**She Seduced Her Husband
and Changed the World**

Mom's Paradox

She seduced her husband and changed the world.

But she remembers only the act, and how great it felt, but nothing about the why.

A story of time travel and a paradox beyond killing your own mother.

"Mom's Paradox" was first published in 2001 in a slightly different form in Men Writing Science Fiction As Women *from DAW Books, edited by Mike Resnick and Martin H. Greenburg*

MOM'S PARADOX

ONE

I WOKE UP AS A WOMAN.

Not that I hadn't been a woman before that morning, before feeling those cotton sheets, smelling the faint scent of John beside me, hearing him snore deeply, the vibration shaking the queen-sized bed like a distant earthquake. It seemed I had a memory of going to sleep as a woman, lying there spent, but not satisfied from the too-short love-making.

I grew up a woman. The memories of my childhood, the pains of dating, of a first marriage, of childbirth were all there.

Yet—

For the first time this morning I awoke as a woman, *feeling* like a woman, as the sun filled the drapes with orange light. What a strange thing, to be a woman, yet have the feeling of waking up as one only this morning.

I lay there, letting John's snoring fill the small bedroom as I tried to place where the strange newness was coming from.

My name was Angie Sheldon. The man shaking the bed beside me was my husband. We had two kids, both just entering high school, a nice house just outside of Denver in an upscale neighborhood, not too many bills, and a decent retirement and college account. I could honestly say I wasn't unhappy with my marriage or with John, just not always satisfied. Yet that lack of satisfaction had never been strong enough to force me to make any changes. I loved John and my kids, so the feeling wasn't coming from there.

Yet I felt wonderful, freeing, almost as if I were alive for the first time just now, this morning.

I focused on more details. I took my creative energy and drive out on my job with a law firm downtown. Both John and I were attorneys, and had met in law school. Now he worked for the District Attorney and I spent my time on business cases for the state's third largest business law firm.

That wasn't it. Nothing felt right or new about the job either. It was just the job I had been doing for years.

But still it was wonderful to wake up a woman.

I eased over onto my side so my back was to John and stared at the dresser with the pictures of our kids, Beth and Danny. I could see them clearly in the morning light. My parents were dead, John's parents still lived in California. Nothing there to cause this wonderful emotion of newness and happiness.

I couldn't remember the last time I had just stopped and looked at my life. It felt as if I was starting fresh this morning. Why?

Because I am starting fresh this morning. Or actually I will be shortly.

The other woman's voice inside my head damned near sent me screaming from the bed. Yet somehow my muscles didn't jerk, I didn't even jump or move, as if I were pinned there, staring at the dresser. But inside my head I was screaming. I could feel my heart pounding, like someone trying to beat her way out of my chest.

Calm down. This is strange enough as it is. Don't make it worse.

I'm dreaming. That's it, I'm just dreaming. I had to be. I tried to calm myself with that thought.

No, you're not dreaming. And neither am I.

I'm going insane!

The panic was a giant ball in my throat. I willed myself to climb out of bed and run toward the bathroom, but my body stayed on its side beside my snoring husband. Nothing I could do seemed to make even my fingers twitch.

You're not insane and you can't move because I have control of your body. And to be honest with you, it feels damned strange. I can also hear everything you think, so calm down, would you?

I'm dreaming. I have to be dreaming.

No, you're not.

I have to be, or I'm going insane. There are no other choices.

Oh, sure there are. A ton of them, just none that you've thought of. And if I don't get you moving soon, some of those choices won't happen.

The newness and good sensation started to drop away, leaving me empty. John had accused me of taking the joy out of just about any situation I got into, but inside I knew I wasn't joyless. I just had a hard time letting go.

No shit. I could give you a hundred examples of how I know that.

I'm going insane. All I wanted to do was scream.

Can't you just relax and go with it? This is strange enough for me without you making it even worse.

Now I knew I had flipped out. "Gone around the bend" as John would say. I was asking myself to relax. This was the strangest dream I had ever had.

I give up.

The good feeling I had woke up with was now completely gone. Suddenly my body jerked into motion, climbing out of bed, shedding my cotton night-gown before I even got across the room. I just left it on the floor. I tried to stop, to pick up the nightgown, but my body was moving on its own. I wanted to scream for John to wake up and help me, but I couldn't.

Thank heavens for some things.

Only on special nights, with the kids gone, had I allowed myself to be nude like this, yet now I was walking out of the bedroom in the morning light, across the hall and into the bathroom. Luckily neither of the kids was awake yet.

Just settle back in there and relax. A little stop here to get rid of what is pressuring your bladder, then we get to the job at hand, so to speak.

The door is open!

As I said, settle down. What, hasn't anyone ever seen you pee?

No.

Oh, man, I just could never believe you were always this uptight, but the more times I do this, the more proof I get.

More times you do what? What is happening to me?

Nothing you're going to remember, so don't sweat it. In fact, I think I'm just going to shut this conversation off for a few minutes until I get you ready.

The blackness crept up from the corners of my mind like a curtain being drawn over everything. I fought it, but everything just got blacker. The last

Some Classic Dean Wesley Smith Stories
Available at your favorite booksellers.

thought I had was that they were going to find me, nude, on the bathroom floor. How embarrassing.

Oh, give it a rest.

TWO

I CAME BACK to awareness looking into John's face. I was back in bed, the bedroom door was closed, and the covers on the bed were pulled back and off.

You're going to have to help with some of this. I don't really have the stomach or the inclination to watch.

"This is a nice surprise," John said, smiling up at me. His hands were firmly on my hips.

At that point I realized that I was wearing my special occasion black nightgown, the one that John had bought for me just after our honeymoon. John had lost his pajama bottoms, and I was sitting on him as he moved under me.

And inside me!

Tell him you always liked mornings.

I wanted to scream, yet at the same time what John was doing felt wonderful. The short love-making last night had left me wanting and excited. At least the door was closed and the children weren't up yet. But I had no idea how I got into the black nightgown and in this position.

Don't question it. Just enjoy it, because I can't watch. Sorry, too weird.

I should stop. This isn't right. What is happening to me? I must be going insane. Voices inside my head telling me to seduce my husband. We have never done anything like this before.

Or in this position.

More information than I need.

John moved a little faster under me. "What got into you this morning?" he asked, his voice husky from the way we were moving together.

Let me give you just a little more help, then I'm going to shut myself out of this. I've had enough counseling as it is.

Suddenly the good feeling I had when I woke up rushed back through me, pushing all my doubts, my worries away like leaves in a strong wind.

I was a woman making love to the man she had loved for years. It felt great.

No better than great, it felt wonderful.

Perfect. I'll be back when this is over.

I seemed to forget where I was and what I was doing.

I wanted to forget.

Everything I had focused on the intense sensations of John inside me, the movement of our bodies, and the pleasure of letting go and just being a woman.

"Is it safe?" John asked, his voice low, his face beaming in the morning light.

I didn't answer him, and I didn't care that it wasn't. I just wanted to keep going, not let these feelings ever end.

The morning seemed to vanish as everything focused down to just John and me.

Then the release that had eluded me last night swept up over my body as I rode John, grinding down into him and forcing him to come with me.

A few moments, maybe minutes later, I collapsed beside him, not even caring that I wasn't covered.

"Wow," John said between gasps.

"Yeah," I managed to reply.

In all the years of being with John it had never been like that. Passion, filled with love and caring and wonderful sensations. Right at that moment I loved being a woman. And I loved being with John.

He leaned over and kissed me, gently at first, then hard. After a few moments he pulled back and smiled. "I have no idea what caused that, but whatever it was, don't fight it."

"Okay," I said, remembering the voice I thought I had heard inside my head earlier. What had I been thinking? Maybe it all came from not being satisfied last night. Right now I felt so good I didn't care.

He kissed me again, then rolled away, and stood. He pulled the blankets back up over me, then grabbed his robe and headed for the bedroom door.

I let the morning light, the wonderful afterglow of the sex, and the warm blankets lull me almost back to sleep.

Looks like it was good for you.

I felt so good I didn't even care I was making up a voice in my head again.

Now that's the attitude, Mom. Relax. Learn how to roll with things.

Mom! Now the panic of hearing a voice swept up over me.

Yeah, Mom. Sorry for the slip. Thank heavens my job here is finished.

What's happening to me?

Like I said, nothing that you're going to remember. I just needed to make sure I was going to be born.

What? Now I was screaming, but again my body wouldn't move, and no sound came out. In the distance I could hear the shower running and John singing.

Calm down. About six timelines over, you and dad did that morning tango you just finished with, and got me as a little accident. *I went on to be one of the major inventors of mind-jumping through time, a cheap but effective form of time travel.*

Time travel? Mind jumping? I had no idea where the voice was coming from.

Of course you wouldn't understand what I'm saying. You never did understand me, or how smart I was. It took me five years of counseling just to get over

being an unwanted child, something you never let me forget, I might add.

I could feel the anger boiling inside me, but I had no idea where it came from.

My anger. Sorry.

The feeling died away.

Anyway, since I was born in only one timeline that we explored, I decided to do the opposite of the old grandfather paradox, you know the one about going back and killing your own grandfather so you can't exist, thus you could never go back and kill him.

I had no idea what the voice was saying. I was going insane. I had to be.

Figures you'd think that. Oh well, the short of it is I jumped back here, into your mind on this timeline to make sure I am born. Otherwise you'd have gotten up a little while back, make breakfast, and been tense and angry all day for no reason anyone could figure out. And I would never happen in this timeline, and time travel would not exist here either. Not that any of that matters to you, or that you will even remember.

I've gone insane. I need help. Maybe professional help.

No, I'm the one who is insane, for even trying to explain the reason of my

existence to her mother. You'd think after all these years I'd know better.

A feeling of disgust and anger filled me.

Oh, sorry, my issues, not yours.

The emotions faded quickly, again replaced with the intense joy of just being alive and satisfied.

I'll leave you feeling happy about the sex and not remembering anything about this conversation. That much I can do for Dad. See you in about nine months. Be nice to me, would you?

The morning sun bathed me and warmed the bedroom as I rolled over and stretched. There was a nagging feeling I had forgotten something, but what did it matter? I just wish we had tried this morning sex thing years ago.

I kicked the covers back and just lay there, exposed to the room, my black nightgown not even covering all of me. I wonder what had gotten into me this morning?

Besides John that is.

The thought had me laughing all the way to the bathroom.

~

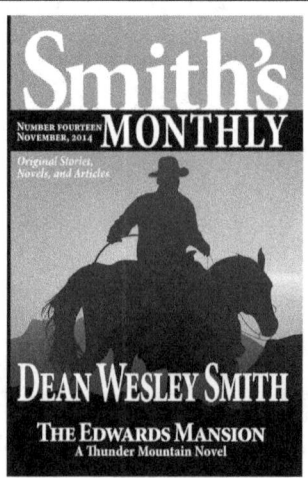

Now Available
from all your favorite booksellers in trade paper and electronic editions.

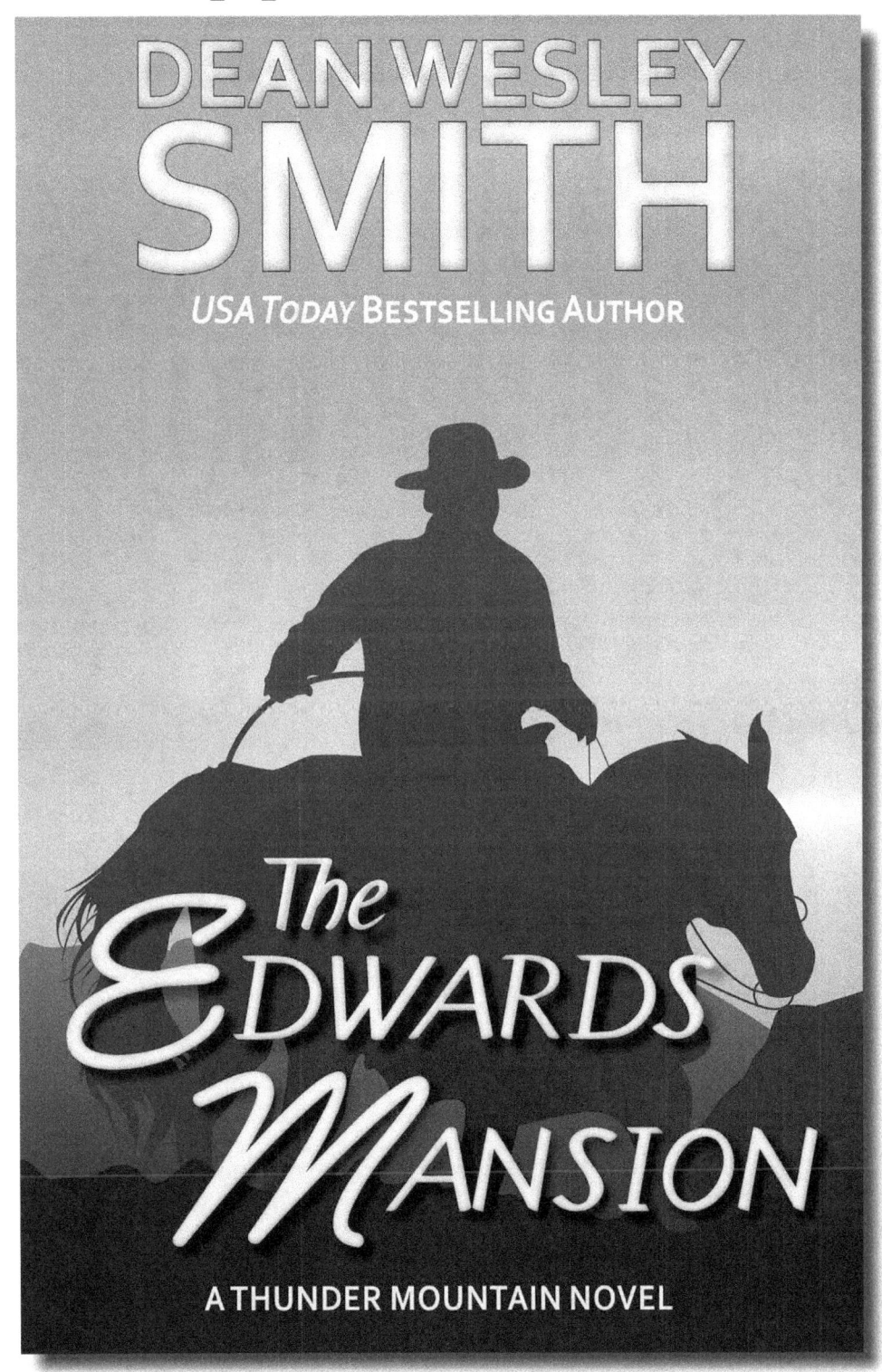

DEAN WESLEY
SMITH

USA TODAY BESTSELLING AUTHOR

The
*E*DWARDS
*M*ANSION

A THUNDER MOUNTAIN NOVEL

DEAN WESLEY SMITH

USA TODAY BESTSELLING AUTHOR

THE LIFE
AND TIMES OF
BUFFALO
JIMMY

1866: Jimmy Gray's parents killed by an evil man, Jimmy's brother wounded, the family treasure in the form of a gold mine deed stolen.

Jimmy finds himself alone and facing a deadly journey west to track and find the man who killed his parents.

Can Jimmy, his first time out of the big eastern cities, learn the ways of the west fast enough to stay alive?

Maybe with a little help from some friends.

The Life and Times Of Buffalo Jimmy:

HEADED WEST

Part One
A Great Loss

THE FIRST SHOT ripped into nineteen-year-old Jimmy Gray's saddle with a sickening thud, barely missing his right leg.

The sound of the shot echoed over the rolling Missouri hills and died into the clear, sunny afternoon air. His horse reared and threatened to bolt even though the shot had not gone through the thick leather, but Jimmy fought it back into control, spinning around completely on ridgeline covered by prairie grass.

A second shot knocked Jimmy's brother, Luke, off his horse.

Jimmy dove for the ground and cover as a third shot narrowly missed him, the sound of the bullet whistling past his ear.

He lay on the ground, face pressed into the soft dirt and grass, trying to breathe. His heart was racing. He had never been so scared in all his life.

He had never been shot at before. He read about such things in dime novels and in the newspapers, but reading about it and having it happen to you were two very different things.

Jimmy and his family were two days ride from Independence, Missouri. He and his brother had just come over the ridge two hundred paces above their family's wagon. Five men had been down there near the back of the wagon, off their horses, from what Jimmy could tell in the quick glimpse before the shooting had started

He hadn't seen his parents.

That scared him even more than being shot at. He just hoped they weren't hurt.

And was Luke hurt? He had to find out.

He had to move.

Jimmy couldn't believe this was even happening. All Jimmy had wanted to see was buffalo. Since his teacher a year ago back in Boston, in his last year of high school, had told him stories of the great buffalo hunts, Jimmy had been focused on little else. The big beasts had become an obsession, his mother had said. His father had only laughed and promised that Jimmy would see his share of buffalo by the time they reached the Wyoming Territory.

His older brother, Luke, had told him as they rode out of camp that the buffalo were no longer in Missouri in 1866, at least not this part of it. They had all been killed or driven hundreds of miles away from the wagon trail, but Jimmy didn't care. He still had his mind set on seeing a buffalo and proving Luke wrong. For all he knew, there could be an entire herd just over the next ridge.

After riding fast away from the well-worn wagon road for a half-mile or so, they had scared up rabbits. Luke, who was twenty, had the family rifle. He had become a great shot and had managed to get three rabbits with only five shots. Jimmy was an expert shot as well. Once

Luke even had admitted he was better than Luke, a real natural with a gun.

Jimmy had helped Luke skin the rabbits and then they had headed back. Luke had been sick since leaving Kansas City and was riding slowly. Jimmy could tell that both of his parents were worried about Luke making the long trip across the country, but Jimmy' father had a job offer at a bank in San Francisco, and had bought a gold mining claim in the mountains near Sacramento, so the family was set on making the trip and starting a new life in the west.

It had been such a perfect, spring day.

Until the shots.

What had happened?

Jimmy scrambled on all fours through the grass, his head low, until he finally managed to reach his brother.

Luke was pushing himself up slightly on his elbows and blood was streaming from his leg. "Get the rifle off my saddle," he said through gritted teeth. "Quick!"

Jimmy glanced around.

Luke's horse had only gone about twenty paces back from the top of the ridge and then stopped. Keeping his head down, Luke ran for the horse, grabbed the rifle from the saddle and brought it back.

There were no more shots at him coming from their wagon, but off his horse, Jimmy couldn't see the trail over the edge of the rise, which meant the men doing the shooting couldn't see him.

Luke had torn off the bottom of his shirt and wrapped it around his leg, but it didn't look to Jimmy as if the bleeding had slowed much.

Luke grabbed the rifle from Jimmy, cocked it to make sure it was loaded, then staying low, hopped the few steps to the top of the ridge, dragging his bad leg behind him.

Jimmy stayed beside him, and at the top of the ridge they both lay down in the grass and crawled the last few feet so they could see the trail below.

Jimmy was shocked at what faced them. He wanted to jump and run, but somehow stayed beside Luke.

Two men on horseback were riding up the hill toward them, guns drawn. Three other men were pulling things from the wagon and scattering them on the ground. Jimmy had no idea where his parents were.

He and Luke were going to die, Jimmy was sure of that.

This was just like all the bad stories he had heard about the western frontier coming true right now.

His stomach was so twisted up, he could hardly breathe.

"Keep your head down," Luke whispered.

Then, taking a deep breath, Luke pulled down on the men like he was shooting rabbits. The shot exploded in Jimmy's ear, since he was so close to Luke.

The lead man went over backwards off his horse like a trick rider Jimmy had seen at the Circus last year in Boston.

The other man's horse reared up, and by the time he could get turned around, Luke fired again.

He must have missed. The second man took off back down the hill toward the wagon. The man that Luke had shot pushed himself to his feet, holding his stomach, and then half-ran, half-staggered back down the hill.

The three men below had their guns out and were firing up at Luke and Jimmy.

"Keep your head down," Luke ordered again. Then he fired back at the men around the wagon. Jimmy watched one of Luke's shots splinter wood off the wagon bed right beside one man.

Luke shot again and another of the men danced as the bullet kicked up dirt and mud right at his feet.

Luke didn't hit any of the men, but his next shot, and the one after, sent them scrambling for their horses.

Jimmy recognized one of the men.

Jake Benson, the man his father had hired to guide them from Kansas City to Independence.

The three men quickly mounted up and joined the fourth. He had picked up the wounded man and was riding at full speed down the trail toward Independence. The horse of the man Luke had shot grazed on the side of the hill. Clearly, they didn't have the stomach for a fight in the open for a horse with Luke having the rifle and the upper ground and all they had were pistols.

Jimmy watched them go, their dust kicking up small clouds behind them.

It seemed to take an eternity for them to vanish over the distant rise.

When would they be back? The question made Jimmy shudder.

The wagon still sat where Jimmy and Luke had left it when they had left to go hunting. It was sitting just off to one side of the muddy tracks of the wagon road, with their two secondary horses grazing while still in harness. But the lunch fire was smoldering instead of burning, and a lot of their personal things had been tossed out into the dirt and dried mud.

After all the shooting, the silence of the wide-open prairie was broken only by the light breeze through the grass.

Tomb-like silent.

Luke sat up, checked his wound, then pushed himself to his feet.

"Get our horses," he said to Jimmy.

Jimmy turned and ran for their two horses, the fear of what might have happened to his parents twisting at his stomach like a bad belly-ache. He grabbed Luke's horse, then mounted up on his own, the hole where the bullet had embedded in the leather of his saddle a clear reminder of just how close he had come to getting shot.

By the time he got back to his brother, Luke's face looked white, and it was clear that he was in a lot of pain.

"Let's find Mother and Father," Luke said, reaching for his horse's reins.

Jimmy made sure Luke could get back on his horse, then started down the hill ahead of his older brother, working to keep his hands from shaking and his stomach under control while trying to look in a thousand directions at the same time for Benson and his men. They would be back. He had no doubt.

The wind whistled lightly in his ears under his hat, the warm afternoon sun glared in his eyes. He forced himself to take shallow breaths as the ride seemed to stretch into an eternity.

It wasn't until he had moved almost halfway down the hill that he saw what he had feared the most. His mother and father were lying in the mud near the rear wheels of the wagon. Neither seemed to be moving.

Jimmy dismounted ten running steps from the wagon before the horse had even stopped.

An instant later he was on his knees beside his father.

He was dead.

His blood had made a muddy pool, his eyes were staring up, unseeing at the blue sky and light white clouds. He had been shot at least twice.

Jimmy stared at the man who had always been there for him. His father couldn't be dead. He was too strong, too powerful a man to die.

An instant later, Luke was on the ground beside their mother.

Jimmy watched as Luke rolled her over. The front of her pretty blue dress was coated in mud and her own blood.

She had been shot in the back.

As Luke rolled her over, she blinked, then opened her eyes.

She was alive!

For a moment, it was clear she wasn't aware of where she was, but as Jimmy moved closer, she looked up at Luke.

"Mother?" Luke said, his voice shaking.

Jimmy touched her arm, trying to give her some comfort as well. He had no idea what they could do.

"Benson," she whispered. "Hide from him."

"He's not here," Luke said. "We chased him and his men off."

She nodded, seemingly satisfied with that. She coughed, blood coming out of the corner of her mouth. She looked up at Jimmy and smiled, then back at Luke. "Take care of each other."

Jimmy watched as she closed her eyes and her body relaxed.

All the life seemed to leave her.

"Mother!" Luke shouted, his voice swallowed by the vast wilderness around them.

Their mother was dead.

They were alone.

Part Two
Moving Forward

JIMMY HAD NO idea how long he had sat beside the wagon road alternating between staring at his parents' bodies and watching the trail and hills for Benson to come back.

Maybe minutes.

Maybe hours.

He didn't know. But finally, the cold afternoon wind made him realize he and Luke had to move.

Luke had crawled a few feet from the bodies and just lay on his back, the rifle at his side. Jimmy couldn't tell if he had passed out, or was just staring up into the sky. The shirt tied around his leg was bright red with blood.

Jimmy found a sheet one of the men had tossed out of the wagon. He ripped out bandage-length strips, then found a bottle of his father's best whisky and, with a quick check for Benson and his men, moved over to his brother.

Luke didn't protest as Jimmy unwrapped the bloody shirt, tore open his pants a little near the wound and checked how bad it was. The bleeding had mostly stopped and the bullet had gone all the way through. That was lucky, but Jimmy still had to get Luke to a doctor and soon.

He poured some whiskey on the wound, as he had seen his father do when Jimmy's mother had cut her hand.

Luke winced, but didn't say anything. He didn't even open his eyes. Then Jimmy wrapped the wound in the clean strips from the sheet.

"We have to get you fixed up," Jimmy said, his voice breaking the silence of the vast plain.

The wind seemed to pull his words away over the swaying grassland almost as he spoke them.

Luke didn't move.

Jimmy pushed himself to his feet and then, without looking at his parents' bodies, he climbed into the back of their wagon and pulled out two of his mother's favorite blankets, then got the two shovels his father had bought in St. Louis and went back out into the sun and breeze. He tossed one shovel onto the ground beside Luke. Then he covered his father with a blanket, then his mother.

"Luke, I'm going to start digging some graves up on the top of the rise. I should be able to see if Benson and his men are doubling back from up there. Rest as long as you need to."

Luke shook his head. "We stay together."

Luke took a deep breath and pushed himself to his feet, using the shovel to balance on one leg. The sickness he had been fighting since they left Boston had really made him weak, and now getting shot had made him much worse. Even though Jimmy was the youngest, he was going to have to be the strongest until Luke got better.

Together, with Jimmy keeping guard and carrying the rifle, they slowly moved up the hill through the grass, Luke using one shovel as a crutch.

At the top, at a place that seemed to overlook the vast plains, they started to dig through the thick sod and into the wet, damp ground.

It would be a good final resting place for their parents.

Jimmy had no idea how long they had been digging, but every few minutes he kept watch, and finally, he saw something. Three wagons were moving toward them slowly but steadily, coming from St. Louis.

"We have company," Jimmy said. "Wagons. Not Benson."

He felt a little relieved. As his father had always said, there was safety in numbers out west. Benson and his men might still attack them, but with other wagons close by, it wasn't likely.

Luke stopped and leaned on his shovel. He was breathing hard and sweating far more than he should have. Bright red blood spotted the bandages on his leg.

"They'll go around," Luke said, and went back to digging.

Jimmy watched his brother for a moment. They had not made that much headway on the two graves, and Jimmy doubted Luke was going to be able to keep going much longer. If they were going to do this right, and give their parents a proper resting place, and be safe from Benson, they were going to need help.

"I'm going to see if they'll lend a hand," Jimmy said. "You rest."

"I don't need rest," Luke said.

"I don't plan on burying you as well," Jimmy said, turning back to glare at his brother. Then with his sternest voice, he said, "Now rest and I'll go talk to these people."

Luke stared at Jimmy for a moment, then nodded and dropped to the ground. A moment later he was lying on his back, his eyes closed, the family rifle in one hand.

In all his life, Jimmy had never felt so alone.

His parents dead, his older brother injured and sick. He was in charge.

How could he be in charge of anything? He was only nineteen.

He first gathered up the killer's horse, then the two horses that he and Luke had been riding. Luckily, they hadn't gone far and were just grazing near the trail. He tied them to the wagon, constantly keeping watch for Benson and his men.

Then he started down the wagon trail, walking beside the deepest ruts toward the oncoming wagons. The three wagons were spaced a good distance apart, and all seemed to be what was called a "small wagon" with square canvas tops, similar to the one his parents had purchased.

A man about his father's age was driving the first rig, moving a team of four oxen gently forward. A woman and two younger children were walking along to one side of the wagon, and a fifth oxen and a horse were tied to the back. The other two wagons also seemed to have families, but they were far enough back that Jimmy couldn't tell for sure.

"What can I do for you, mister?" the man said, stopping his wagon with the lead oxen about twenty paces from Jimmy.

Jimmy stopped as well. He didn't want to seem threatening in any way.

The woman moved up beside her husband and stared at Jimmy, holding her two younger children behind her skirt.

"We were robbed and my parents were killed, sir." Jimmy made himself go on after that sentence. "By the man we hired to guide us to Independence. My brother and I were out hunting. My brother's also been shot and is not very strong, since he's recovering from being sick. If you might stop for a short time, we could sure use the help in burying our parents."

"Oh, my," the woman said before her husband could get out a word.

"Of course we'll help," he said, nodding. "We'll pull around you and stop." He turned to his wife. "Go back and tell the other wagons what we are doing."

"Thank you," Jimmy said. "Very much appreciated." He turned and walked ahead of the wagons back toward the hill. He didn't allow himself to look at the blankets behind his wagon.

"They're going to help," he said to Luke as he reached the top of the hill, picked up his shovel, and went back to digging. "And with them helping, we'll be safer for the moment."

Luke only sighed and didn't move.

Part Three
Independence

IT TOOK TWO days to make the trip into Independence, following the other three wagons as part of their group. Luke had just laid in the bed of the wagon most of the trip, seemingly getting sicker and weaker by the day, even though one of the women from the wagons had nursing training from the war and had cleaned Luke's wound and got it to stop bleeding.

Jimmy had driven the team, taken care of the horses each night, and done what little cooking they needed. Luke didn't eat much, and Jimmy hadn't felt hungry either. He just felt numb.

Luckily, his father had spent a few hours teaching him how to handle the wagon and the horses, but he clearly wasn't that good, and a few simple stream crossings had almost turned disastrous. Henry Basker, the man he had first talked to in the lead wagon, had finally, on what looked like a really nasty downhill crossing, offered to take the wagon across for Jimmy and show him how to do it. Jimmy had never felt so relieved in his life.

Every mile of the trip, he kept expecting Benson and his men to come charging in and kill them all. Jimmy had told Basker and the other two men about Benson and his men, so all of the men on the wagons rode with their guns at the ready.

During the first night of camp, with Luke asleep in a tent beside the wagon, Jimmy had dug through what was left of their family's possessions. Benson had stolen the supply money his father planned to use in Independence and his mother's family jewelry. And worse yet, Benson had stolen the gold mine deed.

The entire family had all been excited about that mine when his father first told them about buying the deed. Ever since Jimmy could remember, people had talked about finding gold out west and never having to work again. Now his father had bought them a real gold mine.

The plan was for his father to work in the bank while Jimmy and Luke worked the mine. Jimmy knew he couldn't get the money or jewelry back from Benson. Those would be gone before they caught up with him. But Benson would hold onto that deed, not knowing how much it was worth, and Jimmy figured that if he found Benson, he and Luke could get the mine back.

To make the deed be worth anything, Benson would have to register his ownership of the deed in Sacramento, just as his father had been planning to do. Jimmy and Luke had to make sure they got to Sacramento before Benson, or get the deed back along the way somewhere.

If Benson didn't come and kill them first, that is.

In his search of the wagon that first night, Jimmy was very relieved to find that Benson hadn't found the false bottom of a family chest his mother had insisted they bring along. In that false bottom, his father had put the money he planned on using to buy them a new home in San Francisco.

Jimmy had strapped a third of the money in a cloth holder to the small of his back under his shirt, then left part of the rest in the false chest bottom, and some more in a false bottom in the wagon floor.

By the time they arrived outside of Independence and stopped the wagon with what looked to be thousands of other wagons, it was around noon of the third day since the shooting.

Jimmy left their wagon camped on a wide plain a mile to the north of Independence next to the Basker wagon, then took Luke into town to find a doctor.

Luke was so sick, he could barely ride, and Jimmy had to stop three times along the well-traveled road to let Luke rest.

Independence was far larger than Jimmy had expected, seeming to spread out over two small hills and fill a broad valley. The wide main streets were so crowded, it was hard to even walk a horse up the middle of them. The streets were muddy and smelled of horse manure. The sidewalks were wood and slippery from spring rains and mud tracked up from the street.

The excitement of being in a new place, a vibrant, alive place like Independence, was shocking. It felt like a large carnival, with lots of noise, loud talking, and construction sounds. Piano music came from the open doors of dozens of saloons, and men fighting in the mud seemed to be common.

Everyone, no matter what age, seemed to have an intense purpose, and no one noticed the two brothers at all, at least that Jimmy could see.

Jimmy, on constant alert for Benson, went into town from the side, staying off the main streets, and tied the horses off on a side street near a saloon. With Luke leaning on him, he managed to walk along the wooden sidewalk and get into a doctor's office beside a general store.

In town, he felt a lot safer with all the people around him, but he still didn't want Benson to know he and Luke were here.

The doctor, a friendly, older man named Davis, stood about as tall as

Jimmy's five-ten, but had a pot belly on him that made him look almost round. He wore glasses and his brown hair was thin and long, combed over to one side.

Doc Davis took one look at Luke, touched his hot forehead, and had Jimmy help him get Luke in a bed in the back of the office, beside two other sick men and a sick child.

"What happened?" Doc Davis asked Jimmy after Luke was resting.

"We were coming with our parents," Jimmy said. "Ambushed by robbers. Parents are dead." He was shocked at how that sounded. It still didn't seem right that they were gone.

"They shot Luke in the leg before we ran them off."

"I'm so sorry," Doc Davis said, putting his hand gently on Jimmy's shoulder.

"Luke and I can get by all right," Jimmy said, taking a deep breath and squaring his shoulders. He pulled a coin out of his pants pocket to pay the doctor. "Will this be enough to get Luke well?" He gave the doctor the twenty dollar gold piece.

Doc Davis looked at it, clearly surprised, then nodded and put it in his pocket. "More than enough. We'll take good care of him, I can promise you that. Do you have a place to stay?"

"I have the family wagon outside of town," Jimmy said. "I'll be staying there."

Doc Davis brushed his thinning hair to one side of his head. "If you need anything, you just come to me. Understand? And I'll let you know more tomorrow on how Luke is doing."

Jimmy nodded. "Thanks, Doctor. I'll be back tomorrow."

With that, Jimmy stepped back out onto the street of the busy western town.

Alone.

His parents dead, his brother sick, and he was alone in a strange town. He had told his friends in Boston he wanted to go west for the adventure.

He just hadn't dreamed it would be like this.

PART FOUR
Luke's Condition

THE NEXT DAY, Doc Davis had said that there was no improvement in Luke's health, and he didn't really know what was wrong.

And he said the same thing the next day as well. "He just needs to rest."

The two days had been filled with rain and cold winds. Jimmy had spent much of the last two days either sitting beside Luke's bed, or searching carefully around town for Benson, walking in the rain with his hat pulled down to hide his face.

Jimmy had decided that he couldn't constantly hide from Benson. It would be better if Jimmy found the killer first, and kept track of him. As long as he was in town, or with the hundreds of wagons camped out on the plain, he would be somewhat safe. But he and Luke would be a lot safer if he knew where Benson was. And if Jimmy did find him, when Luke got better, they would be able to tell the sheriff what Benson had done, and get him arrested.

During the two days, Jimmy had come to know the town of Independence pretty well, including which parts were just too dangerous for him to get near. It seemed even bigger than he had first thought. When he asked one shopkeeper how many people were here, the man had laughed and said, "At what moment?

This time of the year, there has to be a hundred thousand people here and out in that sea of wagons."

How was Jimmy ever going to find one man in a city that size? It seemed impossible. And he didn't feel comfortable going into the saloons, at least not without Luke at his side. So finally, he just decided he would stand with his hat low on his forehead where he could see five or six of the biggest saloon's front doors and watch for Benson.

Jimmy knew he had to play this smart if he was going to get the justice his parents deserved and stay alive doing so. It was like a big game, with life and death as the stakes, and he was doing the best he could.

On the morning of the third day, the sun came back out enough to make the air thick and steamy. The muddy streets mixed with horse manure smelled even worse, if that was possible. Somehow, the town's people had gotten used to the smell, but Jimmy had grown up in Boston, where they paved the streets for the most part, and kept them mostly clean.

Jimmy tied up his horse at his normal spot on the side street just down from the doctor's office. With the sun out, laughter echoed everywhere along the main street. And everyone was moving at a more frantic pace, if that was possible.

Dozens of smaller trains had been leaving every day since he had arrived. A couple of the really big trains, with upwards of a hundred wagons each, were getting ready to head out, and that made him even more worried about what he was going to do next.

He had a wagon and five horses he needed to take care of. The Tasker family had been watching them while he was visiting Luke. He didn't have any help after they left.

"Hi, little brother," Luke said, smiling as Jimmy walked into the back room of the Doc's office. Luke was sitting up in bed, and seemed to have some color in his face.

Jimmy felt his mood soar even more. Suddenly, it felt like the weight of the world had lifted from his shoulders. He wanted to rush forward and just hug Luke, but somehow he stopped himself and just stood beside the bed smiling.

"He's doing better," Doc Davis said to Jimmy. "But for now, I want him to stay right here where I can watch him. He's very weak and a long way from being recovered. And with all the cholera going around, I wouldn't want him to get that in his condition."

"Thanks, Doc," Jimmy said.

Luke smiled. "Yes, thank you, for everything. Especially that young nurse you have helping you."

Doc Davis glared at Luke. "That's my daughter."

Luke's face went back to pale.

Then Doc Davis laughed a deep, rich laugh that filled the room, patted Jimmy on the shoulder again, and left, still laughing.

"He got you with that one," Jimmy said, also laughing.

"Yeah, he did," Luke said. "But she's still cute as a Sunday bonnet."

Jimmy pulled up a chair beside Luke's bed and with Luke leading the questioning, he filled in his big brother on what had happened over the last few days since they got to Independence, what the town was like, what the vast camp for wagons looked like.

The conversation felt wonderful and Jimmy was sure it was the longest the two of them had talked in a long time.

"I've been looking for Benson," Jimmy finally said, worried about what his big brother would say.

Luke looked suddenly serious and worried. "Jimmy, he and that gang of his are cold-blooded killers. I don't want you doing anything until I'm with you."

Jimmy laughed. "You don't have to worry about that. I'm just trying to find him. I won't let him see me if I do."

"Good," Luke said, sighing. "I'll be getting better soon, I promise." He settled down into the bed a little more. He was again looking tired and pale.

Jimmy pushed his chair back. "I'll let you rest and be back later this afternoon." He patted his brother's shoulder. "Glad you decided to stick around."

"Yeah, me too little brother. Me too."

PART FIVE
Finding Friends

JIMMY PULLED his hat down low to hide his face some, then walked out of the doc's office and into the warm, morning air, the spring back in his step. He almost felt like whistling. Pretty soon Luke would be back on his feet and helping him. And that was the best news he had had in a week. He wouldn't be alone.

He moved up the crowded sidewalk to a spot where he could see the front doors of five of the major saloons along the street, all doing a noisy business even this early in the morning. Through the windows of the closest one, he could see two card games going on, and a dozen men standing at a long bar.

He moved to the inside of the sidewalk and leaned against the rough wood wall of a lawyer's office, out of the way of all the hustle and bustle of people filling up their wagons from the dozen general stores along the street. If his mother and father had lived, more than likely he would be one of those people busy filling saddlebags and wagons with provisions.

"Which wagon you working?" a voice asked beside him.

He spun around, ready to run, his heart beating wildly in his chest. A young guy about his age was leaning against the wall. At first, Jimmy thought the blond-headed guy was older, but then his blue eyes told him he was about Jimmy's age. He had his long hair tied back and wore a buckskin jacket that clearly had seen some wear.

"I don't have a wagon here in town," Jimmy said, letting out the air he had been holding and trying to not let the guy see how scared he had been. "Just looking for someone."

The kid laughed. "I told Truitt you weren't competition. But he wanted me to ask."

"Competition for what?" Jimmy asked.

"Working the wagons," the guy said, as if Jimmy should know what that meant. "You got a family?"

"A sick brother in Doc Davis's back room," Jimmy said.

"So you're alone," the guy said, nodding. "So am I. So is my friend Truitt." The guy stuck out his hand. "I'm Zach. Zach Roy."

"Jimmy Tyler," he said, smiling at finally meeting someone besides the doc. "So, what's *working a wagon* mean?"

"Watch," Zach said and pointed at an open-topped wagon being pulled by two horses. The wagon's horses had been tied off just down the street from Hill and Stevens General Store. As Jimmy watched, a young man with chopped up brown hair and pants that were too short for him approached the wagon from along the street side, seeming to wade effortlessly in the mud.

"That's Truitt," Zach said. "Watch him closely. He's a master at working a wagon."

There was no one near the wagon. The owners must have been in the store.

Truitt had clearly timed his arrival near the stopped wagon as another wagon passed close by. As the second wagon went by, Truitt seemed to be knocked against the stopped wagon as if he had been grazed.

He caught himself against the wagon, and then almost faster than Jimmy could follow, Truitt had a bag from the back of the wagon under his arm and was heading across the street and toward a side street as if he'd always had the bag with him, walking as if nothing was different.

"Looks like a bag of beans," Zach said, smiling. "That will keep us eating for a few weeks."

"You're stealing food?" Jimmy said, turning to face Zach.

Zach just smiled and shrugged. "When you have no money, you do what you have to do."

Jimmy started to say something, then stopped. He had come very close to being in Independence without money as well. If Benson had found his father's secret stash, Jimmy would right now be thinking about how to get food and pay Doc Davis for treating Luke.

"You don't have a family?" Jimmy asked Zach as Truitt disappeared safely down the side street with his prize.

"All my family, my parents, my girl died of the cholera in St. Louis a few months back," Zach said, his voice level

and cold. "I promised my dad before he died that I'd head west, carry on with the family dream. So far, this is as far as I've got."

"What about Truitt?" Jimmy asked.

Zach shrugged. "He's alone and won't talk much about it. So, since you're not working the wagons, who are you looking for?"

Jimmy decided that he could trust Zach. He didn't really know him, but he felt like he did, and for now, that was enough.

"I'm looking for the man and his gang who killed my parents. Shot my mother in the back. Two days ride back toward St. Louis."

"Oh," Zach said. "What do you plan on doing when you find him?"

"At the moment, nothing," Jimmy said. "But eventually, when my brother gets well, we'll somehow make him pay for what he's done, report him to the sheriff or something."

"Well, it's a plan," was all Zach said.

PART SIX
Building a Gang

LUKE'S HEALTH seemed to level over the next two days. He didn't get better, but he didn't get worse, either. They had talked a lot about different things, including what to do with the wagon and horses when the Tasker family left. So far, they hadn't come up with any solution.

Each day, while looking for Benson, Jimmy had run into Zach and Truitt. He had come to like them both, but refused to help them work a wagon. He didn't much like the idea of stealing, and at the

Now Available
from all your favorite booksellers
in trade paper and electronic editions.

moment he didn't need to in order to eat and take care of Luke.

It was on the afternoon of the second day, when there weren't enough wagons on the street to make it safe to work them, that a new opportunity arose. Two drunks had staggered out of a bar and gone down a narrow alley to either be sick or pass out. To Jimmy's surprise, the moment Zach and Truitt saw the two drunks, they laughed and said almost together, "Time to roll a drum."

Jimmy decided he actually didn't want to know what that meant, so he stayed in his spot watching the saloon doors while Zach and Truitt moved across the muddy street and to the alley that cut between two buildings. It was too narrow for a wagon and it looked like it held nothing but garbage and broken furniture from a nearby bar.

As Jimmy watched, Zach and Truitt approached the two drunks. Zach said something, then reached down to touch the one drunk. The next moment, the man had a gun in his hand faster than Jimmy could ever imagine being possible. And especially amazing for a man who seemed as drunk as that man looked.

Without losing his aim, the man climbed to his feet to face Zach.

The second man grabbed Truitt and held on while Zach backed against the wall, his hands in the air. Clearly, the two drunks knew what *rolling a drum* meant, and didn't much like it.

Jimmy started across the muddy street, not really sure what he was going to do to help, but Zach and Truitt had become his friends, so he had to help them somehow. His stomach twisted into a knot, but he kept walking, trying to think of anything that might set them free.

As he entered the alleyway, the smell of mold and vomit washed over him and made his stomach even tighter. He could hear one of the drunks threatening to shoot Zach. Some men were fun drunks, others got mean. Jimmy had seen them both in Boston. Clearly, this man was one of the mean ones.

The other drunk held Truitt pinned tight against the wood wall. This situation was going to get downright deadly in about ten seconds if Jimmy didn't do something.

And fast.

"Deputy Roy," Jimmy said loudly, pretending nothing was wrong as he walked toward the man with the gun. "Want me to call the sheriff? Seems you're having a little trouble with getting these two drunks out of this alley. But I will say, this will be a might embarrassing letting these two get the drop on you."

Zach, not missing a beat, laughed. "It sure is."

"You're going to be *dead* embarrassed, mister," the drunk holding Zach said, putting the gun under Zach's chin. "You was gonna rob me."

Jimmy decided right at that moment that he was really starting to hate guns, but he managed to laugh. "And why would you want to go and be hanged for killing a deputy on such a wonderful spring day?"

"This guy ain't no deputy," the drunk said. But even as he said that, he pulled his gun back and pointed it slightly upward. Clearly Jimmy had confused him.

"He sure is," another voice said from the back of the alley.

A moment later, a young guy, really short, and Jimmy figured him to be no more than eighteen years old, even though he looked younger, stepped out of the shadows and moved right up to Zach. He grabbed Zach around the middle and hugged him. "He's my dad. You wouldn't want to kill my dad, would you?"

By this point, Jimmy could tell the drunk was getting really confused. And overwhelmed. Actually, Jimmy was confused as well, but he kept playing the hand he had started.

"Deputy Roy, when did you start letting your son play in the alleys?" Jimmy asked.

"He's not supposed to be here," Zach said, following right along.

Then, while the drunk with the gun stared in amazement at Zach and the young kid holding him like he really was his daddy, another man with long black hair braided into a ponytail stepped out of the shadows and hit the second drunk with a chair leg.

The crack echoed through the narrow alley.

The drunk let go of Truitt and slumped to the ground with a loud moan.

The first drunk spun around, for the first time pointing the gun away from Zach.

The young kid, getting almost airborne, kicked the man's gun hand hard.

The gun went flying into the shadows, landing in something that sounded very wet and very sloppy.

"Ow!" the drunk shouted and held his injured hand against his chest. "Mister, I'll kill you for that."

Zach stepped forward and punched the guy once in the stomach.

When the guy doubled over, the kid with the long braided hair hit him with the chair leg.

The younger-looking kid searched one drunk's pockets while Truitt looked through the others, then all five of them headed out of the alley, across the street, and down a side street, laughing as they walked.

"Thanks," Zach said, glancing at Jimmy. "That was some quick thinking."

"I had a hard time not laughing though," said Truitt, shaking his head. "Deputy Roy. What a hoot."

"Yeah, had me laughing too," said the shorter guy who had kicked the gun.

"Thanks for the help," Zach said to the new men with them. "Who are you two?"

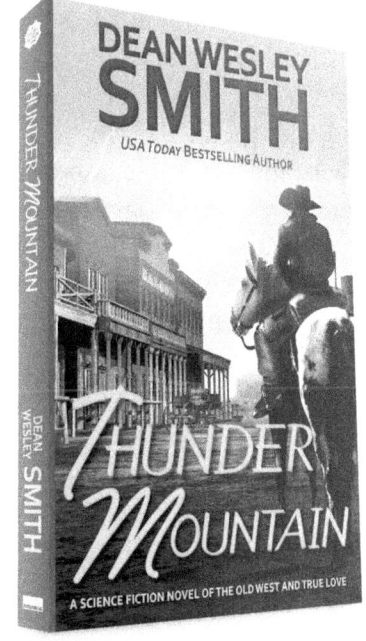

"I'm C.J.," the short one said as they reached a side street and turned toward the edge of town.

"Longfellow Runningwind," the other said, his voice deep and slow.

Jimmy wasn't sure, but he sounded like he had a New York accent.

"Call him Long," said C.J. "Just easier."

"You mind?" Zach asked and Long said no.

Jimmy looked at Long, suddenly realizing that he had just met his first Indian. Or half-Indian, more than likely.

"We better lay low for a few hours," Zach said. "We got beans and some bacon at our camp if you're interested."

Both C.J. and Long looked very interested, both nodding so fast that it was clear to Jimmy that they hadn't eaten today.

Jimmy felt almost embarrassed that he had had a good breakfast at his wagon and had money to buy provisions, at least for a little while. But he didn't say anything. He just felt good having a few friends. That hadn't happened since his last day in school in Boston. He didn't realize until now how much he missed his friends back there.

And how much safer he felt hanging around with them.

Zach and Truitt's camp was a small tent and a lean-to in a small grove of scrub brush near the edge of a small stream. More than likely, this stream would be dry in the summer, but right now, it was flowing good enough to give them some decent water. And they were upstream from the town and the mass of wagons on the other side, which made the water pretty safe to drink.

Truitt dug out some beans and a large pan and filled it with water while Zach started a fire. With the beans, Truitt put in a few scraps of bacon and a pretty good handful of salt. Then, as the beans were cooking, the five of them sat around the fire and talked.

It turned out C.J. wouldn't say anything about his family or his past, but it was clear to Jimmy that the short, blond-haired man had been to school somewhere. He wore wire-rimmed glasses and was constantly cleaning and adjusting them.

None of them wanted to talk about the war at all. Jimmy had learned early on in the trip that talking about the war was always a bad idea. Jimmy had managed to miss the war because he had been too young, and Luke had gone in, but missed most of the action.

Jimmy had also been right about Long. His mother was Sioux and his father white. Long had spent time in both worlds. He had gone to school just outside of New York and had left his mother to get away from the Indian way of life, but had also managed to stay out of the war.

As the beans were being served, C.J. admitted that it was the first meal that he and Long had had that day. They were basically living in that alley, trying to find a way to head west. They had no money, no horses, nothing to their names but clothes and an extra pair of glasses for C.J.

"Well, Jimmy," Zach said, "isn't it about time you tell us who you've been looking for?"

"Yeah?" C.J. said. "Standing out there against that wall for hours certainly draws attention to you."

Jimmy could feel his stomach twisting. "I didn't know I had been that obvious." He had been trying to stay hidden from Benson, and had actually been as obvious as a wine stain on a Sunday-go-to-church shirt.

"Maybe not to most," Truitt said, "but for those of us who watch for any small detail to help us survive, you're one dang big question mark."

Jimmy took a deep breath and managed to laugh. "All right, I'm looking for a man named Jake Benson." He quickly told them the story.

"So, where's your brother?" Long asked when Jimmy finished.

"Doc Davis's office back room."

"He getting better?" Zach asked, actually looking like he cared.

"Not much," Jimmy said. "He's going to need a lot of rest and care."

Suddenly, Jimmy had an idea. His father's voice rang clearly in his head. *Out west, there is safety in numbers.*

"Look," Jimmy said, "I need to go check in on my brother and talk to him about something. Are you four going to be here in an hour? If so, I've got an idea you might all like."

Zach glanced at Truitt, then at C.J. and Long.

"I am in no driving hurry to return to that alley," C.J. said.

Truitt snorted. "I couldn't agree with you more about that. Just stay here for the night."

Zach nodded. "We'll be here."

"I'll be back after I talk to my brother. And don't worry if you hear a horse approaching. That will be me."

"You have a horse?" C.J. asked, surprise on his dirty face.

"Actually," Jimmy said, smiling as he turned away. "I have five of them."

"Oh," was all he heard Zach say.

PART SEVEN
Getting Help

JIMMY DISMOUNTED near where the others were still eating and tied up the horse on a tree limb. Luke had agreed that he should tell his friends about the wagon and have them help.

"How's your brother doing?" Zach asked.

Jimmy was surprised. It seemed that Zach actually cared.

"Very tired," Jimmy said. "We're moving him into a hotel room tomorrow so the Doc can look in on him every day and have the bed in the back free for other sick folk."

Zach and the rest nodded.

"You've got some money," C.J. said, more as a statement than a question.

"Not much," Jimmy said, telling them the truth. "Just what Benson didn't find in my parent's wagon. But enough to buy some provisions and take care of my brother until we decide what to do next."

"So, what's this idea we're going to like?" Truitt asked. "I love surprises, in case no one's told you that yet."

"I might have guessed," Jimmy said, smiling. "I've got a wagon about a mile outside of town. The people who have been watching the wagon and my stock during the day are pulling out tomorrow and I need help."

"You want us to be guards?" Zach asked, looking puzzled.

Truitt just laughed. "We take things, remember?"

Jimmy ignored him. "Actually, I was thinking you could all move out there with me. We can take turns staying with the wagon and stock and I'll pay for all the food and supplies for as long as my money lasts. No more stealing and safer than here or in that alley."

There was silence around the small campfire for a moment. From the distance, you could hear the sounds of pianos and shouting coming from the saloons, getting louder as evening got closer.

"Count me in," Zach said. "On one condition."

"What's the condition?" Jimmy asked, afraid of what it might be. He looked into the blue eyes of a guy he had really come to like over the last few days.

"If you and your brother head west, you take me with you. I promised my dad I'd head west, and this seems to be a good shot at doing just that."

"Me too," C.J. said. "I'm in with that condition."

"Oh, I so love stealing food just to survive, why would I want to join this craziness?" Truitt asked. Then he laughed. "Of course I'm in if you take me with you as well."

They all looked at Long, who just nodded. "I'll join as well. But I have one question. Are you headed for Oregon or California?"

"California," Jimmy said.

Long nodded that he liked that.

Jimmy looked around at the four friends and decided to tell them about the gold mine that Benson had taken.

"A gold mine?" C.J. asked, stunned when Jimmy had finished.

Truitt laughed. "I love surprises and you are sure made of them."

Jimmy smiled. "A real gold mine with a real deed that my father thought might be worth a lot of money. And my father had been a banker, so he would know."

"It seems we have an adventure ahead of us," Truitt said, clapping his hands together in sheer glee.

"You mean better than rolling a drum?" Jimmy asked.

"Far, far better," Truitt said. "Who could ask for more fun? The bunch of us heading west."

Jimmy glanced at Zach, who was smiling wider than Jimmy could imagine him ever smiling.

"Thanks," Zach said.

"Don't thank me," Jimmy said. "It's a long ways from here to Sacramento. And first we have to find Benson and somehow, without getting killed, get that mine deed back."

"If anyone can find him," C.J. said, smiling at Truitt, "we can."

PART EIGHT
The Search Begins

WHILE THE OTHERS had rounded up what few possessions they had from their camps, Jimmy had ridden out and gotten two other horses, then brought all four of his new friends back to the wagon, with Truitt riding behind Zach and C.J. behind Long.

By nightfall, they had had a fire going near the wagon and tents pitched and Truitt was working on what smelled like a wonderful stew. He was clearly a cook, and had gotten excited over all the spices and staples Jimmy's mother had brought along.

Jimmy was surprised at how good horsemen Zach and Long were. Both clearly knew and loved the animals, and how to treat them with respect.

By the time the evening had ended, Jimmy was feeling great about his decision. And he really liked being around them. They were all very different, but all of them were on their own and they all knew that they had a better chance of getting west if they worked together.

The next morning, with Long and Truitt watching the wagon while hundreds of other wagons around it were pulling out, Jimmy and Zach and C.J. headed back into town to help Jimmy move Luke to his room in a three-story hotel that smelled of perfume and baking bread.

Jimmy paid for an entire month of room and food. Twelve dollars. The hotel owner was pleased to see the money upfront and promised to help Luke as much as he could, especially with Doc Davis looking out for him as well.

It turned out that Jimmy had needed the help moving Luke. Luke was so weak, he could barely walk, and climb-ing the long staircase from the hotel's big lobby to his second floor hotel room tired him so much, he fell asleep almost at once after he got into bed.

"That's normal," Doc Davis told the three of them in the narrow hallway outside of Luke's room. "I have arranged for two meals a day to be sent up to his room, and his bed pan emptied. I doubt he's going to be making it out too much for some time. I'll check him every day as well."

"Thanks, Doc," Jimmy said. "Very much appreciated."

"Just take care of yourself as well," Doc Davis said. "Stay dry and don't go getting chilled. You don't want to be in there on a cot with your brother, do you?"

"Not a chance, sir," Jimmy said.

After Doc left, Zach asked Jimmy, "You want to sit with your brother a while?"

Jimmy shook his head. He didn't need to do that. Luke was as well taken care of

as anyone could be at this point. He just had to rest and get better.

"Then let's go see if we can find Benson," Zach said. "We have a gold mine deed to get back."

For the first time in what seemed like a long time, Jimmy felt as if his life was actually moving forward. And even though it was starting to rain slightly again, he was smiling.

They had no luck that day finding Benson, and after checking in with Luke, they headed back to the wagon, where Truitt had cooked an amazing meal of bread and stew.

Long, in the meantime, had brushed the two horses left there and checked them over for any problems. He had also fixed part of the tongue on the wagon that had cracked while crossing the last stream outside of Independence. He had also helped the Taskers with a repair before they pulled out.

It seemed to Jimmy that every one of them had a special skill that fit well with the other's skills. And Jimmy had no doubt he was just beginning to see all their special talents.

PART NINE
A Plan

IT WAS FINALLY, on the fourth afternoon that the five of them were together, that Zach came back with news about Benson from a small hotel and saloon on the edge of town.

And it wasn't good news.

It seemed that Benson had been there for a week or so, camping out west of town and drinking every night with three or four friends.

"Is he still there?" C.J. asked.

"Nope," Zach said. "The sheriff chased Benson and his friends out of town. It seems they robbed an elderly couple."

"Any idea where he might be heading?" Jimmy asked.

Somehow, in the days since reaching Independence, Jimmy realized he had gone from being the scared kid hiding out from the killer of his parents to a person who wanted to track the killer and make him pay. He wasn't sure when that change had happened, but it sure had. And now, after getting this close to the killer, Jimmy didn't want to lose him now.

"From what the bartender I talked to told me," Zach said, "Benson was bragging that he had a gold mine deed in California and was headed there to work it."

"My father's mine," Jimmy said. He could feel his anger boiling, and right now all he wanted to do was hit something. But instead he forced himself to take a deep breath and try to think.

"I'm afraid it probably is," Zach said.

"How far of a head start does he have on us?" C.J. asked, clearly puzzling out what to do next as well.

"Three days," Zach said. "He left at the same time as those two big trains."

"More people to rob and kill along the way," Jimmy said.

The others just nodded at that.

"I'll meet you all back at camp," Jimmy said, feeling just about as low as he had felt in a week. "I need to tell Luke what we found out. We'll talk about what to do tonight over dinner."

A few minutes later, Jimmy turned into Doc Davis's office.

"Everything all right with Luke?" Doc asked

"Far as I know," Jimmy said. "I'm just headed there now, but I have a question to ask you. How long you think it will be until Luke will be able to travel?"

"West?" Doc Davis asked.

Jimmy nodded.

"At least two months, maybe more to be really safe," Doc said. "Or maybe not this year at all. It depends on how fast he recovers."

"Thanks, Doc," Jimmy said and left without another word. He had known that, but he needed the Doc to confirm it. Now he had no idea what they were going to do.

He was feeling sick to his stomach, not because he was now safe from the man who had killed his parents, but because it looked like that man was never going to pay for what he did.

By the middle of the summer, who knew where Benson would be. It had been hard enough finding him in a town the size of Independence. With the entire west to search, it would be impossible.

Luke was sitting up in bed, sipping on some soup, and he seemed to be stronger.

"Hi, little brother."

Jimmy didn't say anything, just pulled a chair over closer to Luke's bed and sat down.

Luke stared at him, frowning, then said, "You found Benson, didn't you? I'm ready to talk to the sheriff."

"Not really," Jimmy said. "He and his gang of killers were chased out of town three days ago, heading west, bragging that they had a mine to work in California."

Luke sighed and put the soup on the nightstand. "I was afraid of that. I've been laying here the last few days thinking about what to do if you did find him, or if he had left. I've got a plan."

Jimmy felt a sense of relief. His mother always said that Luke was the thinker between the two of them. Jimmy was the one who rushed in for the adventure.

"Do you trust the boys you met here?" Luke asked.

"I trust them," Jimmy said, nodding. "They've been helping me guard the wagon and it was Zach who found out where Benson went."

"Do they all want to go west?" Luke asked.

Jimmy nodded. "All of them do."

"Sell the wagon and all the equipment," Luke said, his voice firm and in control. "You'll never catch him with a wagon."

"Catch him!" Jimmy shouted. "I'm not leaving you!"

He pushed his chair back and stood. His stomach was clamped into a knot. No way could he leave Luke.

Luke held up his hand and kept talking, his voice level. "Let me finish. You need to buy three more horses and leave me one in the stable here. And leave me enough money to pay for a year of this room and board and Doc Davis and a little extra. The other two horses will carry supplies for you. Then the five of you head out to track Benson."

"No," Jimmy said firmly. "That's not a plan. I'm not leaving you."

"Jimmy, you know Doc Davis won't let me travel. And if I try, I'm going to be dead in two weeks. You just keep track of him, don't show yourself, and I'll meet you in Sacramento next July 4th. Then we'll deal with that killer together. It's the only way we can make him pay for what he did to Mother and Father."

Jimmy just shook his head and said nothing. He hated this idea.

"You can't help me by sitting here, you know that?" Luke said, staring at Jimmy. "You did a great job getting me to Doc Davis on your own. You also have to know I believe in you to even suggest that my little brother travel clear out west without me?"

Jimmy nodded. "But I can't lose you."

Luke laughed and patted the bed. "I'll be right here. We'll only be apart until next summer."

Jimmy said nothing. The idea of going west alone terrified him more than he wanted to admit.

More than facing Benson, actually.

"Besides," Luke said, smiling, "You've got your friends to help out, and I've got Doc Davis's daughter to keep me company. Better than your ugly face."

"I can't argue with that," Jimmy said, managing a smile.

"Think about it," Luke said. "But you know I'm right. You have to go, at least to keep track of Benson until I can help you get that killer to justice."

Luke scooted down in the bed and closed his eyes with a sigh. "I envy you the adventure, little brother."

"When you're well, we'll have adventures together," Jimmy said.

"You have a deal," Luke said. "Now get out of here so I can get some sleep. And get a good price for the wagon and the equipment. Make Father proud."

Jimmy left, pulling the door tight behind him.

By the time he had finished a very slow ride out to the wagon, he knew that Luke was right.

There was no choice.

To stop Benson, or even keep track of him, Jimmy and his new friends had to go and go soon.

They had to chase Benson into the wilderness.

PART TEN
Headed West Again

JIMMY FINALLY GOT his wish to see a buffalo ten days out of Independence. It was May 7th.

It had taken two days for the five of them to sell the wagon and equipment and buy three more horses. During the first days on the trail, Long had pointed out some plants that were poison, and others that were good to eat. It seemed to Jimmy that there was a lot to learn about Long. And he had a lot to teach them about survival in the west.

Before they left, Jimmy had paid for three months in advance for Luke's hotel room and food, and gave Doc Davis another payment for his services. Then he gave some money to Luke, enough for Luke to pay for a year in the hotel and supplies to get west next spring.

Jimmy had left a few of the family's most personal things with Luke in the hotel room, and had given his father's rifle to Zach. He seemed to be the only one of them who wanted to touch it. Jimmy said it would come in handy for hunting. Everything else, Jimmy sold to buy camping gear and supplies that they packed on the extra horses and in their own saddlebags.

After all that, he didn't have much money left, but he didn't tell anyone but Zach.

The goodbye with Luke had been hard for Jimmy, but after a few days on the trail, Jimmy's mood had lightened and he had started looking forward to the adventure ahead.

On Long's suggestion, they didn't push the horses, but instead just walked them along at a steady pace, often between wagons in the long trains. Jimmy had figured that Benson was only five or six days ahead by the time they left Independence. Considering the eighteen different legs of the trip that lay between Independence and Sacramento, and how far they all had to travel, that wasn't very far.

Zach had said that since Benson and his men didn't have any money when they were chased out of town, more than likely they would join onto a train to find food and rob some unsuspecting family.

So each night, they camped near a different train camp, not only for protection, but to get to know those in the train to make sure Benson wasn't among them. The last thing they wanted to do was pass him without knowing it.

For the first leg, which was about a hundred miles from Independence to the Kansas River ferry, the trail was packed with wagons and people walking. At times, the trail seemed more like a busy city street than the main wagon road west.

But on the second leg, a two hundred mile stretch northwest across grasslands to the Platte River, the wagons seemed to spread out some, even inside the same train. It usually took a wagon about two weeks to make that leg, but they made it in six days, traveling at a steady pace, passing wagon after wagon, all with friendly faces waving at them as they went by.

Jimmy was starting to get a better idea of the vastness of the country. As far as the eye could see, it was green grasslands and low hills. The air was clean and fresh, especially after a rain. The only real excitement they encountered during the first days out of Independence was getting across a couple of swollen streams. It was clear that wagons had been lost in those streambeds, from the looks of the ruined equipment scattered downstream. Some family's dreams hadn't lasted very long.

When they reached the South Fork of the Platte River, the trail turned back westward and followed the south bank. The river was wide and brown and seemed to flow slowly and gently along. By this third leg of the trip, the wagons were really starting to spread out more and more, and sometimes it was impossible to tell where one company ended and another started. And there were more and more travelers in groups of two or three wagons, easy pickings for a man like Benson.

At one point, C.J. asked Long about Indians in this area. Long had pointed to the north. "Pawnee territory. To the south is Cheyenne. We're moving between them, so no problems."

Jimmy was glad to hear that, and glad even more that Long was with them. Not only did he know where the Indian territories were, but he had found some great roots that Truitt had used in some wonderful tasting stews.

The next morning, Long pointed at a dried brown pile to one side of the trail. "Fuel for a fire," he said. "Buffalo chips."

That had gotten them all excited and searching along the rolling hills around the river for any signs of actual buffalo. But they didn't see any that day. However, Long was correct about the dried chips being great fuel for the campfire.

Finally, on the tenth day out of Independence, a man from one of the wagon trains they were slowly passing came riding hard and fast back toward his wagon from a ridge to the south. "Buffalo!" he shouted when he got close enough.

The cry went up and down the wagon train like a brush fire.

"Looks like we might be eating meat tonight," Truitt had said, smiling at Jimmy.

Jimmy was so excited, he could hardly keep his heart from beating right out of his chest,

"Can a rifle like this stop one?" Zach asked Long, pointing to Jimmy's father's rifle tied to his saddlebag.

"In the heart, right behind the front legs," Long said. "Two or three shots, maybe. But don't shoot a bull. The meat is too tough. A small cow is the best."

Zach nodded.

Then Long turned to Jimmy. "I will camp below that rock ledge with the packhorses until you return."

"Not interested in seeing a buffalo?" C.J. asked.

"I have seen far too many of them," Long said, then took the packhorses and moved slowly off toward the rocks.

"Let's go find some buffalo," Jimmy said, smiling at his friends.

With that, they headed at full ride toward the hill where the man had come from. Two other men were right ahead of them, and Jimmy had no doubt many others from the train would be following.

As they crested over the rise, at first Jimmy couldn't see anything different. Then it dawned on him that part of the shallow valley to his right was covered in brown instead of waving green grass.

Buffalo!

What looked to be thousands of them. The stories were right. It did look like a sea of buffalo.

"Oh, my," Truitt said, awe in his voice.

Jimmy just stared. The buffalo were majestic creatures. Jimmy could see a number of larger bulls, and hundreds of smaller calves, grazing near their mothers. Even from a distance, he could tell they were bigger than any cattle he had ever seen. The bulls looked to be almost as big as their horses, not as tall but much wider.

A half dozen men rode past them, heading for the buffalo, rifles out and ready.

Jimmy glanced over at Zach. "Think you might be able to down one of those?"

Zach looked stunned, but then he smiled and nodded. "My dad said I was the best shot he had ever seen. I just have to get close enough."

"Let's go," Jimmy said. "C.J., Truitt, we'll try to cut out a small cow from the herd, let Zach get a clean shot."

"Right with you," C.J. said.

With that, Jimmy spurred his horse into motion down the hill toward the herd, following the men from the train. His heart was racing and he was having trouble catching his breath. Never, in all his life in Boston, did he think he would ever be doing something like this. What would his friends back there think if they could see him?

What would Luke think?

The buffalo were spooked by the men riding at them, and turned to run, in mass. The sound was almost deafening, louder than a train pulling into a station. And even on the horse, Jimmy could feel the ground shaking from that many large animals running at once.

Jimmy led them to the right, while the other men went to the left side of the herd. He had his eye on one medium-sized cow that was on the edge of the herd. He pointed at it and beside him Truitt shouted, "Got it, boss!"

Then C.J., seemingly completely fearless, did something that Jimmy would have never thought of doing. He took his horse into the herd, running with it, trying to cut the cow farther away from the herd.

It seemed to be working until suddenly shots echoed through the air from the other side of the herd.

The buffalo got even more frantic, running faster and harder.

And the entire herd turned toward them.

Jimmy found himself and his horse surrounded by buffalo, all running at top speed. He and his horse had no choice but to run with the herd.

He didn't dare stop.

He tried to ease his horse sideways, but there was no place to go. He was completely penned in by stampeding buffalo that smashed against his legs and his horse.

It was like riding while the ground around him was moving at the same time.

To his left, C.J. was stuck as well, a look of total concentration on his face as he tried to keep his horse on its feet. Jimmy couldn't see either Truitt or Zach, and hoped they were out of the herd and behind them.

"Ease back!" Jimmy shouted at C.J., pulling his horse back just enough to slow him, but not turn him. He didn't dare try to stop fast or turn. In the thundering of the herd, he could barely hear his own yell.

As he slowed just a little, the buffalo started moving around him, running forward, opening up spaces as the herd started to pass him.

C.J. glanced over and saw what Jimmy was doing, then started to do the same thing.

It seemed to take forever for the herd to pass Jimmy completely, but actually it must have only been a few seconds. As he made it into the open behind the herd, he let out the breath he must have been holding. He was sweating and his heart was beating so hard, it felt like it might explode.

If his horse had gone down in that herd, he would have died a horrible death.

He glanced around. Zach and Truitt were following a distance back, looks of worry on both of their faces.

The herd passed C.J. and the four of them stopped and tried to catch their breaths.

"I thought you two were dead for sure," Truitt said, shaking his head and laughing.

"I thought we were too," Jimmy said. He held his hands on his pants legs so that the others wouldn't see them shaking.

"Let's not do that again," C.J. said, sweat pouring down his face. He took off his glasses and tried to clean them, but his hands were shaking too much, so he gave up. "I think next time, I'll just stay with Long and the horses."

"Great buffalo hunters we are, huh?" Zach said, then he laughed. After a moment, all four of them were laughing.

Jimmy was just glad that all four of them were still alive so that they could laugh.

PART ELEVEN
A Real Hunt

SINCE THEIR FIRST experience with buffalo, they had seen a half dozen other herds before reaching the South Fork crossing. Some of the herds were smaller, some closer to the trail. But Jimmy's great desire to see them had worn off completely. He now had a huge respect for the big creatures.

After spotting the third herd, Long had finally agreed, after much pushing from Zach and Truitt, to help them to get some meat for dinner. As far as C.J. was concerned, he never wanted to see a buffalo again and he said he would be glad to watch the horses.

Long showed Zach a rock to sit behind with the rifle just down a shallow valley from the herd. "Shoot a small cow or large calf as it runs past. That will be more meat than we can carry."

Zach had nodded and looked worried when Long took his horse away, walking it slowly back to let C.J. hold it.

Then Long told Jimmy to go to the left of the herd, Truitt to the right, and he said he would stay directly behind them. "We move up to them slowly," Long said, "then when I give the signal, wave your hat and shout."

"We'll drive them directly at Zach," Jimmy said, glancing down the valley ahead of the herd where Zach crouched behind a rock.

"The beasts will turn slightly left, following the valley, and will pass beside Zach's position," Long said. "They are lazy creatures by nature and will not run up a hill unless they are forced to."

Jimmy just hoped, for Zach's sake, Long was right about that.

A few minutes later, they were all in position and Long gave the signal. This time, Jimmy had no plan on getting too close to the herd, and he noticed that Truitt stayed a safe distance away as well.

The herd of large beasts rumbled into motion, moving toward Zach. Again, Jimmy couldn't believe the noise and how much the ground shook.

For a moment, Jimmy thought Long was going to be wrong and Zach was going to have to depend on hiding behind

a rock to save his life. But then, as Long had said they would, the herd turned left, giving Zach a clear and close shot at the nearest creatures.

Zach leveled the rifle on one small cow and fired twice.

The cow went nose down, tumbled once, and then lay there, not moving.

Long motioned for C.J. to bring Zach's horse and the packhorses, and all of them moved toward the dead buffalo.

Jimmy was amazed at how ugly the creature was up close. And Long had been right, they were very smelly beasts, like a rancid stew left out in the sun for too many days. Their hair was patchy and bugs crawled all over them.

Long gave Jimmy, Truitt, and Zach step-by-step instructions on how to get the meat out of the beast, how to pack it, and so on. By the time they were finished, all three of them had to take a swim in the cold brown water of the river just to get the smell off.

But that night, the buffalo steaks that Truitt cooked were wonderful. Jimmy figured it was almost worth it.

Almost.

PART TWELVE
A Big Storm

THE NEXT AFTERNOON they reached the South Fork Crossing.

All Jimmy could think about was that it wasn't possible to cross that wide a river. It had to be at least a half-mile across. It looked more like a lake than a river. He could swim, but not that good.

"We're going across that?" Truitt asked.

"All of them are," Jimmy said, pointing at the two hundred wagons that were camped along the banks of the river. "We can make it."

"I'm not much of a swimmer," Truitt said, clearly not happy with the idea.

"Neither am I," C.J. said.

"Your horse can swim," Long said. "Just stay in the saddle."

Truitt looked at Long. "Oh, sure, easy for you to say."

As the five of them sat and stared at the ford from the high bank, at least twenty wagons were in the water at one point or another in the crossing. And more were camped on the other side.

From what Jimmy could tell, none of the wagons seemed to be in too far over their beds, and none of the horses seemed to be swimming. That, at least, was a good sign.

They spent the rest of that day camped with the wagons, making sure Benson wasn't among those waiting to cross. Then, the next morning, they went into the water.

As Jimmy pushed his horse gently into the slowly moving river, he wasn't sure what was more frightening, riding in a herd of buffalo or crossing a river a half-mile wide. At that moment, he almost wished he was back with the buffalo.

But the river turned out to be shallow all the way across, and he didn't even get his boots wet. That afternoon, after checking the wagons camped on the other side for any sign of Benson, they headed away from the river into the fourth leg of the long trip.

From what C.J. told them, it was just over one hundred and eighty miles from the crossing to Fort Laramie. More than likely, that would be where they would catch up to Benson.

The trail from the crossing cut across a shallow range of hills and started up the North Fork of the Platte River.

The hills around them now were rocky and higher, and the brush thinner. And by this point, the wagons were really spread out. Sometimes they would ride for a few hours before catching up to a stopped band of wagons.

"We're in Sioux territory," Long said on the third day. "We should camp at night with a wagon company for safety."

Jimmy had no argument with that.

Jimmy wanted to ask Long many questions about his mother's people, but figured now wouldn't be the time. Maybe later in the trip. Right now, Long looked very serious and focused on the rocks and hills around them and Jimmy let him concentrate.

On the third evening as they were moving along the river, it seemed as if the sky around them and above the mountains just suddenly turned a pitch black. It had rained off and on for the entire trip, but no storm before had looked this bad.

Zach pointed at the coming clouds. "I think we need to take cover."

"I agree," Long said. "That will have some strong winds and lightening with those clouds."

"How about up that canyon there?" Truitt pointed to a rock-lined canyon "We should be able to anchor our tents pretty well there."

"It's not with a wagon company," Jimmy said. He didn't much like the looks of the coming clouds either, but he also didn't like the idea of camping alone in Sioux territory without a lot of people around them. And at the moment, there was no wagon company within sight along the trail.

"The Sioux will take cover as well," Long said. "They consider a storm like this one bad medicine."

"Can't argue with them there," Truitt said as a rumbling of thunder echoed out over the river.

With one more look at the clouds, Jimmy said, "Let's move before we get soaked."

At a full gallop, they turned away from the trail and headed up the rocky canyon, following a shallow stream. There were numbers of side canyons off the main one, but Long led them to what seemed like an alcove water had cut into the rock. The walls of the canyon would shelter them both from most of the wind and the lightening.

They secured the horses, then madly worked to pitch and secure their tents. Jimmy had just finished and crawled inside when the first gust of wind really rocked his tent and a moment later the rains started.

Chances are, it was going to be a very long night.

He must have dozed because the next thing he realized, lightning and thunder were shaking the ground around him, and water was pouring into his tent.

He grabbed his saddlebags and got out into the storm quickly. In one flash of lightning, he saw that the small stream they had camped beside was quickly rising.

"Water!" he shouted. "Everybody up and out!"

Another very close strike of lightning spooked the horses and he barely got to them in time to hold them from trying to break away.

"We need to get out of this canyon!" Long shouted over the thundering of the storm.

"And fast!" Jimmy shouted.

He could only see the others through the pitch black pouring rain when lightning lit up the canyon. But from what he could see, the others were scrambling to gather up their gear and get to the horses.

The water around them was coming up faster than Jimmy could have imagined possible. He decided to leave his tent and bedroll. He doubted he could get to them in the rising water anyway.

He managed to get a saddle on his horse while the others worked frantically in the pouring rain beside him. By the time he got the gear on one of the pack-horses and got mounted, the water had risen so fast, it was up to his waist.

Somehow, he got his horse and the packhorse headed downstream, but now both horses seemed to be swimming in the strong current and it was everything Jimmy could do to just hang on.

A lightning strike showed a side canyon ahead that looked mostly dry. He tried to turn his horse in that direction, and somehow the horse got footing and pulled out of the water, with the pack-horse following.

Lightning strikes, one right after another, gave him just enough light in the rain to work his way up the canyon to a high, wide shelf area that would be above any flooding.

There he dismounted and tried to hold the horses as tight as he could against the shelter of the rock wall.

The rain pounded on him as he knelt down. He was so cold, he was shivering and his fingers were numb.

Around him, the storm raged, as if the Earth itself was mad at him.

He stayed pressed against the rocks, trying to hold the horses from bolting with every close lightning strike and thunderous clap.

None of the others had made it into this side canyon.

More than likely, they had been swept downstream and into the big river and were dead. Even if they could swim, no one could survive that swirling torrent in the rock canyon for very long.

It was going to be a very long night.

He had lost his friends.

Mother Nature and the west had clearly won this battle.

And again, he was completely alone.

PART THIRTEEN
Alone Again

THE MORNING LIGHT was barely allowing Jimmy to see the narrow side canyon around him. The air was bitingly cold, and Jimmy was soaking wet from the long night in the rain. He needed to get dry and warm quickly, before he got sick. He knew, without a doubt, that this kind of cold and wet could kill a man out here in the wilderness faster than any wild animal.

Faster than a killer like Benson.

Jimmy had to get dry and warm up as soon as he could, somehow.

In the faint light, he slowly eased himself and his two horses down off the rock ledge he had reached during the flood. The canyon was no more than a hundred paces across and the walls were as tall as three Boston banks. The stream flowing through the bottom of the canyon now was only a fast torrent, not at all dangerous-looking. But he could see the watermarks up the rock walls where the water had been last night in the flash flood. He

had been lucky to survive. He had no idea how the rest of them could have.

Yesterday, there had been an easy path through the rocks. Now the way down to the main canyon and the wagon trail was completely blocked by boulders and brush and walls of mud. In one place, the water was flowing under some boulders that were far too big to get a horse over. It was clear he wasn't getting down the canyon and back to the river that way, at least not with two horses. He was going to need to find another way out.

He took a deep breath and shouted, "Zach! Long!"

His shout echoed among the rocks and then died under the sounds of the stream.

Nothing.

No one shouted back.

He had to keep believing they were alive. He had lost his parents, and left his sick brother Luke in Independence. He couldn't lose his friends as well. He had to find them.

Or at least find their bodies.

He shivered and felt light-headed. The cold and wet was clearly getting to him. He had to keep moving, find a way to get dry.

He headed back up the side canyon, sometimes wading in deep mud, other times climbing over rocks, looking for any trail up and over the steep rock walls. Finally he found a path that he could get the horses up to a ridgeline and then work his way around and back down to the river.

At the top, in the morning sun, he stopped, took off his wet clothes and wrung the last of the cold water from them, letting the sun warm him as best it could so early in the day.

He had some mostly dry extra clothes in his saddlebag, so he put those on, then put on his light coat, and then put back on his heaviest coat. He would be sweating this way soon enough, but that was what he needed to do to get warm.

An hour later, as the warmth of the sun had him warmed back to normal, he headed back down into the wide valley that ran along the side of the North Fork of the Platte River. It took him almost three hours to go the few miles down to the trail, the riding was so rough.

No wagon companies were in sight in either direction. With one look at the wagon trail, Jimmy knew why. Every stream that flowed out of the hills above the river had flooded last night in the storm. And now the trail was cut with deep gashes, sometimes up to the height of ten men deep. Those streams would take time to work wagons through or around. The next company through here was basically going to have to build a lot of new trail.

The river itself flowed dark brown with mud and much higher than it had yesterday. There was all kind of debris floating in the river, and as Jimmy watched, the canvas top of one wagon floated past.

Jimmy rode back to the mouth of the canyon he had been trapped in, then on foot he searched the length of the huge gash in the ground from the canyon wall to the river's edge, looking for any signs of his friends.

Nothing.

More than likely, they had been swept into the river. Maybe a couple of them had made it out downstream.

He headed down the trail they had come up yesterday. The going was slow, as he had to pick his way over one washed-out gulley after another. But finally, he reached a half dozen men working out ahead of a wagon company, trying to find or build a new trail through the area.

Jimmy talked to all of them, asking if they had run across any boys about his age along the river.

"Nope," one man said. "Just a number of dead horses and cattle floating past. Sorry."

Jimmy sure hoped those horses were from a company of wagons up the river farther. He didn't want to think about any of them being his friends' horses.

By the middle of the afternoon, he gave up his search and turned back west. He might as well go on to Fort Laramie. Maybe the rest of the group would be waiting for him there. More than likely, if they had searched for him and couldn't find him, that's what Zach would have them do.

They would be there. He had to believe that.

PART FOURTEEN
Benson Shows Up

FINALLY, ALONE AND tired, Jimmy came face-to-face with the killer of his parents.

With the light just barely tinting the sky on the morning of the second day after the flash flood, Jimmy had worked his way into the settlement beside the military buildings of Fort Laramie.

There were a large number of saloons spaced with even more general stores than Independence had. He knew the stores sold expensive supplies for those who needed them at this point of the trip west. This would be the last major re-supply stop until the west side of the Nevada Territory. Entire wagon trains full of supplies had left Independence ahead of the main rush of settlers to stock these stores.

The town was laid out on a gentle slope, and to one side were hundreds of Sioux Indians camped in groups of lodges. Long had told them that his people would be here, trading with the settlers, but Jimmy was still surprised to see that many camped that close to the town and the military buildings.

On the other side of the town were a good three hundred wagons filling a hillside and a wide valley. Smoke drifted lazily through the crisp, clear air from all the morning campfires.

Jimmy had rode into the mostly still-dark town, moving down the main street looking for any sign of his friends or their horses.

Nothing.

Luckily, he had saved what was left of his father's money when scrambling for safety in the flood. He needed a new tent and bedroll. He pulled his horses up to a general store that was just opening.

Suddenly, the man he hated the most walked out of the saloon right beside the store.

Jake Benson stood right there in front of Jimmy on the wooden sidewalk, not more than twenty paces away.

Jimmy sat in his saddle, stunned and frozen. That man had shot Jimmy's mother in the back. Jimmy could feel his anger building like a pot ready to boil. He wanted to run at Benson screaming and shouting and just beat the man to death with his fists, but he knew he wasn't big enough or strong enough to do that to Benson.

And besides, Benson had a gun and his men were with him.

"Just follow him until I can join you," his brother Luke had said. *"Then we will take care of him together."*

Jimmy made himself take a deep breath, then he dismounted and eased around to the other side of his horse so he was hidden from Benson. He had been lucky the killer hadn't spotted him.

Jimmy's hands were shaking, his breathing shallow and swift. Benson scared him to death, and made him fantastically angry at the same time.

Benson laughed at something another man coming out of the saloon said. Then Benson and his three men mounted up and started toward the edge of town, heading west. There was no sign of the man Luke had shot.

Jimmy mounted back up as well. Staying far enough back as to barcly still see the four men in the distance, he rode along behind them.

An hour later, it was clear that Benson and his men were on the wagon trail, moving at a steady walking pace, following a company of wagons that had just pulled out.

Jimmy turned around. At least he knew where Benson was headed.

West.

For a gold mine.

Now Jimmy had to find his friends. He could afford to wait around Fort Laramie for three or four days and still catch up with Benson. The killer and his men had had a five or six day head start on him out of Independence and Jimmy had caught him this time. He would catch the killer again, he had no doubt.

Jimmy couldn't let Luke and his parents down. He had to keep following Benson, even if he had to do it alone.

The sun was cresting over the hills as Jimmy got back into town and tied up his horses in front of a general store. As he was about to climb up onto the wooden sidewalk and go inside, he glanced down the street.

Zach!

Jimmy couldn't believe it. His best friend was standing against the wall of a saloon with his back to Jimmy. Zach was clearly watching the trail coming in from the east, the trail that Jimmy had come in on three hours earlier.

Jimmy wanted to shout and jump for joy. He couldn't believe Zach was still alive. He headed down the sidewalk with a smile on his face that hurt it was so big.

He walked up behind Zach and then said in his most serious voice, "Is Truitt working wagons again?"

Zach spun around, then, smiling, he grabbed Jimmy by the shoulders and shook him. "You're alive. I can't believe it. You're alive. C.J. said you would be."

"And you didn't believe him?" Jimmy asked, smiling just as hard.

"We searched that entire area, but we couldn't get back up the canyon, and by the time we went around to an area on top of the hills to look down into the canyon, there was no sign of you."

"We?" Jimmy asked. "Is everyone all right?"

Zach nodded, smiling. "Banged up a little, and the horses have some cuts and scrapes. That stream just dumped us out onto the bank of the river like so much garbage. Long has been taking care of the horses and they're going to be good as rain. But we lost some of our provisions and gear. We've been living on what's left of the buffalo meat, camped down near the wagons since yesterday."

"Well," Jimmy said, "Let's go get everyone. I think I have enough left of my father's money to get whatever new gear we need. I lost some of mine as well."

"You managed to save your father's money from the flood?" Zach asked.

"Sure did," Jimmy said, "and a packhorse."

Then Jimmy got serious. "This morning I saw Benson."

"Where?" Zach asked, clearly stunned. "What did you do?"

Jimmy patted his best friend on the shoulder. "Let's head back to the camp. I'll tell everything over breakfast. We have plans to make and a gold mine to get back."

Zach laughed. "Oh, I can't tell you how much I love the sound of that."

"Yeah, me too," Jimmy said. "Me too."

PART FIFTEEN
A New Team Member

WITH LONG TENDING to the slightly injured horses, the four of them went back into town that afternoon to get supplies for the trip west. It was going to take every dime of the money Jimmy had left to re-supply, especially in Fort Laramie.

As Jimmy was helping Truitt and C.J. carry gear out of one store, he came out to find Zach, who had been guarding the horses, sitting on the edge of the wooden sidewalk next to a young man who looked to be around Jimmy's age of twenty. The man was writing in a notebook. He had on a tall black hat and his long dark hair flowed out from under the back of the hat.

Across the street, two drunks were taking wild swings at each other and then falling into the mud. As Jimmy watched, the guy seemed to be writing down what he was seeing, stumble-by-stumble, blow-by-missed-blow.

Zach glanced up to see Jimmy watching.

Now Available
from all your favorite booksellers in trade paper and electronic editions.

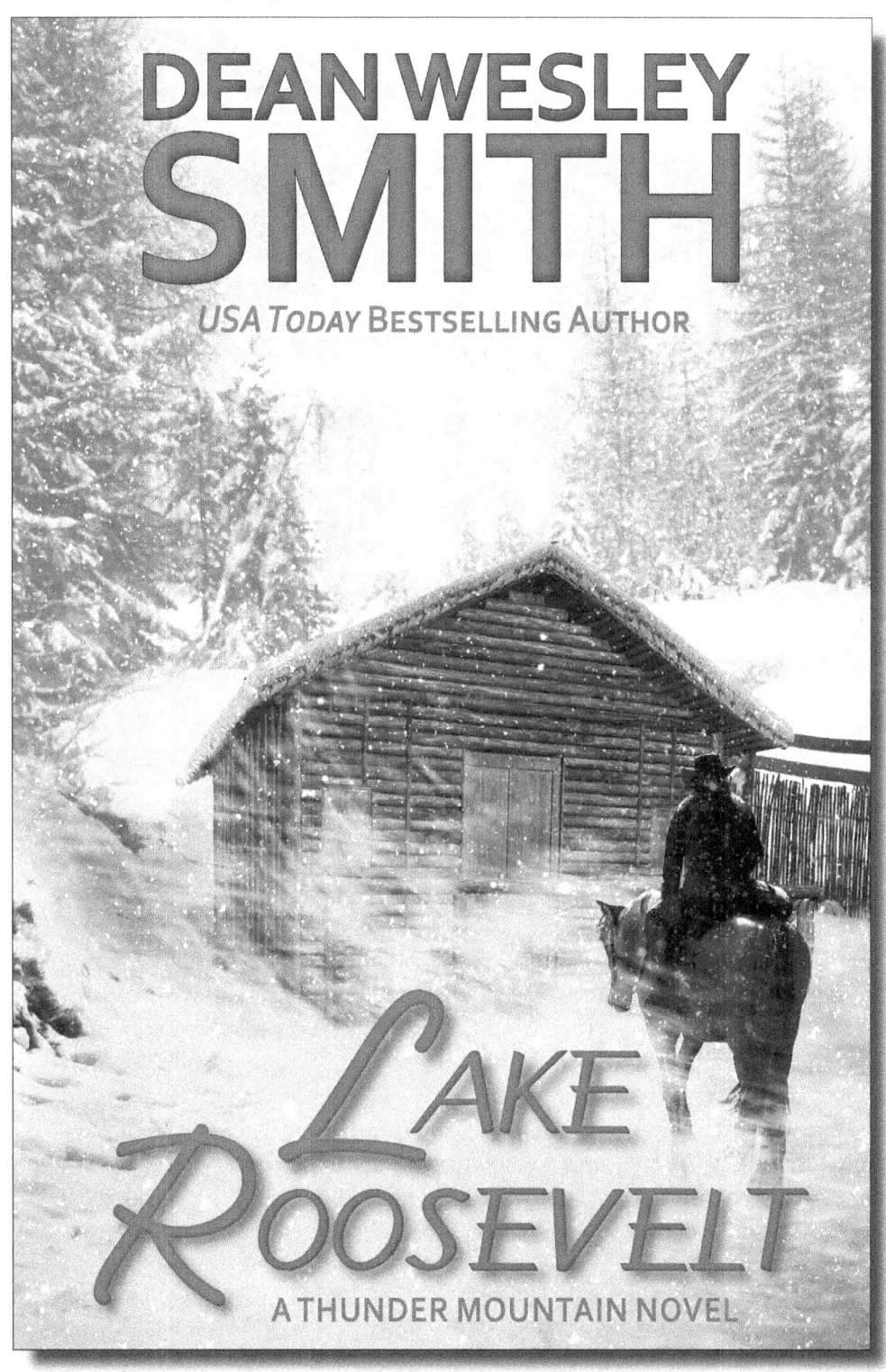

DEAN WESLEY
SMITH
USA Today BESTSELLING AUTHOR

LAKE ROOSEVELT

A THUNDER MOUNTAIN NOVEL

"Meet Joshua Mark," Zach said. "Future journalist and storyteller."

"Call me Josh," the man said, glancing up at Jimmy. "You two got separated in the big storm, didn't you?"

Jimmy glanced at Zach, who shrugged. "I didn't tell him."

"Saw your meeting this morning," Josh said, still writing down what was happening with the two drunks across the street. "Figured it out for myself."

"Pretty sharp," Jimmy said, surprised. "You with one of the wagon companies?"

"Nope," Josh said. "I'm just trying to head out west. I'm going to be like Mark Twain and write down stories about the west and then sell them."

Jimmy stared at the side of Josh's face as he wrote down how the fight had ended, with one drunk falling against a horse rail and knocking himself out. This guy was clearly very, very smart. Jimmy had had a number of years in school, but he couldn't write anywhere near as well or as fast as Josh was doing.

"Who's this?" C.J. asked as he came out of the store and dropped down on the edge of the wooden sidewalk beside Josh. He noticed what Josh had been doing and said, "Hey, can I read it?"

"Sure," Josh said, handing C.J. the pages held together with a strip of leather. Josh pointed to a place on one page and said, "Start there."

"You have family?" Jimmy asked, starting to like this guy more and more every second. He was clearly very smart, maybe even smarter than C.J., if that was possible. And they were going to need smart if they were to do anything with Benson when they caught up with him again.

"Nope," Josh said. "Just me. Parents died, no one else."

"You got a horse?" Zach asked.

"Nope," Josh said. "I was just going to walk along with one of the trains, maybe work for some food along the way when I could. That's how I got this far."

Jimmy motioned that Zach should follow him back into the general store. As Zach stood, C.J. said, "This is really good. You have more like it?"

"I sure do," Josh said, smiling.

Inside the store, Jimmy turned to Zach. "Are you thinking what I'm thinking?"

"We're headed into some really rough country," Zach said. "We're better off if there's more of us riding together."

"And the mine?" Jimmy asked.

"I have a hunch," Zach said, smiling, "that there's going to be more than enough work and gold for all of us."

"I agree," Jimmy said, thinking about what it would take for Josh to join them. He likely had his own gear, and they had an extra horse. They only needed one packhorse.

Jimmy looked at Zach. "Let's ask him if he is interested in joining us."

"Who's going to join us?" Truitt asked, coming up with a handful of spices in cloth bags and a block of salt.

"The man outside with the tall black hat," Zach said. "He's as sharp as a drapery tack."

"The guy doing the writing?" Truitt asked, glancing out the front door.

Jimmy nodded, looking for any sign that Truitt might not like the idea.

"Great by me," Truitt said, turning around to go back to shopping. "I have a hunch that where we are heading, we're going to need all the help we can get."

Jimmy laughed. "That settles it, then. Three votes win."

Zach pointed back out the door at how C.J. and Josh were laughing over something. "I'm betting you'll get a fourth vote real easy."

That night, around a warm campfire of buffalo chips, Truitt cooked them a great meal and the six friends talked late into the darkness.

By the end of the evening, Jimmy was very glad they had met Josh.

By mid-morning of the next day, they were headed west.

Four of the eighteen legs to reach California were behind them.

The easy four.

PART SIXTEEN
They Make Hard Progress

THE VASTNESS of the West was overwhelming to Jimmy, not in a bad way, but with a feeling that kept generating excitement. Every day he marveled at one sight or another, from small things like the sight of an animal he had never seen to stunning rock formations.

And the smells seemed to constantly change, from dry sagebrush to wetlands along the river.

They had traveled through the fifth leg up the river to the ford of the North Fork of the Platte River, making a steady pace for seven days. The trail was much, much rougher, and the wagon companies were clearly having more trouble with the pull.

They were doing fine, walking most of the time to rest the horses.

In a couple places, the trail was a full day's ride away from the river, so they had to watch their water more carefully.

At Independence Rock, all of them carved their names on the rock, along with thousands of other names. Jimmy couldn't believe so many people had gone past this place.

This was a rough trip for even someone in as good of shape as he was. And it was clear that if his brother had tried to make even these early legs, it would have killed him.

The seventh leg took them up to the top of the South Pass and over the Continental Divide. The air, the higher they climbed, got colder at nights, and twice over the four days up to the pass, it snowed on them during the night.

They walked the horses even more, and moved shorter distances because none of them were used to the higher altitude. Jimmy found it amazing that all the mountains around them were still covered in white.

He had never seen anything so beautiful in all his life. Pictures and paintings just didn't do it justice in any fashion.

And the smell of the pine in the crisp morning air just made his head spin in happiness.

The main trail then angled north to Fort Hall , then back south to the split in the Oregon and California Trails forty miles to the south of Fort Hall.

Fort Hall was small, with few saloons or general stores. Considering that it was a major spot on the trip, it wasn't much to see.

There were a few Snake Indians camped near town, and very few wagons. It was the last place to really buy supplies on either the California or Oregon Trails, but most wagons didn't need anything here and just camped for a night, then pressed on.

"We're about halfway to California from Independence," C.J. said in the morning as they rode out of Fort Hall.

"The easy half," Josh said.

Jimmy didn't like the sound of that at all.

Forty miles later, they reached Raft River, where the Oregon Trail split from the California Trail.

The southern California trail went along the Raft River for a while, then went up and over a few ranges until finally dropping down on Goose Creek.

It was on June 14th, as they worked their way along a small stream called Goose Creek, just inside the eastern edge of Nevada, the union's newest state, that everything changed.

The trail ahead went around a low ridge and it was from that direction that the sounds of gunfire came.

Close, very close.

Then a woman screamed.

Jimmy froze, wondering if that was what his mother had sounded like when Benson killed his father.

Then there were more shots and another scream.

"Get down!" Zach shouted.

All the boys dove from their horses and scrambled for cover in a small grove of trees near the spring.

Jimmy had no idea what was happening, but it didn't sound good.

Again, the woman screamed loud and long.

All Jimmy could think about was that they had to do something to help her.

Anything.

His mother hadn't had anyone to help her.

The woman's next scream echoed over the hills and then died out in a horrible way with one more shot.

Too late to help her. That was all he could think.

Jimmy glanced around at his five friends. What had they gotten into this time?

PART SEVENTEEN
Death Comes to the West

THE WOMAN'S SCREAMS were frightening in how sharp and clear they carried over the wide Goose Creek valley.

Jimmy jerked around in the saddle of his horse, trying to figure out where the shots and screams were coming from as Long, who had been leading the six of them at a steady pace, immediately dismounted and pulled his horse toward a grove of tall trees beside the stream.

Jimmy did the same, realizing just how big a target he was sitting up there on the horse.

So far, the vastness of the West had scared and overwhelmed him, a flash flood had almost killed him, and he had barely escaped being trampled by a buffalo herd. Yet that woman's scream sent more chills through his blood than anything he had heard since leaving Independence.

Around him, the Goose Creek valley looked like a peaceful place, a wonderful green strip of life in the otherwise brown hills. Large leafy trees bordered the creek, and kept the area cool from the heat of the day.

Keeping his head low, Jimmy followed Long deeper into the trees, finally stopping and tying up his horse on a large log.

All six then hunkered down together, listening. Not even a slight breeze broke the silence of the valley and the gentle sounds of the stream. Jimmy could hear his own heart pounding in his chest and he tried not to pant too loudly.

Two more shots rang out over the trees.

Jimmy could only think about what had happened to his mother, how she must have screamed when Jake Benson shot his father in the back. Jimmy wondered if his mother's screams sounded as chilling before she was shot as well.

The scream came again, then another few shots. Finally, the valley settled into an uneasy silence.

Like the silence at a funeral.

Jimmy pushed the thought away and turned to Long and the rest of his friends. Long knew the West and distances and seemingly everything else about survival out in the wilderness. Jimmy had come to count on him and his special talents.

"Indians?" Jimmy asked, his voice barely above a whisper.

He forced himself to breathe and try to keep calm, not let his total hate of guns and the sound of those screams get in his way.

"Bannocks in this area," Long said, nodding, his long black hair flowing around his shoulders. "They are a mean group."

Josh, their newest member, shook his head, his notebook and pen clutched tightly in his hand. "That doesn't sound like the type of guns the Bannocks would have."

All five of them turned to stare at their newest member. Clearly, besides writing stories, Josh knew guns. That was a talent that Jimmy would have to keep in mind in the future.

Long nodded, then whispered. "Josh is right. We need to take a look."

"Can you tell where the sounds are coming from?" Zach asked. His hands squeezed their only gun, a hunting rifle that used to belong to Jimmy' father.

Jimmy could tell that the sounds of the woman screaming had bothered Zach a lot as well. Usually Zach was the calm one. Now he was squeezing the butt of the rifle like it was a dishtowel he was trying to wring water out of.

"Just over the ridge to the right," Long said and Josh nodded in agreement.

Jimmy glanced at Josh. "Can you tell how many different guns were fired?"

"Three," Josh said. "One rifle, two revolvers."

Even Long looked impressed.

"Glad you're along with us," Truitt said, patting Josh's shoulder.

Josh smiled and nodded thanks.

Jimmy glanced around at his five friends and decided they needed to act. This was the west, after all.

"Truitt, you and C.J. stay with the horses. Be saddled up and ready to come riding fast with all of them if we shout for help."

Truitt nodded.

Zach checked quickly to make sure the rifle was fully loaded. Between bloodthirsty outlaws, stampeding buffalo, and deadly weather, the West was proving itself to be no parlor game.

"Go slow and stay quiet," Long said softly as he headed out for the small rise to the right of the stream.

To Jimmy, it seemed to take them forever to get to the top of that hill, picking their way first through the trees, then up the gentle incline through the sagebrush, moving slowly and carefully, staying in behind Long.

But in reality, it couldn't have been longer than a minute.

Just before they reached the top, the crackling of a large fire could be heard from the other side, then a man laughing.

The sound made Jimmy catch his breath.

It was the sound of evil. Pure evil.

Long motioned for them to spread out beside him, and then they crawled the last few feet on hands and knees to the top of the ridge as the hot sun beat down on their backs.

Beyond the top of the hill, Goose Creek doubled back into the sheltered alcove of a small valley. The main trail stayed in the larger valley. In the shelter between the two ridges, someone had built a small ranch with a slanted-roof barn and a cabin. A garden had been planted beyond the cabin, and behind the farm was a large grove of trees, so thick that Jimmy could barely see down through them. It looked like a wonderful oasis in the vast desert and rough lands of the Wyoming Territory

The house was starting to burn, black smoke billowing up into the clear morning sky. The crackling of the flames was getting louder as more and more of the house caught fire. Sparks flew into the air before vanishing.

And there were three bodies scattered around the burning building.

Jimmy was stunned and sick to his stomach at what he saw. Clearly the family that had lived in the house had been shot down.

Four horses were tied up near the barn right below them, and the sounds of men talking came from the barn.

Jimmy looked at the horses. He knew one of them.

Benson!

The man who had killed Jimmy's parents had now killed another family.

PART EIGHTEEN
The Unthinkable

JIMMY KEPT HAVING trouble breathing as he stared at the scene below them. He forced himself to take slow, deep breaths and try to think.

He had to do something.

Beside him, on their stomachs as well, Long, Zach, and Josh just stared.

Josh kept making long swallowing motions, like he was trying to hold his breakfast down. Jimmy had no doubt Josh was taking in every detail. He seemed to have a real skill for seeing things that others didn't, and then putting those details in his stories. This wasn't going to make good campfire reading, that was for sure.

Four men came out of the barn, laughing, leading two horses.

Benson.

All Jimmy could do was stare at the man who had killed his parents.

Something had to be done.

But any movement that they made down the hill at the men would just get them all killed as well.

Zach muttered something Jimmy couldn't hear and then pulled the rifle to his shoulder. He took aim, then lowered his rifle, stared at the scene below, then took aim again at the four men.

Jimmy reached over and put a hand on the gun.

When Zach glanced at him, Jimmy shook his head. It wasn't the time, and even though Zach was a good enough shot that he might get one or two of the killers, the other two would kill all the rest of them. That wasn't the way to do it. They had to come up with something else.

Zach looked like he was going to object, then finally nodded and lowered the rifle, his face white, his breath coming in gasps.

Jimmy forced himself to turn back and stare at the homestead and death below them, trying to see anything that was possible to do.

"Ideas?" he whispered to the others.

All three shook their heads.

Jimmy studied the trees behind the house. They would allow someone to get close, but then what?

Those men deserved to be hanged.

The thought echoed through his mind and Jimmy knew what they had to try to do. One at a time, they needed to pick off these men, separate them, bring them to justice. Even though he had promised his brother he wouldn't do anything until they were together, he couldn't wait any

longer. Too many people were getting killed.

He turned to Josh. "The rope on my saddle, and Truitt's rope. Run and get both of them as quickly as you can. And bring all the horses and the other two up here right behind us. The sounds from the fire should cover the noise."

Long nodded in agreement.

Josh looked puzzled, then without a word scampered away.

Zach whispered to Jimmy. "What are you thinking?"

"We have to stop those men before more people get killed," Jimmy said, his voice barely in control. In all his life, he couldn't remember being this angry. "And the only way we're going to stop them is one at a time."

He quickly outlined his plan to Zach and Long.

Long and C.J. were the best two riders, so they would be the decoys. And C.J. had his special rock sling that might come in handy as well while he rode. It would be up to Jimmy and Truitt, with Zach standing guard with the rifle, to make the plan work.

Jimmy turned to Zach after he nodded agreement to the plan. "If you have to, can you really shoot a man?"

"I don't honestly know." Zach said, glancing down at the four men where they stood talking near the bodies of the family they had slaughtered. "But if I can't, I can at least give you cover."

Jimmy nodded. "Good enough. But it's going to be better to not fire a shot. The idea is to not let these men know what happened to one of them."

Zach nodded and went back to squeezing the stock of the rifle in nervousness.

Jimmy had no doubt they were in way over their heads with this plan. They were six basically green men taking on four deadly killers in the middle of the wilderness, with no chance of any help. More than likely, this was going to turn out badly.

But they had to try.

Jimmy just couldn't let more people be killed.

Zach and Jimmy went back over the hill to talk with the rest, leaving Long to stand guard.

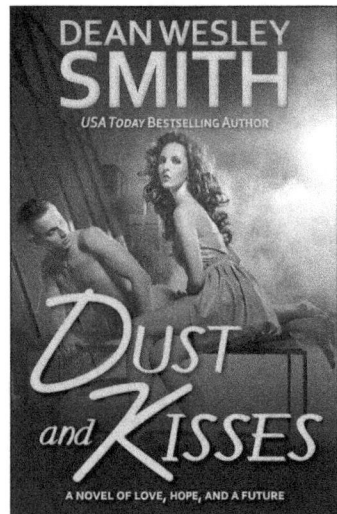

"We have to move fast," Jimmy said after explaining the plan. "We will meet three miles off the trail in the trees just after dusk tonight, where we camped last night. Make sure none of the killers are following you."

Everyone nodded. Jimmy could tell they were all as afraid as he was, but all were willing to risk this.

Jimmy and Truitt each took a coil of rope. Jimmy put his over his shoulder so he could drop it quickly if he had to run. Then heading along the top of the hill, he and Truitt worked their way over and down into the trees behind the homestead.

Jimmy could see that Zach took up a position behind a rock on the hillside where he could see both Jimmy and Truitt. He was such a good shot that from there he could easily knock a man off his horse if he needed to.

And if he could.

Jimmy just hoped he wouldn't have to.

Silently, Jimmy moved from tree to tree through the grove along the stream, until he found a good tree beside an animal trail, then quickly went up it with one end of the rope. He hadn't climbed a tree in years, but it was a skill he hadn't forgotten.

About ten feet up, he settled into the crook of a branch, then quickly got his end of the rope around the tree trunk. Then he made sure he was braced and the rope was in place.

Truitt, on the other end of the rope in the tree on the other side of the trail, nodded that he was ready. They had the rope up high enough that anyone riding under it wouldn't notice it.

Jimmy gave Zach up on the hill the ready sign, and Zach turned and gave it to Josh.

Jimmy knew that if this didn't work, they might be trapped in these trees, and if that happened, he and Truitt would soon be dead.

Through the trees, Jimmy could see the killers getting ready to mount up.

Less than ten seconds later, with a blood-curdling war cry, Long and C.J. came riding around the edge of the ridge, their heads down, their horses going at full speed. Long had untied his hair and it flew out behind him like a cape.

And C.J. had wrapped himself in one of Long's Indian blankets and put some dirt on his face to make himself look more Indian, even with his glasses. To the four killers, it must have looked like Long and C.J. just appeared out of thin air not more than fifty paces away.

C.J. lifted up in his saddle only long enough to twirl his rock sling and hit one man solidly in the side with a rock.

The guy swore as he went to the ground, trying to get his gun out of his holster.

C.J. and Long rode past the killers on the other side of the burning homestead and headed into the trees behind the house where Jimmy and Truitt waited.

Benson had his gun out the quickest and fired, but the shot missed both C.J. and Long as they pushed into the trees and flashed right under Johnny and Truitt and the rope they held between them.

All four killers quickly mounted up and rode after Long and C.J., just as Jimmy knew they would. They didn't dare let any witness, even Indians, live to tell what they had done to that poor family.

C.J. and Long, once they got out of the trees down the stream, would split up and circle out over the hills to the north. Jimmy had no doubt that they could get away. They were both fantastic riders and had fast horses. Jimmy was far more worried about what he and Truitt were about to try. If they missed, one or both of them would be more than likely dead.

The man that C.J. had hit with his sling was a little slower mounting up than the other three and was trailing the other killers by a good twenty paces.

Benson and two of his men flashed past under Jimmy, the sounds of their swearing and horses' hoofs covering the sounds of the house burning.

Both Jimmy and Truitt timed the rope drop perfectly as the fourth man rode under them. The idea was to knock him off his horse, tie him up, and take him away before the other three got back.

The rope caught the man squarely across the upper chest. Perfect!

Jimmy had braced himself in the tree and had the rope wound around the trunk once, but the impact of a man being pulled off a horse at full run yanked Jimmy shoulder-first into the trunk. The rope burned in his hands as he fought to hold on.

Somehow, he did.

The killer swung up high in the air as the horse kept going, then dropped back.

The killer did a half turn in mid-air and landed on his head and shoulders on the trail.

There was a loud crack that echoed through the trees as the man hit.

Jimmy dropped the rope and climbed quickly out of the tree. His hands were shaking so badly, he could barely hang onto anything. Truitt's face looked white and his eyes were wide as they both scrambled to tie up the killer.

But by the time they had his hands tied, it was clear to Jimmy that they didn't need to do more. Jimmy dropped the rope and backed away like he was backing away from a snake.

Truitt did the same, muttering softly, "We weren't supposed to kill him."

"Get moving!" Zach shouted softly from up the hill.

"Let's go," Jimmy said, glancing up at Zach. "They might be back at any moment."

"What are we going to do?" Truitt asked, a sound of panic in his voice.

"Hide him, just like we planned," Jimmy said. He felt like he was about to be sick, but they couldn't stop now. They had to stay on the plan, even though the killer was dead.

Truitt nodded, took a deep breath, and seemed to come back into his eyes.

Jimmy quickly slipped the rope under the killer's arms, then at full run they dragged the man's body away from the trail and the burning building, deeper into the trees, using the rope around his chest to pull him like a sled. Near a rock ledge and the edge of the thick forest, they dropped the killer's body into a depression beside a tree, then frantically tossed some branches and dead grass over him.

Jimmy walked ten steps away and looked back. He couldn't see the body at all.

Truitt was still standing over the body staring at the killer.

Jimmy moved back over to his friend and put a hand on his shoulder. Truitt clearly had no problems taking things, or playing tricks on people, but he had never been near death.

"It was an accident," Jimmy said, trying to convince himself as much as Truitt. "Let's go."

Truitt nodded, took a deep breath, and turned. "I'll get his horse." He ran back toward the trees where the man's horse had stopped and was grazing.

With one last look at where they had hidden the killer's body, Jimmy headed back through the trees. He grabbed the two horses that Benson had planned on taking from the homestead. Benson wouldn't get them.

Not this time.

Jimmy glanced around at the dead family. Right now, he couldn't do anything for them. They would come back after the other killers had gone.

As fast as he could, Jimmy climbed back up the hill, pulling the two horses behind him.

A few moments later, Zach and Truitt joined him with Josh and their horses. There were four of them and they now had seven horses.

"The fall killed him?" Josh asked, his face white, his hands twisting the notebook.

Jimmy nodded. "Broke his neck."

He was having a lot of problems with the fact that they had killed someone. But right now, he couldn't think about it. He had to get himself and his friends out of there and to safety.

"Let's get riding."

"Yeah, I'd like to be a long ways from here when Benson gets back," Zach said, putting the rifle in his saddle and mounting up quickly.

C.J. and Long were riding at full speed north. Jimmy, Truitt, Zach, and Josh, with the extra horses, would ride at the same speed south, then wait until almost dusk to circle around back to where they had camped last night.

With luck, they would all be there.

PART NINETEEN
Back Together

THEY HAD ALL arrived in camp safely, with Long coming in last because he had wanted to make sure where Benson had gone. Long had the ability, because he was part Indian, to move silently and get amazingly close to things without ever being seen.

He told them that Benson and the other two killers had waited for their man for a while at the homestead, poked around a bit, then finally started down the trail at a good speed, clearly trying to put distance between them and the burning homestead.

Long said that there had been a lot of swearing and that Benson thought their "friend" had taken the horses and headed back up the trail, leaving them.

Or maybe the Indians had gotten him.

Good news to Jimmy. They did not suspect they were behind them.

Jimmy still posted three guards that night, and they hadn't built a fire. They didn't dare let Benson find them, not after what Benson had done to that family.

Jimmy hadn't slept much at all, and the only time he managed to fall asleep, he had a nightmare of the dead killer and the family standing and politely applauding. It was a horrid nightmare that woke him up sweating and made him take over guard duty an hour sooner than he was supposed to.

He couldn't believe he had killed a man. Even as an accident, did that make him as bad as Benson? He tried to push that thought away, but it kept coming back over and over all night long.

The next morning, Long scouted ahead and finally found Benson and his two remaining men moving west down the California Trail. They seemed to be pacing behind a small wagon company.

An hour later, they headed back and arrived back at the homestead and slowly dismounted. The building was still smoldering, sending a thin line of smoke into the clear blue sky.

"We need to bury these folks," Zach said, picking up the shovel the boy had been carrying when he was shot in the back.

Jimmy nodded and looked around. The ridge where he and the others had watched yesterday would be perfect. "Up there, where they can stand watch for all time over their homestead."

Silently, all six boys went looking for what it was going to take to dig three graves, get the bodies up the hill, and get this done.

Two long hours later, they were all hot and sweating, but they had the family in the ground with crosses over each grave. It reminded Jimmy far too much of when he and his brother had buried his parents.

Benson had to be stopped.

"I wish we knew their names," C.J. said.

"The Goose Creek family," Josh said. "As long as we remember them, they will live on."

"No way to forget this," Truitt said. "I'm going to be having nightmares for months."

"Yeah, me too," both Jimmy and Zach said at the same time.

"Should we do anything about him?" Zach asked, pointing to the trees where the body of the killer was.

"Let the animals have him," Long said, disgusted.

"He was a human," C.J. said, taking his glasses off his face and wiping sweat from his forehead. "He deserves something."

"He killed this family," Zach said, pointing up the hill at the graves they had just dug. "He doesn't deserve anything."

"We'll put some rocks on him," Jimmy said, staring up into the trees. He was having enough trouble with the death of the killer. He couldn't have the thought of animals getting the man in his mind.

"I'll help you," Truitt said.

All six boys helped, and in fifteen minutes they had the man under a cairn of rocks. They didn't mark the grave.

As they came out of the trees toward the barn, a stage came into sight from the west, pulled by a team of six horses.

During the trip west, they had passed a number of large wagons and stages going east. All of the stages had been Butterfield Stages, carrying mostly letters and a few passengers who didn't mind getting tossed around inside a stagecoach for a few thousand miles.

The stage pulled up in a wide area just off the trail and the boys went down to meet it.

"What happened?" the driver asked, his hand on his gun. His co-driver had his rifle up and ready.

Jimmy understood their fear. The house had been burned down, and these two men had no idea that Jimmy and his friends hadn't done it.

Jimmy told them what they had found, and then who had done it. None of them said a word about what they had done to Benson's man yesterday.

"We buried the family up on the hill," Jimmy said.

"There are three men tucked in a few miles behind a wagon company about a half day up the trail," the driver said, clearly relaxing, taking his hand off his gun. "Not much we can do."

"Out here, there's not much anyone can do," Zach said.

"Ain't that the truth," the driver said.

Jimmy described Benson and the driver nodded. "That was the man. It's too bad, too. The Bennetts were good people. Thanks for burying them. You boys stay away from those three."

"We will," Jimmy said to the driver, even though he knew they wouldn't.

Josh and C.J. got the Bennett's full names from the driver. Josh wrote them down carefully, then the two of them went back up the hill to put the names on the crosses.

Jimmy asked the driver if he could send a letter along to someone in Independence and the driver said sure. Jimmy wrote a quick note to his brother Luke, care of Doc Davis, and gave it to the driver. He offered to pay for the letter's

delivery, but the driver just tucked it in his pocket. "You've paid for the letter by burying our friends."

The stage left and they all paid their last respects to the family on the hill. Then, as they were back near the barn silently getting ready to mount back up, Long held up his hand. "Do you hear that?"

Jimmy strained to hear something besides the wind in the trees and the distant sound of some fast water in the creek. Nothing, but Jimmy had come to accept that Long could hear and see things that none of the rest of them could. It was an amazing special ability.

Long handed his horse lead to Zach and went back toward the smoldering house, quickly and silently.

Finally, Jimmy heard what Long had heard.

A faint whimper.

Something was alive back there.

But how could that be possible?

Long and Jimmy went to the right of the cabin, Zach with his gun out went to the left. C.J. had his rock sling out and was right behind Jimmy.

On the other side of the burnt-out building, they all stopped.

Jimmy held his breath, listening to the sound of the stream and the faint wind in the leaves of the trees.

Then the sound came again.

A whimper.

Long turned and moved around behind a few trees. There, he pulled open what looked like a sod-covered door on a root cellar that none of them had noticed tucked behind a tree next to the hill.

Inside, sitting on the stairs, was a young boy, about seven years of age.

He blinked at the bright light, then covered his head and started crying.

It took an hour or so for the boys to get the child calmed down and some water and food in him. He said between sobs that his name was Arthur.

Jimmy knew they certainly couldn't take Arthur with them, but they also couldn't just leave him either.

Jimmy pulled Zach aside. "We need to get the kid back to Fort Hall."

"That's a hundred miles back," Zach said. "I can do it."

"Or find someone in a wagon company who will take him," Jimmy said. He didn't much like the idea of Zach not being at his side. There had to be a better choice.

"A wagon train is unlikely," Zach said. "Fort Hall with the military is his best bet. Unless we can catch up to that Butterfield Stage." He didn't sound hopeful, and Jimmy doubted they could. Those stages moved fast, and kept going, changing horses all the time.

Jimmy stood thinking for a moment, staring at the three crosses on the hill above them. He knew that Zach was right, and he was the best person to do the ride because he was the most responsible of all of them.

"Take along the two horses that we rescued," Jimmy said. "They belong to the kid now anyhow. They might help him get a home. And give him the killer's saddle and gear. Truitt can go with you."

Zach nodded.

"If you don't catch us by Virginia City," Jimmy said, "we'll wait for you there." Virginia City was on the other side of Nevada from where they were, up against the Sierras and the final mountain passes over into California. At a good speed, they were still three weeks away from there, but with Benson moving slowly ahead of them,

Jimmy doubted they would be moving very fast at all.

Zach nodded. "If we ride solid, it won't take anywhere near that long. We should be back with you by the time you are down on the Humboldt. Maybe ten days."

"That's what I was figuring," Jimmy said.

Twenty minutes later, Zach and Truitt headed back east with the young boy saddled up on one of his horses.

The other four continued west, using the killer's horse as a packhorse. They still had three killers to track and try to stop.

CHAPTER TWENTY
On a Killer's Trail

THE NEXT DAY, Jimmy, Long, Josh, and C.J. caught up with Benson and his men again just after the trail crested over a slight range of hills and dropped down onto Dead Horse Creek.

The hills were covered in sparse dry grass and sagebrush. Only the areas along the creek were green. This area felt a lot more like a desert to Jimmy than anything they had come through, giving them almost no protection from the hot sun. The rock bluffs along the stream were brown, and sometimes towered a good hundred feet into the air above the shallow creek.

The coach driver had been right, Benson and his three men were following a few miles behind a small wagon company with only eight wagons. Only having eight wagons was just asking for problems. Usually the companies were far larger when they left Independence.

More than likely, this was just part of a larger company that had slowly split apart over the long months of travel.

Long scouted ahead, watching Benson and his men, as the rest of them stayed back and out of sight. Jimmy was convinced that Benson planned on robbing the train at some point. The questions were when and where.

And more importantly, how could Jimmy and the rest of them do something to stop it? This time, he didn't want to kill any of them. The accidental killing of one of Benson's gang bothered Jimmy a lot. He wasn't about to let his friends become like Benson and his gang.

That evening, the train made camp up against a tall rock bluff, with the wagons in a loose circle to protect the middle of the camp. Benson and his men camped back a few miles near a bend in the stream in some small trees.

Jimmy had the boys get off the trail and make camp on top of the bluffs above the wagons and far enough away from the company that their fire wouldn't be seen.

"So, how are we going to stop Benson from robbing that wagon train?" Jimmy asked after they had a fire going. The sun was still an hour from setting and Jimmy figured they had just about that much time to do something.

Josh held up some weeds. "This might do it," he said.

C.J. pushed his glasses down his nose and stared at the weeds in Josh's hands. "You want to poison them? That's called locoweed and it drives cattle crazy."

Jimmy had never seen anything like it, and he was surprised that both Josh and C.J. knew what it was. It had been along the trail for miles.

"My people use it in special ceremonies," Long said. "It makes you see things that cannot be seen. It will not kill taken in small amounts."

Jimmy laughed, then stared at Long. "Think you can get some of that into Benson's and his men's food if we gave you a diversion? That ought to keep them from robbing anyone tonight."

Long nodded. "They are cooking beans and coffee they took from the homestead."

"What do you need for a diversion?"

Long moved over toward the rocks without saying a word, then moving faster than Jimmy could see, he grabbed into a hole and picked up something. When he turned around, Jimmy could see it was a very angry, very large rattlesnake. The rattle on the end of its tail was making an intense noise. "Their horses will not like this," Long said, holding up the huge snake he held behind the head.

"I don't like it," C.J. said, backing away.

Long held the snake with one hand while he watched Josh chop up some of the weeds into tiny bits, then smash them between two rocks until he had a fine powder. Long held out his empty hand and Josh brushed the powder into his hand.

"Follow me," Long said. "I will show you where you can watch their camp."

A few minutes later, Jimmy, C.J., and Josh were hiding behind rocks as Long worked his way down toward the killer's camp. The three were sitting around the fire, clearly getting ready to eat. Their three horses were tied up in the trees about thirty paces from their fire.

Long got close, tossed the snake into the middle of the horses, then ducked down behind a large rock near the three men. Jimmy would have been scared to death getting that close to those three

killers like that, but clearly Long had very little fear of them.

Their horses went crazy, rearing back against their ties, trying to get away from the angry rattlesnake.

All three killers reacted as one, jumping up and running for the horses.

Almost like a ghost, Long appeared near their food and drink and put powder in both, then vanished back behind a rock.

It was everything Jimmy and Josh and C.J. could do to not laugh. They ducked down to make sure they weren't seen, and after a few minutes, Long joined them.

The four boys watched the killers eat. At first, nothing seemed to be happening. They cleaned up their camp, put out their fire, and got ready to ride out as it started to get dark. Clearly, they were still planning on robbing the wagon company.

Then Jimmy noticed that one of the killers tried to get on his horse and missed, falling into the dirt. The other two laughed and pointed and laughed.

"The plan seems to be working," Josh said.

"But not enough," Jimmy said as the three rode laughing toward the wagon company.

CHAPTER TWENTY-ONE
One More Plan

"CAN WE GET to a place above the wagons without being seen?" Jimmy asked as the three killers rode off. He couldn't let Benson and his men kill more innocent people. He just couldn't.

"What are you thinking?" Josh asked, looking worried.

"No plans yet," Jimmy said. "But I'm open for all kinds of ideas. We can't let those monsters kill an entire company of people."

"I agree," C.J. said, patting his sling. "I just wish Zach had left the rifle."

Jimmy felt his stomach clamp at that. They were unarmed against three armed killers.

"This way," Long said, vanishing back into the darkness.

It took them a good thirty minutes on foot to get to the bluff over the wagons. By that point, there had been shots and women screaming.

The sound had made Jimmy' blood go cold and his heart race. This couldn't be happening again.

Not again.

A half-dozen cook fires lit up the area under them, making it seem like a bright day among the wagons. Benson had killed what must have been the train's leader, and two of the killers were holding two women with guns to their heads. The rest of the families were standing helpless, just watching. The killers were weaving back and forth like they were drunk, and laughing at anything.

There had to be twenty men and women in that train, plus another ten children.

Jimmy knew that most of them were going to die unless they did something, and did it fast.

Jimmy signaled that they should move back from the edge, then turned to C.J. and Josh, the two smartest of them all. "Any ideas?"

"We have surprise on our side," Josh said. "They don't know we're here."

"And we have the darkness to help us," C.J. said. "We can spook them into running since they have so much Loco weed in them."

"I can do a very frightening Bannock war cry," Long said. "If I ride through the shadows near their horse making the cry, they might think they are surrounded by Bannock."

Jimmy nodded. "Especially if we are pelting them with rocks at the same time."

C.J. laughed and whipped out his homemade sling. "They won't even know what hit them."

Three boys with rocks against three men with guns.

Jimmy had no doubt they were going to have to be very lucky to get away with this attack.

Very lucky if they lived, actually.

He couldn't believe that for the second time in three days he was going to attack Benson and his men. It was crazy.

"Long, when we hear you coming, we'll start throwing," Jimmy said.

"Five minutes," Long said, nodding and then vanishing silently into the darkness back toward their camp and their horses.

Jimmy went on. "C.J., you take the younger killer, Josh, you take the other one. "I'll take Benson. Make sure you are in a sheltered place with a lot of rocks to throw when they start shooting. And if your man leaves the light, we all run."

Long and C.J. nodded.

"This is going to be fun," C.J. said, laughing.

Josh just shook his head.

Jimmy would have never called this fun. Crazy, yes, deadly, yes, but never fun.

They all spread out along the top of the cliff, picking up fist-sized rocks as they went.

Jimmy found at least a dozen and put himself behind a large rock that allowed him shelter, but if he leaned out and forward, he could clearly see the camp below.

His heart was beating so hard, he was sure Benson could hear it.

"Okay," he said softly to himself. "Make each throw deadly."

At that moment, an echoing Bannock war cry filled the air, sending shivers down Jimmy's back. It seemed to hang in the night air, echoing off the rocks like there was more than one call.

Long was right, that was something that would frighten enemies and friends alike.

Long came flashing into the light, past the fire, and back into the darkness. All three killers spun around, guns aimed into the darkness, but they had so much locoweed in them, they barely stood up.

Jimmy took a deep breath, stood and threw the rock at Benson as hard as he could.

Benson was standing in the middle of the camp, near a fire, staring after the ghost-like image of Long.

The rock fell a few feet short, bounced once and slammed into Benson's shin.

Benson snapped forward and grabbed his leg, swearing and clearly in pain.

In all his life, Jimmy had never felt such a thrill as that moment. Maybe C.J. was right.

Maybe this would be fun.

An echoing Bannock war cry again filled the air, sending more shivers down Jimmy's back. The people in the wagon company dove for cover under the wagons as the three killers stood their ground under the rocks from above.

All three killers started firing up at the cliff face, but their aim was random and far off target.

Long flashed past the camp again, coming in closer behind the men, screaming out his war cry.

Jimmy missed with his second rock, but his third throw hit Benson squarely in the chest and knocked him to his back in the dirt.

Before he could get up, Jimmy hit him with another rock, this time in the back, sending him back to the ground.

The gunfire had stopped.

The two killers came running toward Benson, heading past him at a mad dash for their horses. They were clearly as scared as a grown man could get.

Long's war cry again filled the night air.

Jimmy was throwing as hard and as fast as he could, letting his anger at Benson power his arm.

A rock from C.J.'s sling caught the youngest of Benson's men in the arm, clearly breaking it. The other man was bleeding from a head wound and limping from the attack that Josh had waged on him.

Jimmy kept throwing, fast and hard, not letting the man who had killed his parents have a moment's rest.

To the men below, it must have seemed as if the dark night sky had opened up and just dumped rocks at them.

Long screamed out the Bannock war cry again.

It made Jimmy shiver, and even Benson's horses reared up at the sound.

Jimmy's aim was getting better. He hit Benson squarely in the shoulder as he climbed to his feet, spinning the man around and forcing him to drop his gun.

Benson scrambled on all fours for his gun as Jimmy hit him in the back with another rock, sending him to his stomach.

Finally, Benson scrambled up, turned and limped behind his men for his horse.

Jimmy managed to hit him one more time in the back of his leg before Benson got mounted and rode at full speed west, out of the camp, following his two men down the California Trail.

There was silence in the wagon camp.

Jimmy knew that Long would follow the killers for a distance, terrorizing them, making sure they didn't turn back on the wagon company.

Below them, the stunned people of the wagon company scrambled for their weapons and got ready to defend themselves as well. It was going to take a little explaining as to why they wouldn't have to.

"Well," C.J. said from somewhere in the darkness. "Shall we go down and say hello?"

"I don't see why not," Jimmy said, laughing, feeling better than he had felt in a long, long time. They had beat Benson once more.

Now Jimmy knew they could somehow do it again.

And again.

Until the killer was finally brought to justice.

Jimmy looked down at the stunned people staring upward into the darkness, waiting for more rocks to come flying, then laughed again. "It seems they might owe us a dinner."

PART TWENTY-TWO
Headed Toward Danger

MORE THAN THREE weeks had passed since Zach and Truitt had rejoined them from taking the young boy back. It had been the longest and hottest three weeks Jimmy could ever remember. They had followed slowly, very slowly, behind the wagon train that Benson and his men were shadowing.

Long reported that one of Benson's men, the one with the broken arm, seemed to be getting weaker and weaker, which got a cheer from everyone. It had been C.J., with his special sling, that had hit the man in the arm with a rock.

They were all proud of the fact that they had rescued an entire wagon company from Benson and his killers. To Jimmy, after not being in time to save the family at the homestead, saving the fine people of that wagon company had felt wonderful.

The people of the company had been very appreciative as well, wanting the boys to ride along with them the rest of the way to California.

Even though there were some pretty girls Jimmy's age with the company, all of them had decided to move on, to stay close behind Benson and his men.

The trail across most of Northern Nevada wound in and out of the desert scrub and rocks beside the ever-smaller flow of the Humboldt River. They had had to cross the river seven times, but the flow was so small, the crossings hadn't ever been a problem.

As C.J. and Josh had told them, ahead was the Humboldt Sink, where what was left of the river just vanished into desert.

And beyond that, the hardest leg of the trip, the Forty Mile Desert.

Every day along the Humboldt, the temperatures were unbearable in the afternoon, so they had adopted a travel method of getting up before dawn and moving in the early light, then by noon finding a shelter of either brush or rocks and resting during the hot hours.

Long kept great care of their horses, making sure they were fed and watered the right amounts, but even with the good care and decent grass, the heat was clearly taking a toll on them. A week earlier, Long had shifted the horse C.J. was riding to a packhorse because it couldn't carry C.J.'s weight and his gear anymore.

Along the river, Jimmy was stunned at how many broken-down wagons littered the trail. At each wagon without people, Jimmy had them search for water bags and smaller supplies that might come in handy. They had found a few water bags and a canteen.

With what Jimmy understood they were facing, trying to carry extra water might just be what saved their lives.

Years and years of dead stock bones, bleached white, littered the sides of the trail as well. There weren't that many wagon companies ahead of them yet this summer, since they were traveling by horse, but even so, there were already dozens of fresh dead animals beside the trail, most of them torn apart by packs of wild dogs Josh said were called coyotes.

Jimmy couldn't imagine what it was going to be like when all the wagons behind them got here, in the heat of August. The entire trail would smell like death almost every step of the way.

They had had to pass at least four solo wagons with families. They had broken down and been left by their companies who had had no choice but to move on.

They had stopped to see if they could help at each family, but there was really nothing they could do. The families all seemed to have water and food. Jimmy figured that with luck, the families would join up with another company coming along, either with their wagon fixed or walking the rest of the way. Otherwise, if at some point they didn't move forward, those families, children and all, would just die in the extreme heat of the desert.

As each day went by, and the farther they got down the Humboldt, the more graves there were, all with names roughly scratched into wooden crosses.

Josh started to write down all the names and locations, but after a week on the Humboldt, there were so many, he gave up the task as too depressing.

Two days away from the Humboldt Sink, Josh read them all a passage from his favorite writer, Mark Twain, who had been out west a few years earlier and had written about the Forty Mile Desert.

Twain said, "It would hardly be an exaggeration to say that we could have walked the forty miles and set our feet on a bone at every step."

"Okay, no more of that," Truitt said, shaking his head. "We still have to cross that thing."

With the intense heat, all the bones and graves along the Humboldt, and forty miles of sand ahead of them, Jimmy could imagine Twain being very, very right about what they were facing.

Jimmy sure wasn't looking forward to that leg on this adventure.

PART TWENTY-THREE
Knowing What's Ahead

THE WAGON COMPANY that Benson was following camped for three days on the edge of the Sink, so they were forced to camp back down the trail a half-day's ride to make sure they weren't seen.

Just sitting, not moving, bothered Jimmy more than anything. But Long said it was a good thing, since they were resting the horses, and gaining all their strength before crossing the Forty Mile Desert.

With the wagon company camped like that, Long was able to get much closer. It seemed, from what Long overheard, that some of the men of the company had died during a river crossing early in the trip, and now there were only five men and three older boys in the seven wagons, with a dozen young children and ten women.

Long said Benson and his men were pretending they were going to help the company across the desert.

"Not likely," Jimmy had said. "It's only a matter of time before those people meet a very sad end."

"Unless we can do something to stop Benson," Josh said.

"I'm open to any ideas," Jimmy said.

They talked about it for most of the evening and all of the next day, but no one could come up with anything that would allow them to stop Benson and not get killed.

The wagon company was camped right out in the open, above the water, with no place around the wagon camp to surprise Benson with any kind of attack. And at night, the company had two men standing guard at all times. Usually one of them was one of Benson's men, or Benson himself.

Finally, they all agreed to try to warn one of the men of the wagon company when he got away from the train. It was the best plan they could think of.

Jimmy and Long, just before dawn on the second morning, met one of the younger men from the train while he was out trying to gather wood for a fire. He wasn't much older than they were, and looked very tired and worn out. His clothes were tattered and he looked underfed. Fighting wagons along this trail could do that to a man.

After they had told him about Benson and his two men, the guy had only nodded. "Thanks for the warning, but we don't trust them either. We won't let them get the drop on us." He patted the six-shooter he had tucked into his belt.

"If you need our help, we're camped back down the trail," Jimmy said.

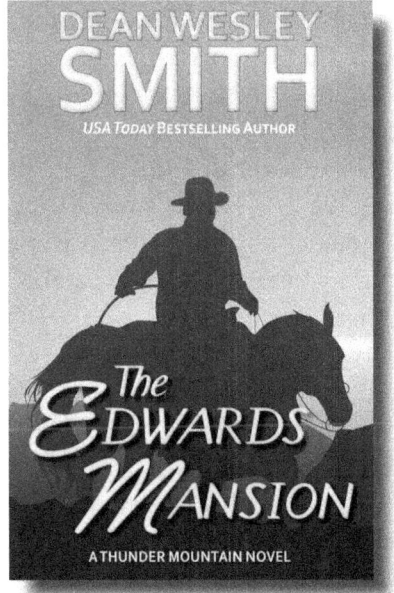

Two Thunder Mountain Novels
Available at your favorite booksellers.

The guy nodded. "We won't. Thanks again, though."

"Just don't tell Benson we're behind you," Jimmy said.

"Oh, trust me," the man had said with a shake of his head, "I don't even talk to those men."

With that, he walked back toward the wagon company carrying an armload of sticks.

Jimmy had no doubt that the warning wouldn't help. If Benson followed his true nature, that man would be dead very shortly.

But there was nothing he or the rest of them could do, so they went back to waiting.

Jimmy wasn't so sure how rested they were getting in the extreme heat. The air just seemed to take any energy he had out of his body, and it wasn't until long after the sun went down and the air cooled that he even started to feel like moving at all.

One night, around the campfire, Josh and C.J. filled them all in on what was coming for them in the desert.

"Most companies start across the desert at night," Josh said, "leaving the camp near the Sink to cross the fifteen miles that it takes to even reach the drop down into the Forty Mile Desert."

"It's well over fifty miles from the last water to the Truckee River," C.J. said.

Together, they all worked out a plan.

Jimmy hadn't liked the sound of anything that was coming.

Fifty-five miles in sand, without water.

They were going to have to be very, very ready for the crossing.

Finally, coming back just after dawn on the third morning, Long reported that the wagon company, with Benson and his men helping them, had started to make

the crossing. "They left one wagon behind," Long said, "but no people."

"We go tonight," Jimmy said. "Let's move up to their old camp and get ready. That will give them a full day's head start. We don't want to catch them somewhere out there in the middle of that sand."

"Good idea," Truitt said. "They won't be stopping, that's for sure."

"Neither will we," C.J. said. "Stopping in that desert is the quickest way to die."

"Sounds like a good time," Zach said, shaking his head.

"Before we leave," Jimmy said, "we need to make sure every water bag is full, every canteen."

"I'll have the stock well watered," Long said. "But we're going to need every drop we don't drink for the horses to get them across as well. And we'll have to pack extra grass."

When they reached the campsite beside the Sink, they could clearly see the six wagons kicking up dust far out on a vast open expanse of light brown sand.

They found shelter under some trees and settled in.

For Jimmy, the heat of the day seemed to drag on and on.

California was just over those mountains in the distance. Somewhere, between here and Sacramento, he needed to get his father's gold mine deed back from Benson.

He just didn't know how yet.

All of them tried to stay in the shade as long as the sun was out, and from where Jimmy was sitting, by mid-afternoon, he could no longer see the dust trail from the wagons.

Tomorrow, instead of resting in the shade, they would be moving in the heat. Once you started across the desert, there was no stopping.

A lot of things had happened on the trip west, but right now, what faced them frightened him more than anything had frightened him before.

But they had no choice.

If they stopped, they died.

PART TWENTY-FOUR
Starting Across Hell

AS AN ALMOST full moon came up over the hot desert, they broke camp. Every canteen, every water bag was brimming full. Then, with each of them taking one last, long drink from the fresh water near the camp, they started off.

"Stay between the wagon wheel ruts," Long said, taking the lead as he usually did. "Safer in the dark."

Jimmy was last in line and was leading one packhorse.

Zach led another packhorse behind Long.

Then it was C.J., Josh, and Truitt in that order.

They kept close to each other and after a while Jimmy noticed that his eyes had adjusted and he could see pretty well in just the light from the moon.

They moved steadily.

As the night got cooler, Long had them pick up the pace. They needed to cover as much ground as possible when it was cool and dark.

They made the fifteen miles to the edge of the desert without any problems. The moon was directly over their heads as they reached the edge of the Forty Mile Desert.

They stopped for a few minutes rest on the top of the ridge before dropping down the steep incline to the desert floor.

At first, Jimmy didn't understand what he was seeing. The trail was framed all the way down the slope to the level desert floor with piles and piles of white.

Then it suddenly dawned on him what he was actually looking at.

Bones.

Thousands of animals' bones lined both sides of the trail down the hill like a horrid decoration of a nightmarish garden path.

"Ready?" he asked everyone, tearing his gaze away from the bones.

"Not really," C.J. said.

"We've come this far," Truitt said, "we can't let forty miles of sand stop us."

"One at a time down this slope," Long said, mounting up and starting down between the rows of white animal bones gleaming in the moonlight.

Long made it to the bottom fine, and so did Zach with his packhorse.

Truitt went next, then Josh, both signaling they were at the bottom with a whistle.

Jimmy sat on his horse at the top, watching C.J.

Everything seemed to be going fine until suddenly, about halfway down, C.J.'s horse stumbled and went down, dumping C.J. into the deep sand.

C.J. rolled down the hill and came up spitting sand.

Long and Zach, on foot, quickly climbed back up to him while Jimmy led his horses down slowly from the top.

C.J. was fine, but his horse had broken a leg.

They got the supplies and water off the horse and distributed to the other horses. Then C.J., with Long's help, saddled their best packhorse with his gear.

The horse with the broken leg had been one Jimmy's father had bought in

St. Louis. For some reason, it suddenly felt as if he was going to lose another member of his family.

He felt sick.

As Jimmy watched, and Long turned his back, Zach did the hardest job he had ever had to do.

He led the horse over to where there was a large pile of white bones that were piled almost waist high.

Then, with one clean shot from the rifle, he put the suffering horse down.

Just like with much of what they had had to do on this trip, there just wasn't a choice.

It was life, or it was death.

And to Jimmy, here in the Wild West, there didn't seem to be much between the two.

PART TWENTY-FIVE
Into the Desert

FOR THE NEXT two hours, as the sun started to color the sky in reds and browns, they rode in silence, moving at a fast pace across the flat sand while it was still cool. Then, just before the sun came up, Jimmy had them stop and rest and water the horses.

"From here," Long said, "we go slowly."

Long and Truitt and C.J. took care of the horses while Jimmy and Zach and Josh checked to make sure all the water was secured, protected from direct sun, and not leaking. With the day they had ahead of them, they were going to need every drop.

C.J. figured they had gone at least twenty-five of the over fifty-five miles to the Truckee River.

The easy half was all Jimmy could think.

The next thirty miles, the sun would bake them as dry as an overcooked biscuit, as Truitt would say.

As the sun crested the distant ridge, they started out again, the horses wading slowly in the soft sand.

The farther they got into the desert, the more bones and remains of wagons they found. Some of the remains had been there for years, others were fairly new. Jimmy had no doubt that by the time the summer was finished, and all the wagon companies behind them had crossed this, there would be many, many more broken dreams littering this nightmarish place.

It seemed that Mark Twain's description of this desert was very accurate.

At one point, C.J. pointed out a pile of bones ten feet off to one side of the trail. It took Jimmy a moment to realize what he was looking at in the hot sun.

Human bones.

Maybe three people, their bones piled like firewood, their skulls gaping at the sand around them.

And from that point on, they saw more and more human bones. Out here, the people who were still alive didn't dare stop and bury anyone. They just left them beside the trail and pushed on.

They had no choice.

They now stopped every hour to rest and feed and water the horses. Jimmy drank what he thought he should to make the water last, but it never felt like enough.

With the sun moving higher in the sky, the temperatures climbed, making him feel like he was standing far too close to a raging fire.

The glare off the sand was blinding, and waves of heat just radiated up like the sand itself was on fire.

Now Available
from all your favorite booksellers
in trade paper and electronic editions.

To Jimmy, the short stops seemed almost worse than moving forward, but he knew they had to do them, to pace this journey.

At one point, about an hour after dawn, they came across a bubbling hot springs, the water so hot that steam filled the air around it even in the dry heat. There was no reason for even trying to cool and drink the water, since it smelled like sulfur.

Josh said that someone reported that there used to be a sign here that said, "If you can't go forward, you won't survive going back."

"The sign is a myth," C.J. said. "But more than likely the meaning is very true."

Truitt said something about now knowing where the devil lived as they went past the bubbling, hot sulfur water.

CHAPTER TWENTY-SIX
One Down

JIMMY WATCHED TRUITT sway for a moment side-to-side in his saddle like he was on a boat in high waves, then tumble off his horse and land with a thud in the hot, desert sand.

"Truitt's down!" Jimmy shouted to the others ahead of him, panic filling his gut like a bad meal. He jumped off his horse and scrambled in the deep sand to where his friend lay. He felt like he was running through deep water, the sand was so soft. It fought him every step.

He knelt beside Truitt, the hot sand burning through his pants. Carefully, he turned his friend over and brushed the sand away from his mouth and eyes, moving Truitt's brown hair off his fore-

head at the same time. Truitt's skin was red and he was breathing shallowly.

"Truitt? Can you hear me?"

Truitt moaned, but didn't open his eyes.

They couldn't lose Truitt. Not now. Not here.

Long ran up with the rest and knelt in the sand. He quickly unscrewed a canteen and poured a little water on Truitt's forehead. The sand and dirt turned to a thin mud and dried in streamers down his cheeks almost instantly in the intense heat.

Long glanced over at Jimmy. "Open his mouth."

Jimmy pried open Truitt's mouth with his fingers and Long poured the water in slowly. Truitt choked for a moment, coughed, then drank.

After a moment which seemed like an eternity, it was as if Long had given him a magic medicine. Truitt blinked, opened his eyes, looked at the five men hovering over him, and then asked in a soft whisper, "What happened?"

Long gave him another drink of water, then stood. "Heat."

He pulled out a piece of buffalo jerky from his belt pouch and handed it to Truitt. "Chew on this and drink."

Truitt made a face, but did as Long said. None of them liked how salty Long's jerky was, but they all trusted Long when it came to anything having to do with survival out in the west. And right now, here in the middle of the Forty Mile Desert, the most dangerous stretch of the California Trail, they really needed his special skills to stay alive.

"Everyone, water and jerky," Long said, taking a drink himself and then taking out a piece of buffalo jerky. Long had spent nights smoking the jerky back after leaving Fort Hall, and Truitt had complained that Long had used a lot of their salt provisions for the process.

All Long had said was, "We will need it salty." He hadn't explained, and no one had asked. It was now, in the heat, that for some reason, Long wanted them all eating the salty jerky.

After they got out of this, if they got out of this, Jimmy would ask him why.

Jimmy moved away from Truitt and stood beside the horses, letting his wide-brimmed hat protect his face from the glaring sun. He then did as the others, working on the jerky and washing it down with water. They had carried into the Forty Mile Desert as much water as they could, but they were going through it alarmingly fast.

Long and Zach gave water to the horses. Joshua and C.J. sat in the shade their horses offered, drinking and chewing on the buffalo jerky.

Truitt had managed to move over beside C.J. in the slight shade of one horse and was looking better by the minute.

Jimmy turned and looked back the way they had come. The drifting sand made it impossible to see anything but the distant low hills. In the other direction, ahead, through the haze of the hot summer day, were the mountains of the Sierras. They looked to be both invitingly close, and impossibly distant.

And somewhere, just ahead of them, Jake Benson and his two remaining men were moving with a wagon company. Benson had killed Jimmy's parents, shot his brother, and then had killed another family back on Goose Creek, on the east side of Nevada.

At night, Jimmy was still haunted by the man they had accidentally killed at that homestead, but during the day, Jimmy just didn't let himself think about it. That man had been one of the men who

had killed Jimmy's parents, and the family on the homestead, and who knew how many others. Yet Jimmy still hated the fact that the man had died. That wasn't what they had planned.

And the accident had given him many, many nightmares over the past weeks. He had no doubt, it was going to haunt him for a lot longer.

He pushed the thought away. Right now, Benson and his men were ahead of them, in the desert, pretending to help a small company of wagons. More than likely, Benson was going to rob and kill the fine people in the wagons somewhere in the middle of this horrible desert, but there was nothing Jimmy or any of the others could do about it. They had even tried to warn the people, but had been ignored.

"Keep eating and drinking," Long said. "We'll rest the horses for another ten minutes."

Jimmy nodded. Even though Jimmy was mostly in charge of the group, when it came to the horses, Long was in charge. He knew how to keep them alive and moving west, and that was all that mattered.

Jimmy looked at the distant mountains and wondered if he would ever see them. They had a long way left to go to get across this desert, and their water supply was going down fast. Without water, what happened to Truitt would happen to them all in the intense heat.

Very quickly.

CHAPTER TWENTY-SEVEN
More Trouble Ahead

AFTER THEY RESTED and had eaten the jerky and drank enough water,

Long said to Jimmy. "We need to walk from here. The horses can't carry us much farther in this deep sand and in this heat."

Jimmy agreed.

Long had warned them all this would happen. It was part of their plan So, on foot, they started out again, leading their horses.

Each step felt to Jimmy like he was sinking in quicksand, as the desert wanted to not let his boot go. He tried to stay in the wagon tracks, but often missed and stumbled, using the reins of his horse to keep himself from falling face down.

Every step drained more and more energy.

Every mile was a torture.

It wasn't even the hottest time of the day yet, yet the air felt like he was inside a hot oven.

An hour later, as they crested a slight rise in the desert floor about three hours after dawn, they could see the seven wagons that Benson had been "helping" across the desert.

They were stopped dead in the trail and there were no signs of people or the oxen and horses that had been pulling them.

Jimmy wanted to stop short, let Long scout ahead and see what was happening, but both C.J. and Josh said, "We can't stop. We have to go past them."

Jimmy glanced at Long, who clearly agreed with C.J. and Josh.

If they stopped, they died.

If Benson was still with those wagons, they were going to have to take the chance and walk right past him.

Jimmy didn't like that idea at all.

In fact, that idea scared him almost as much as this desert did.

"We ride the next mile until we're past those wagons," Jimmy said.

Long agreed and had everyone give their horse a drink.

Back in the saddle, even moving slowly, it didn't seem to take them long to cross the next mile of desert.

Jimmy now wasn't focused on the sun, but on what was ahead. He hardly took his eye off those wagons.

There was no sign at all of life.

Nothing was moving, not even the canvas tops of the wagons, since there was no wind at all in this forsaken place.

The closer they got, the more likely it was looking that Benson and his men had robbed the poor wagon company, killed everyone and left.

Twice so far, in the thick sand, the trail had gone around what had been a stopped wagon company some years before. Those wagons had been weather-beaten and the white bones of stock and people littered everywhere. Now this wagon company had stopped right in the middle of the trail as well, and it didn't look as if those wagons were ever going another foot forward.

There were no oxen or horses left with the wagons to pull them.

As they got close enough to see details, it became clear that what they were seeing was a massacre.

Benson and his men had struck again.

All the men and boys were scattered around the wagons, some laying face down in the sand, others face up. They were clearly all dead. A couple of them had guns in their hands, including the man Jimmy and Long had talked to.

It seemed he had been wrong. He had let Benson get the drop on him.

Jimmy had no idea why they hadn't heard the shooting. Maybe sound didn't carry well over the sand.

"No women," Zach said as they got closer.

Jimmy was surprised he hadn't noticed that. There weren't any women's or children's bodies in sight at all. Maybe Benson and his men had taken them.

Then Long pointed to one man's body and Jimmy recognized him as one of Benson's men. It was the one with the broken arm. It looked like he had just passed out and died right where he lay. Or maybe one of the wagon men had shot him.

Long led them in a wide circle around the wagons, starting what would become the new trail through the sand.

It wasn't until they passed the last wagon in line that Truitt shouted, "The women!"

At first, Jimmy didn't see them. Then, as Truitt turned and rode toward the wagons, Jimmy finally saw movement. It was a child moving his arm.

The women and children were laying in the sand in the shade under the lead wagons. None of them seemed to have been shot, but the heat of the first three hours of the day without water had done its worst on them.

All of them moved closer, leading their horses to what little shade the wagons gave them, then dismounted.

Jimmy found one woman who looked to be about his mother's age. She was barely able to talk and he gave her a small sip of water. Her chapped lips struggled with the drink, but after a moment, some life returned to her eyes.

"Give everyone else some water," Jimmy said to the others, "see who is alive, who isn't."

"Don't give them too much water at first," Long said. "In their conditions, it will make them sick."

The boys spread out to the women and children laying under the wagons, waking them, giving them water.

"Jake Benson?" Jimmy asked the woman. "Did he do this?"

She nodded. "He and his men turned on us in the middle of the night. They said we were slowing them down. They robbed us, shot the men, then took all the water, stock, and money. They left us here to die."

Jimmy felt sick to his stomach. Benson was the most cold-hearted creature that had ever pretended to be human. How could anyone do this simply for money?

Jimmy gave the woman another small sip, then stood and went to talk to Zach and C.J.

"We have to get these women and children to the Truckee," Jimmy said.

"I can't see how we can," C.J. said.

"But we can't leave them," Zach said, echoing exactly what Jimmy was thinking.

"I know that," C.J. said. "But taking them may mean that none of us make it. We're still a long ways from that river."

Jimmy nodded. The sun was pounding on them. It felt like he had gotten far, far too close to a fire and there was no place to get away to.

"How far?" Jimmy asked.

C.J. shrugged. "From my guess, we are still a good fifteen, maybe twenty miles away from the river, through thick sand."

"And Long is going to want us to walk to save the horses," Zach said.

Jimmy didn't like the sound of that. "Find out how many women and children there are. And have Long check how much water we all have. Then we'll all talk. We're all risking our lives with this, we all need to be a part of this decision."

The rules of the west were that each person took care of themselves, but Jimmy had no doubt that he couldn't let these woman and children just die here. He was going to help them somehow, save them from what Benson had done.

He just hoped it didn't cost them all their lives.

PART TWENTY-EIGHT
Tough Decision

"CAN WE JUST rest here in the shade of the wagons until the sun goes down and make a run for it?" Truitt asked as all six of them gathered together.

Jimmy had been wondering the same thing.

Long, C.J. and Josh all shook their heads.

"The heat on this desert would drain all of our water, even if we were resting," Josh said.

"Look what three hours did to the women and children," C.J. said. "And that was what one of them told me was their plan."

"We would never make it to the river without water," Josh said, "even at night."

Long agreed. In his steady voice he said simply, "We can't stop. We must press on and soon."

"How many are there?" Zach asked.

"Eight women still alive and all claim they are able to walk," Truitt said. "A dozen children, six of them too young to walk in this deep sand."

Jimmy turned to Long. "How much water do we have?"

"After what we have given to the women and children, we will be out of water before we get to the river, even if we went without them."

That made all of them stand in silence in the hot desert sun, just thinking about the huge risk they would take if they continued to help this wagon company.

Jimmy nodded, then looked around at his friends. "Is everyone agreed that we try to save these woman and children? I vote that we do."

All five of his friends nodded as one.

Jimmy laughed. "You know, we're all crazy."

"That seems clear simply by where we are standing," Truitt said.

Everyone laughed, but it was worried laughs. Jimmy was scared at the idea of what they were about to do. He knew the rest of them were as well.

"Everyone take a small drink," Jimmy said, "then give a small drink to the horses as well. After that, get the six kids who can't walk tied onto the horses so if they pass out, they won't fall off. We need to get moving."

Jimmy glanced in the direction of the hot sun as everyone spread out. It couldn't be much past nine in the morning. They had the hottest part of the day still hours ahead of them, and fifteen to twenty miles of sand to wade through.

And nowhere near enough water to get six of them, eight women, seven horses, and a dozen children to the Truckee River.

But they were going to try.

And with luck not die in the attempt.

PART TWENTY-NINE
An Attempt

THE NEXT TWO hours went slowly as the sun climbed higher and higher in the sky, sucking every bit of moisture from anything alive.

Long led the group, leading the only packhorse. The strongest woman among the survivors was leading Long's horse

right behind him. A young boy was tied to the saddle, his head and back covered by a light shirt.

Jimmy, with a young girl on his horse, followed. A girl about Jimmy's age named Caroline walked with him, or behind him, as they tried to stay in the wagon wheel tracks to make the walking easier. It was Caroline's younger sister who was on Jimmy' horse.

Caroline was a blonde with flashing blue eyes. Her light skin was blistered by the sun, even though she wore a wide-brimmed hat. Her once blue dress was tattered, faded, and dirty. Jimmy liked her at once, but he wasn't sure why.

She seemed strong and was able to keep up. They didn't speak hardly at all, since that would have taken too much energy. But Jimmy found himself enjoying her company as much as it was possible in these circumstances. And thinking about her and wondering what she was like certainly kept his mind off of the heat and the deep sand.

After two hours, Long gave a little water to each horse, then had each of them take a very shallow drink. Jimmy had put him in charge of the water and told everyone to not drink unless Long told them to.

Jimmy was trusting Long to know when they had to drink to keep them going. Josh was also making a few suggestions to Long from things that he had read, and Long was sometimes following his suggestions.

Again, it was taking all of them and all their skills to survive this.

They didn't stop for longer than a few minutes at any point. There was just no point in resting. Every minute stopped was one minute longer it would take them to reach the river.

Before the next quick stop, Zach shouted from the end of the procession and Jimmy looked around.

A woman had fallen face first into the sand and two other women were not able to move her. It was the woman that Jimmy had given a drink to under the wagon.

Jimmy had Caroline hold his horse and he went back to see what could be done. But by the time he waded through the sand to where she was, C.J. was standing up shaking his head. "She's dead."

Two other women were still kneeling in the sand beside the dead woman.

Jimmy looked at the dead woman for a moment, the thoughts of his own mother filling his mind. Benson would pay for this. For everything he had done.

Jimmy turned his back on the dead woman. "Let's get moving."

He knew his voice sounded cold and mean, but he didn't dare allow himself to look back at her body just laying there beside the trail with all the other bones of travelers and horses and oxen.

They weren't crossing just a desert. They were crossing a graveyard.

An hour later, they were slugging up a low ridge. The sand was so deep, that even staying in the wagon wheel tracks from companies that had gone before, the horses sank up to their knees in the sand.

Every step for Jimmy seemed like torture.

Long stopped them halfway up the impossible slope and had them all drink tiny sips of the water they had left. Now they were completely out of water, and the sun was still high in the sky, baking them.

Jimmy just hoped there wasn't far to go. He could tell his energy was draining quickly, and beside him, Caroline was stumbling far more often than she had when they started out. He wasn't sure how many more miles any of them could go.

Over an hour later, they crested over the top of hill. The wagon trail went downward with a much harder base sand between some thin sagebrush. The going was easier, a relief since they were going downhill and not wading in such deep sand.

In the distance, in the bottom of the valley below them, there was a tall stand of cottonwood trees that seemed to curve off into the distance toward the mountains beyond. Jimmy had learned that distances out west were very hard to judge. He had no idea if those trees were just a mile away, or ten miles away.

But what those tall trees meant was water. The river was there, under those trees.

They just had to get to them.

PART THIRTY
The River

AS C.J. CAME over the ridge behind Jimmy and saw the trees, he shouted, "Three miles left! Just three miles!"

Caroline looked back at C.J., then ahead at the trees. "Can he be right?"

Jimmy smiled. "When it comes to this trail and where we are, C.J. and Josh are always right. They've read everything about this trip that has ever been written. I have a hunch that Josh will eventually write his own book about all this as well."

"Three miles," Caroline said, her voice cracking in what sounded like a sigh. "I can make three miles."

She was right. Jimmy knew he could as well.

They walked on side-by-side in silence through the baking heat.

Long kept their pace steady and didn't speed up at all, even though it was downhill and they could see in the distance their goal. Jimmy knew that they could still lose people and horses in these three miles.

Three miles was a very long distance in this kind of heat.

But Long also didn't call a rest break half way down the gentle slope. At this point, there was no point in resting. They had no water left. They either made the last few miles, or they died very close to their goal.

Another woman behind Jimmy fell, but this time she hadn't died. Just passed out.

"I know what that's like," Truitt said, shaking his head.

Long and Zach simply lifted the woman up and draped her over Zach's horse in front of a small child. If she ended up dying, they would find out at the river and not before.

The last half-mile had to be the longest half-mile Jimmy had ever walked.

The cottonwood trees bordering the river were looming high in front of them now, and the blue of water reflected the sun like a mirror. But they were still a half-mile away under baking sun.

Every footstep felt like sheer agony, and Jimmy seemed to use every ounce of his energy with every step, yet the sight ahead kept him moving, taking another step forward and then another step.

Caroline was walking beside the horse and her sister, and it was clear that at times she was using his saddle to hold herself up from falling.

A few times during that last half mile, Jimmy turned to see how the others were doing.

They were all stumbling like he was, but they were all looking ahead at the water.

Long kept them going at the same speed all the way to within three hundred paces from the river, then he turned and shouted back, "Get the children off the horses without trying to stop the horses, then give the horses their heads."

Jimmy had no idea what Long was worried about with the children. All he wanted to do was stagger at the water and drink. But he didn't have enough energy to ask Long why. He just acted.

They all did.

Somehow, he and Caroline got her sister untied and off the horse without stopping. The little girl was completely limp in Jimmy' arms. Then Caroline tossed the reins back up over the horse's head so that it could go as it wanted.

Just as Jimmy had thought about doing, his horse made a dash at the river, splashing into it right behind Long's horse.

Caroline and Jimmy almost got run over by Truitt's horse as it went past, also headed for the water.

"Everyone drink slowly at first, just small sips." Long shouted, then turned for the river himself.

Jimmy somehow carried Caroline's small sister the last few hundred paces to the water's edge, then laid her gently on the wet rocks beside the water.

As Caroline was giving her sister a handful of water, washing the young girl's face, and taking a handful herself, Jimmy walked into the water and fell face first into the wonderfully cold, clear river.

Never, in all his life, had anything felt so wonderful.

Beside him, one after another, everyone did the same.

PART THIRTY-ONE
Back into the Desert

JIMMY CRESTED OVER the ridge and looked at the deadly Forty Mile Desert. Its rolling sand seemed to stretch forever.

He and his friends had just made it across that desert. They had barely escaped the intense heat and lack of water the first time across.

Now they were riding back into the desert.

Again.

Into the very good chance of death.

Again.

Jimmy felt more scared this time than the first time. Now he knew the dangers, and how close, very close, the desert had come to killing them all.

He remembered the intense agony of every step, the thirst, the feeling of fighting off losing consciousness and just falling into the hot sand.

Yet, within five days of beating the desert the first time, they were going to challenge it yet again.

This kind of stupidity he was sure was what got people killed in the west. And up until now, all of them working together had been pretty smart. At least, they had survived.

Challenging the Forty Mile Desert a second time wasn't smart.

After making it across the desert the first time, they had stayed for three days on the banks of the Truckee River, camping with the women and children they had rescued.

Jimmy had not minded camping next to the river that long since the time allowed him to get to know Caroline a little better.

She was his age and her father had been killed in a river crossing in the Wyoming Territory. It was just Caroline, her mother, and her little sister trying to make it to a homestead they had in California. She had no idea what they were going to do next, now that their wagon and all their supplies were lost.

For the first two evenings, Jimmy and the rest of his friends had talked among themselves about giving up on their chase of the killer, Benson, and helping the women over the mountains and into California.

But by the third day, they still hadn't decided what to do.

Jimmy's goal was to track Benson and stop him, get the deed to the gold mine back, and make Benson pay somehow for killing his parents and all the other people he and his men had killed along the trail from Independence.

But at the same time, Jimmy couldn't leave these women and children alone without food or supplies.

Joshua had suggested they just stay near the river helping the women recover for a few days and an answer might present itself, but then, when pushed, he had just smiled and not said any more. He clearly had a plan, but he wasn't sharing that plan with any of the rest of them, no matter how much they pushed him.

His only comment was simply to say, "It's too crazy to talk about yet."

None of them had seemed to mind the stay at the river either. The shade of the big cottonwood trees and the coolness of the river kept them all comfortable.

Truitt spent his time learning how to cook new recipes from the women, which was just fine by Jimmy and the rest.

Zach struck up a friendship with a girl named Sandra, and they spent a couple evenings walking along the river bank after dinner.

Longfeather was just happy that they were giving the horses time to rest. His passion was clearly those seven horses, and keeping them well.

Josh spent most of his time with his feet dangling in the cool water writing in his notebook, and every time he finished a story, C.J. got to be the first to read it.

It was also Josh and C.J. who had enough reading to know some basic medical help for the older women who were slow to recover. Long as well had a few wilderness cures, as he called them, and they all three learned from one of the older women on how to treat sunburned skin.

So it was three days well spent, as far as Jimmy was concerned, even though they might be getting farther and farther behind Benson.

On the evening of the third day, the wagon company that they had helped save from Benson back on Goose Creek arrived at the river, all of them splashing into the water just as they had done when they had arrived, even though it turned out they hadn't run out of water.

They were all happy to see each other again, and over dinner that night, Jimmy told the new arrivals what Benson had done to the women's wagon company.

They were all shocked, and said they had wondered what happened when they saw the men and wagons.

It was at that point that Josh told everyone about his plan. With enough men and horses, Josh thought they could go back and rescue the women's wagons.

Jimmy hated the idea.

Hated it.

Period.

The last thing he wanted was to go back into that desert.

Ever.

If he had to go back east to get his brother, Luke, he would go north and go on the Oregon Trail before crossing that desert again. As far as he was concerned, Josh had lost his mind.

But the men from the second wagon company who had just come off the desert thought it was possible, and the light in Caroline's eyes at the thought of having her family things back made Jimmy keep his mouth shut and think about it.

After talking with Long about the horses, and thinking about it for a few hours, he knew Josh was right.

He still hated the idea.

But he knew it was a good idea to go back into the desert for this reason.

Two days later, after the new wagon company's horses were well rested and watered, they set Josh's plan in motion.

Zach, Long, and Jimmy took all seven of their horses and loaded them with water bags and canteens and enough food and salty jerky to last for a day.

Three men from the new wagon company also went with them with nine of their horses. The plan that Josh had come up with would save five of the women's wagons.

If it worked.

They left after dinner, as the air was starting to cool near the river.

As Jimmy rode out of camp with a wave from Caroline, his only hope was to see her and the river again.

PART THIRTY-TWO
The Plan

THE RIDE BACK to the women's wagons, on rested horses, actually didn't take very long. Going through the first time, it had seemed to take forever to walk from the wagons to the river. But being fresh, rested, and on horseback, riding fast and after dark, the ride back out into the desert took less than four hours.

That eased Jimmy' worries a little, but not much.

They were back in the middle of the sand and there were still a bunch of things that could go wrong.

Very wrong.

When they reached the women's wagons, the sun was not even starting to color the morning sky, but the moon gave them more than enough light to work by.

They emptied the personal possessions of the women from two of the most damaged wagons into the five wagons that seemed to be in the best shape. They shifted some of the load around so that two of the wagons were much lighter than the other three. Two wagons had to be pulled through the sand with just two horses each. The heavier wagons would have four horses in harness.

They moved the men that Benson had killed, and the two dead women, and laid them out to one side of the two wagons they were leaving behind.

Then, with a few words from one of the older men, Jimmy and C.J. and Zach covered the bodies with a little sand and put a makeshift cross near them. It was the best they could do for the dead in the little time they had dared spend.

Jimmy knew it was much more than most people who died on this desert got.

They didn't bother even covering the body of the dead killer. He wasn't worth their time as far as Jimmy was concerned. Jimmy was just glad that Benson only had one man left in his gang.

With everyone riding in the wagons, they headed back to the river before sunrise.

So far, the plan seemed to be going perfectly.

So far.

But the Forty Mile Desert was the most deadly stretch of trail that Jimmy could ever imagine. He wasn't about to go underestimating it now. Just being out on it again was crazy.

Zach drove one of the two light wagons with Jimmy riding along, since they were the two most inexperienced with wagons. Between the two of them, they managed to stay close to the wagon in front of them.

Long drove the other two-horse light wagon.

The men from the wagon company, with the experience of getting wagons all the way from Independence, drove the other three.

It got hot, very hot, sitting up on that wagon seat as the morning wore on and the sun climbed overhead.

Jimmy managed to keep his face in the shade of his hat and his hands and arms out of the sun as much as possible.

The sand kicked up by the horses pelted his skin like fine shot from a gun, and his eyes felt like they were coated in sandpaper.

Both he and Zach were constantly washing their eyes out.

The lead wagon driver drove the horses at a good pace and stopped every hour to rest them. Every hour they also rotated the horses between teams of two on the light wagons, and teams of four on the heavy wagons.

They all drank their fill of water, and gave the horses as much as they wanted as well. They had brought enough water with them to drink at that pace for a day. But if something happened to slow them

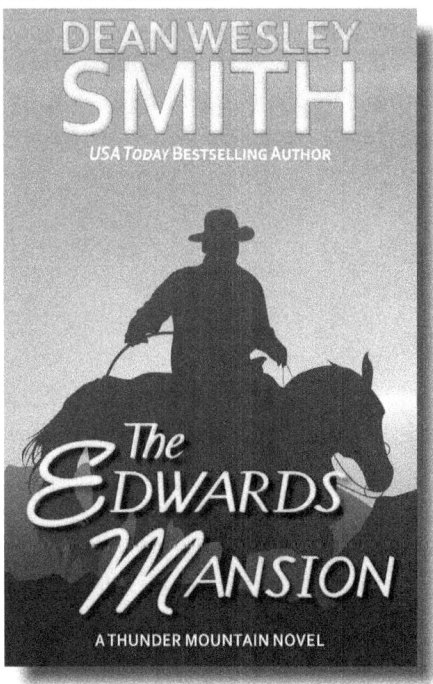

down, they were going to have to cut back quickly.

Much to Jimmy's relief, nothing happened.

They crested over the rise above the river in just under ten hours, and were welcomed back into camp near the river with a wonderful dinner, just twenty-four hours from the time they had left.

The smile on Caroline's face that evening when she saw her family's things was worth the trip back into the desert for Jimmy. She had even kissed him on the cheek to thank him, and then she made sure that he promised to come by their new homestead outside of Sacramento.

It was a kiss that Jimmy would always remember, and a promise he planned on keeping.

PART THIRTY-THREE
Back on the Chase

THE NEXT DAY, Jimmy waved at Caroline one last time, and then he and his friends left the Truckee River and headed up into the hills for Virginia City. They still had to somehow find Benson again, and stop him from killing any more people.

And they had to get the gold mine deed from him.

The closer they had gotten to California and the gold fields of Northern Nevada and the Sierra Mountains, the more they had talked about finding gold and striking it rich. It was great campfire talk almost every night now.

As they crossed over the ridge outside of Virginia City, Jimmy wasn't sure what he had been expecting, but it sure wasn't the large booming town that faced them.

Virginia City seemed almost as large as Independence, and covered a wide hillside as well as stretching down into two valleys. There were mine tailings in giant piles in dozens of locations among the buildings, and there wasn't a tree to be seen anywhere near the town.

Dust from horses and wagons drifted over the town like smoke.

The place looked very hot, and very alive. Even from a mile out, they could hear the piano music from the saloons, and occasional gunshots echoed off the mountains behind the town.

"We need to find a place to camp," Jimmy said as they all sat on the ridge staring at the town.

"Most of the mining claims are down the valley to the south," Josh said.

"And right in the middle and under the city itself," C.J. said. "If we go west, beyond the town, and over those low ridges, we should find fresher water and a place to camp."

They talked for a minute about how they should go into town.

Long felt that it might be asking for trouble if he went right into town without first seeing how the residents of Virginia City treated Indians.

Jimmy didn't like that, but after Long insisted, he went along.

Long and Truitt turned west, leading the packhorse. The two of them would go around the large city, while Jimmy, Zach, C.J., and Josh rode into town. They would all meet near dusk a few miles outside of town on the Carson City wagon road that connected the two towns.

Twenty minutes later, the four of them rode into the center of Virginia City, Nevada, the most dangerous town that existed west of the Mississippi, looking for a deadly killer.

PART THIRTY-FOUR
The Search Goes On

JIMMY HAD BEEN stunned at the excitement, the energy, and the feel of Virginia City when they rode in that first day. It was very much like Independence, only with far more drunks and fighting. The mines and mine tailings seemed to be everywhere, bright brown scars on the rough land. The mineshafts riddled the ground right under Main Street.

Over half of the buildings along the main streets were two-story wood structures, and more were going up all around. Clearly, since there were no trees nearby, they were hauling in the lumber from some distance.

Long had been right to stay out of town. Jimmy soon discovered that a few years earlier, there had been a massive misunderstanding that had led to the building of Fort Churchill by the Army and then the Pyramid Lakes Indian battle. Feelings around town were still running hot on what had happened, so it was better that Long had just stayed on the sidelines.

There was no sign at all of Benson or his one remaining man.

They met back up with Long and Truitt, then made camp on a river a few miles upstream from Fort Churchill. The location gave them fresh water and was up against a rock wall that could be defended if for some reason they were attacked. Jimmy had a hunch that they would be using the camp for some time to come. It was going to take time to search for Benson.

Then, early the next day, with Long and Josh staying in the camp, the rest again went in search of Benson.

C.J. had suggested that they would cover more ground if they split up, so Jimmy and Truitt went into Virginia City. Zach and C.J. headed in the other direction for Carson City.

Unlike the search in Independence, this time more than Jimmy knew Benson on sight. They also knew who Benson's riding companion was, and what the men's two horses and saddles looked like.

That first day of the search was long and hot, and left Jimmy feeling frustrated. Suppose Benson had gone ahead and stayed on the trail and went on over the mountains to Sacramento. Now, after all the time on the river, he might already have the gold deed registered in his name. That night, Jimmy talked to the rest about his worry and suggested that maybe they should split up, with some of them riding for Sacramento.

None of them had agreed with Jimmy's fears. They were all convinced that Benson was still in the area. As C.J. had said, "It's certain he's here somewhere."

Josh said, "It wouldn't be in his character to move on. He's going to drink and spend the money he stole from the women's company before he leaves here, just as he has done every time before."

Jimmy still wasn't sure, but he felt better that at least they all agreed that staying and searching was the right thing to do.

So the next day, Jimmy and Zach and C.J. and Truitt stayed together instead of going two different directions. C.J. figured it was better that they cover one town per day completely and Jimmy had agreed. They planned to split up in each town.

As it turned out, it didn't take long to prove C.J. and Josh correct. Benson had stayed.

It was in Virginia City, as they rode into town just after dawn, that Jimmy spotted Jake Benson, the man Jimmy hated more than any man alive. Benson's horse was roped in front of a saloon and the murderer was just walking down the sidewalk as if he had no care in the world.

"That's Benson," Jimmy said to his friends, pointing at Benson's back.

"So that's what the poisoned snake looks like," Truitt said.

"Deadly and mean," Zach said.

Zach and Truitt had never seen Benson before, since they had been taking the only survivor of Benson's Goose Creek killings back to Fort Hall when Jimmy and the others saved the wagon train.

"That's him," Jimmy said, not even trying to hide the disgust in his voice.

They quickly dismounted and tied up their horses in front of a general store.

"Now what?" Zach asked.

"We follow him," Jimmy said. "From now on, he never leaves our sight. Any time of the day or night. We just have to wait for the right moment."

The others nodded and they all moved after Benson down the main street.

Jimmy could barely contain his anger. Right in front of him was the man who had killed his mother and father. And many others along the trail from Independence.

Jimmy had to stop Benson, but he had no idea how.

And it was clear that the others wanted to stop Benson almost as much as Jimmy did, after burying that family on Goose Creek, and those men and women in the desert.

Benson had left a trail of bodies in his wake and it seemed that Jimmy and his friends had been doing nothing but cleaning up after him and digging graves. If Jimmy had anything to say about it, that was going to stop right here in Virginia City.

Benson just kept walking, his boots rumbling on the wooden sidewalk like it didn't matter. He was almost swaggering.

It was clear to Jimmy that Benson believed no one was after him for all that he had done. That was good. Even after being chased off from that wagon train back on Goose Creek, Benson didn't feel threatened, which meant they still had surprise on their side.

"Split up," Jimmy said. "Truitt, you and Zach pace him down the other side of the street."

Truitt and Zach crossed over between two wagons while Jimmy and C.J. stayed behind Benson.

Jimmy had no idea what they would do now that they had found him, but one thing was for certain, they weren't going to lose sight of him again. They would be on him like a tick on a yard dog until Benson did something that would allow them to act.

Benson walked most of the length of the booming mining town, going by saloon door after saloon door. The wooden sidewalk ended and he kept on going downhill, out of the main part of town, passing some smaller buildings and a few large tents that housed different businesses.

Then finally, near the lower south edge of town, Benson turned into a small wooden-planked building that had a painted barber pole hanging on the front wall. The building was no bigger than a shack and had been built up against a rock bluff. It had a tin roof. Jimmy couldn't imagine how hot that must make it inside the little shack in the middle of the day. Even with the front door standing open, Jimmy doubted Benson would be in there long.

"Stay here," Jimmy told C.J. "I'll be back.

Then, as if on a mission, he walked past the front of the shack and got a quick look inside, keeping his hat low on his head.

He then circled around, went back up the other side of the street, and met the others off to one side of the street in the shade, where Benson couldn't see them.

"It's only Benson in there with a barber," Jimmy said. "Any ideas?"

Zach shook his head, as did Truitt.

But C.J. smiled. "I just might have something we could do. But if it fails, we might get shot."

"After watching that scum of the earth walk up the street like he had done nothing," Jimmy said, "I'm willing to take some risks. That man in that building killed my parents."

Zach nodded. "And a lot of other innocent people. After seeing how he left those women out in the desert to die, I agree. We have to stop this animal."

"All right," C.J. said, nodding. "But my plan is going to take some rope and a blanket."

Jimmy glanced around. There was a general store about a half block back up the street. He had maybe just enough money left for what C.J. needed. "You three stay here," he said. "How much rope?"

"Thin and strong and about thirty feet."

Jimmy nodded and turned toward the store without even asking C.J. what his plan was.

"Get a shovel, too," C.J. called after him. "With a long handle."

PART THIRTY-FIVE
The Plan

JIMMY TRUSTED C.J., but he sure hoped this plan would work as he headed for the general store at a fast walk. They had rope on their horses, and blankets and shovels back in their camp, but that would take far too long to get. He was going to have to spend the very last of his father's money for this. He sure hoped it worked.

It took him less than five minutes and he was back with what C.J. said he needed.

C.J. took the shovel, gave the blanket to Truitt. Then he quickly explained his idea on how they could capture Benson and maybe get him to the Virginia City Sheriff. After they captured Benson, the boys would have to ride to catch the women in the wagon train. The women could then testify to the Sheriff about what Benson had done to their men. Jimmy was sure the women hadn't made it too far up into the Sierras yet.

"This is crazy," Zach said, smiling at Jimmy. "He has a gun and clearly doesn't mind killing people."

"I know," Jimmy said. "But we got to try."

"I'm not saying we don't," Zach said. "I'm just saying that this is crazy."

"No argument from me," Jimmy said, smiling back at his friend.

"You know," Truitt said as they headed across the street, "that if this works, we're going to have to come up with a name for it."

"Let's see if it works, first," C.J. said, clearly worried, even though it was his idea.

Near the barbershop, with the rope trailing behind him in the dirt, Jimmy walked past, again keeping his face from being seen clearly.

Inside the barbershop, he could see Benson still sitting in the chair and the barber working at Benson's beard and hair. Both were looking away from the door.

As Jimmy got to the other side of the barbershop and out of sight of Benson and the barber, he stopped and eased the rope right up near the front step up into the small shack.

On the other end of the rope, Zach pulled tight. To Jimmy, the rope seemed clearly obvious tucked against the bottom of the step, but C.J. had assured them that if they got Benson to come out fast and hard, he wouldn't notice it.

Truitt unfolded the dark wool blanket that Jimmy had bought and moved over against the barbershop front wall, his back to the wooden planks, the blanket held in both hands.

Then, when he was ready, it was C.J's turn.

C.J. stepped up so he could be seen through the front door of the small shack.

"You Jake Benson, mister?" C.J. asked, leaning on the shovel like he always stood that way.

Jimmy was impressed that C.J. sounded so calm, like none of this mattered.

"Yeah, what's it to ya, kid?" Benson said from inside.

Jimmy felt a chill go up his spine. He hadn't heard that voice since before his parents were killed. He hadn't liked it then, he didn't like it now.

"I was told to come down here and tell you that he's taking your horse and gear in payment for what you owe him."

"Who!" Benson shouted.

The shout echoed off the tin roof.

Jimmy could hear from the scraping sounds that Benson had stood up. Both Jimmy and Zach made sure they were braced and ready with the rope.

"He didn't give me his name," C.J. said. "Black beard, brown hat, black mare with a silver braid on the saddle."

C.J. had just described Benson's remaining riding companion.

With that, C.J. stepped back a few steps into the middle of the street, allowing room for Benson to come straight out of the building.

"I'll kill that snake," Benson shouted as he stormed out of the barbershop, putting his hat on as he came.

Jimmy and Zach instantly yanked the rope up as Benson stepped for the street. The rope caught him in the shin and Benson went forward hard, face down into the dust.

Truitt moved faster than Jimmy thought possible, sprawling on Benson from behind with the blanket, covering the killer's head and arms.

Zach and Jimmy moved in and quickly wrapped more of the rope around Benson's legs.

But Benson was clearly fast and angry. He was bucking Truitt like a wild horse out of control.

From under the blanket, Benson's hand and gun came out and he fired once.

The shot barely missed Jimmy and ricocheted off some rocks down the street.

"Get his gun!" Zach shouted.

Jimmy, as hard as he could, smashed his boot down on Benson's gun hand.

The gun spun away in the dirt.

Benson screamed and bucked Truitt even harder under the blanket, but couldn't stand because Zach has his legs tied up.

C.J. stepped up, and with a swing of the shovel, hit Benson on the head through the blanket.

Now Jimmy understood why C.J. had wanted the shovel.

Suddenly, Truitt was lying on an unmoving pile of man and blanket.

Jimmy's heart was beating so fast, he could hardly breathe, and he was sweating like he had never sweated before.

Truitt pulled the blanket off and stood while Zach wrapped even more rope around Benson's legs and tied it off like he would a steer.

They had captured Benson.

Jimmy couldn't believe it.

CHAPTER THIRTY-SIX
Now What?

"EVERYONE ALL RIGHT?" Jimmy asked.

"Yeah," they all said, but it was clear that Truitt was out of breath and more than likely bruised up from his ride on Benson's back.

Jimmy moved over and picked up the gun, holding the heavy hunk of metal in his hands.

More than likely, this was the gun that had killed his parents, shot his mother in the back, killed the family at Goose Creek, and the men in the desert.

Jimmy looked at the gun, then at the man out cold in the dirt of the street.

"Shoot him," C.J. said. "Don't let him ever kill anyone again."

"We wouldn't blame you," Truitt said, "after what he did to your parents."

"This man do something to you boys?" the barber asked from the door of his shop.

"Killed my parents," Jimmy said, his voice surprisingly calm for how his stomach was feeling. "Shot my mother in the back."

"Oh," the barber said.

"And then he killed a family back on Goose Creek," Zach said. "And some men in the middle of the desert, leaving women and children to die just so he could steal their money and stock."

The barber nodded. "You know, a lot goes on in this street that I just don't seem to notice."

Then the man turned and went back into his shack, cleaning, pretending to not look out the door.

Truitt laughed.

Jimmy was just glad that the barber wasn't going to try to stop them. Jimmy stared at Benson, then at the gun in his hands. He really wanted to kill Benson. More than he had wanted to kill anything or anyone in his entire life.

But he wouldn't do it.

He was still bothered by the man they had accidentally killed back on Goose Creek. Killing Benson would give him nightmares for the rest of his life.

And besides that, it wasn't the right thing to do.

He shook his head, still staring at the heavy gun in his hands.

"No, I'd be just like him if I killed him," Jimmy said. "For whatever the reason."

Jimmy unloaded the revolver and then laid it on a rock beside the barbershop. Picking up another large rock, he smashed the gun over and over, feeling the anger toward Benson with every blow.

The gun was shattered and bent and in pieces when he finally stopped.

"No one is going to be killed by that gun again," Jimmy said, panting at the work it had taken to destroy the gun.

"There isn't a big enough piece left to throw at anyone," Truitt said, laughing.

Jimmy turned back to see the rest of them all smiling at him. Along the street, a small crowd was gathering to watch.

To Jimmy, it didn't matter. Benson would never kill another person with that gun.

CHAPTER THIRTY-SEVEN
Trying to Get the Mine Back

BENSON MOANED and tried to push himself to his feet, seeming to realize slowly that his hand was injured and his feet tied.

Jimmy moved over to Benson, who looked up at him from his hands and knees.

"Remember me?" Jimmy asked.

Benson blinked a few times, then suddenly he remembered. "The Tyler kid."

Jimmy nodded. "Good, I was hoping you would remember, since you killed my mother and father."

Benson snorted and said, "We're a long way from Missouri, kid." He turned around so that he could work to untie the ropes around his feet.

"Before my mother died from the two bullets you put in her back," Jimmy said, "she told me and my brother it was you. Now I would like my father's gold mine deed back that you stole."

Benson snorted again. "Tough woman, your mother."

Benson kicked the rope loose and tried to push himself to his feet, wincing

at the pain in his hand as he braced himself with it.

With all the anger that had built up over the past few months, Jimmy stepped forward and stamped down hard on Benson's gun hand again, smashing it into the ground.

The tough man screamed and fell back into the dirt, clenching his broken hand.

"I'm going to kill you, kid," Benson said through clenched teeth, his eyes closed in pain as he rolled in the dirt.

"Not with that hand you're not," Jimmy said. "So, my father's gold mine deed, please."

"You going to have to kill me before you get that gold mine deed back, kid," Benson said.

"Oh, we're going to do much worse than that," Jimmy said.

Jimmy glanced at C.J. who was standing in the street behind Benson. "Want to help our guest rest for a few more minutes?"

"I would love to," C.J. said, smiling.

When Benson moved to sit back up, C.J. stepped forward and hit Benson from behind on the side of the head with the flat base of the shovel. The clang echoed down the street and the few of the town's people who were watching and listening made laughing noises as Benson flopped out cold in the dirt.

"Remind me next time we're digging," Truitt said to C.J., "that you're deadly with a shovel."

"Thank you," C.J. said, smiling and pretending to bow like he was performing in a Wild West show.

"Truitt, keep an eye out for this guy's riding companion," Jimmy said.

"Yeah, real good thinking," Truitt said, moving up the street closer to town.

Now Available
from all your favorite booksellers
in trade paper and electronic editions.

He jumped up on a rock so that he could see over the growing crowd.

By now, people were watching from both sides of the street and close enough to hear everything that was said. Jimmy didn't care. At this point, he had nothing to hide.

Zach wrapped the rope around Benson's feet again, and tied it off solid. It would take a knife to get that rope off the next time.

"Remind me to not get you men mad at me," the barber said from his doorway.

Benson's damaged hand was flopped in the dirt. It was clearly broken at the wrist and already starting to swell.

Jimmy, with his mother and father's dead bodies in his mind, stepped forward and smashed Benson's gun hand again with the heel of his boot.

Bone snapped loud enough to echo down the street.

Around them, the crowd made a gasping noise.

"Oh, that's got to hurt," C.J. said.

Jimmy smashed Benson's hand once more, grinding it under the heal of his boot just to make sure the man would never use that hand for anything, let alone firing a gun to kill anyone.

To Jimmy, what he was doing didn't feel good. But it felt right.

CHAPTER THIRTY- EIGHT
A Second Attempt

THE PAIN OF the second stamping woke Benson up and he screamed again, clutching his forever-useless hand to his chest and rolling in pain in the street.

Finally, after what seemed like a long time of cursing and shouting, Benson sat up and tried to untie the ropes with his one good hand.

Jimmy kneeled down to face the man who had killed his parents.

"Now, the deed to the gold mine that you stole from my father after you killed him and my mother. Where is it?"

Jimmy made sure his voice was loud enough for anyone in the crowd to hear.

"Never," Benson said through the pain.

"It's all right for you to kill anyone you want," Jimmy said, shaking his head and laughing. "But you can't take a little pain?"

Benson glared at Jimmy.

Jimmy decided to try another way to get the mine. "You know, all those women and children you left in the Forty Mile Desert without water are going to be really happy to see you."

Jimmy made sure his voice was loud. He wanted everyone to know what this man had done.

Benson again just glared at him.

Jimmy went on. "Especially since you gunned down their fathers and husbands and stole all their water and stock. What do you think they're going to tell the sheriff when they see you?"

A couple people in the crowd gasped.

"They're dead," Benson said, trying to spit at Jimmy and missing.

"No," Jimmy said, "actually, they are all alive. My friends and I were behind you, and we saved them. And they are all very willing to tell the sheriff what you did. Now, where is my father's gold mine deed?"

"Never," Benson said. "I said never, kid, and I mean never. You're going to die for what you have done to me."

"Oh, you're going to shoot me in the back like you did my mother?" Jimmy asked, not bothering to hide the anger in his very loud voice.

Benson tried to spit again, but nothing seemed to come out of his mouth.

"Listen," Jimmy said, "you think what we did to you here is bad, in front of all these fine people?"

Benson twisted around, suddenly realizing that a crowd had gathered to listen and watch and no one was helping him.

Jimmy went on. "You'll discover this is nothing. We're going to dog you every step you take, every moment of every day and night and make your life a living nightmare until we get my father's gold mine deed back."

"Just try it, kid. You'll make it easier for me to kill you."

"Just remember I warned you," Jimmy said.

Jimmy stood up as Benson struggled to untie the ropes around his ankles with one hand.

Jimmy nodded to C.J., who smiled and once again hit Benson on the back of the head with the flat of the shovel.

Benson went over sideways in the dirt.

The crowd cheered this time.

"He's going to have one very nasty headache," Zach said, laughing.

CHAPTER THIRTY-NINE
Doing the Right Thing

JIMMY QUICKLY SEARCHED Benson, not enjoying the feel of touching the man at all, but he had to look for the gold mine deed.

Nothing.

"Search him to see if I missed it," Jimmy said to Zach.

Zach found only a few coins that he pocketed. But no gold mine deed.

"So, we going to turn him into the sheriff?" C.J. asked.

"I think that's what he deserves, don't you?" Jimmy asked. "Then we have to go see if we can catch the women's wagons before they get too far up the Truckee. They will need to stand witness against him for what he did to their husbands and fathers."

"Good answer, kid," a voice said from the crowd as a man stepped forward.

Jimmy turned to see the sheriff of Virginia City walking toward him. He was a tall man, very thin, with rough skin on his face and a scar on his forehead. But the smile on the sheriff's face told Jimmy that he was in no trouble.

"Sir," Jimmy said, "are you willing to hold him until we get the women to come and testify against him?" Jimmy asked.

"We know he's killed at least ten men in Nevada," C.J. said.

Again the crowd gasped.

The sheriff stood over Benson and shook his head in disgust, then turned to Jimmy. "You boys bring witnesses to a crime this man committed and we'll put him on trial. Nevada Circuit Court rides through here in three days."

"Thank you, Sheriff," Jimmy said, smiling.

The sheriff glanced around and motioned for two men to come help him carry Benson. "Better stop at Doc's office to get him to take care of the hand," the sheriff said, smiling. "Looks to me like he caught it between two rocks."

The crowd just laughed.

Jimmy felt very, very relieved.

It was over.

Jimmy and Zach went back up the street until they found Benson's horse and searched his saddlebags. No mining deed. But they did find a few things that would help them, and a little more money tucked down in a hidden pocket.

"Now how do we find it?" Truitt asked as Benson was led off to jail.

"We find Benson's friend and follow him back to their camp," Jimmy said. "It must be in his gear at his camp."

They searched all afternoon through the city, and never spotted Benson's friend.

But to Jimmy, the mine didn't seem to matter that much at the moment. They had stopped a killer.

And Benson would be tried.

And Jimmy would get to see Caroline again.

It surprised him how much he wanted to see her, be around her.

That night, they celebrated around their campfire.

Jimmy knew that his brother Luke would be proud of what he had done, the lives they had saved by stopping Benson.

It felt very, very good.

Josh made C.J. tell him three times what had happened so that he could write it all down, and then made C.J. promise that the next day he would take Josh into Virginia City to see the area in front of the barbershop, so he could get it right in the story.

Jimmy just sat there and enjoyed his friends.

Enjoyed making it west.

He had set out to have an adventure and it had been far more than he had ever wanted. But they all had survived and helped others.

Since losing his parents, it was the best night Jimmy had had.

~

Coming Next Issue in Smith's Monthly
The Full Thunder Mountain Novel
that is the Origin Story for all the Jukebox Stories
MELODY RIDGE

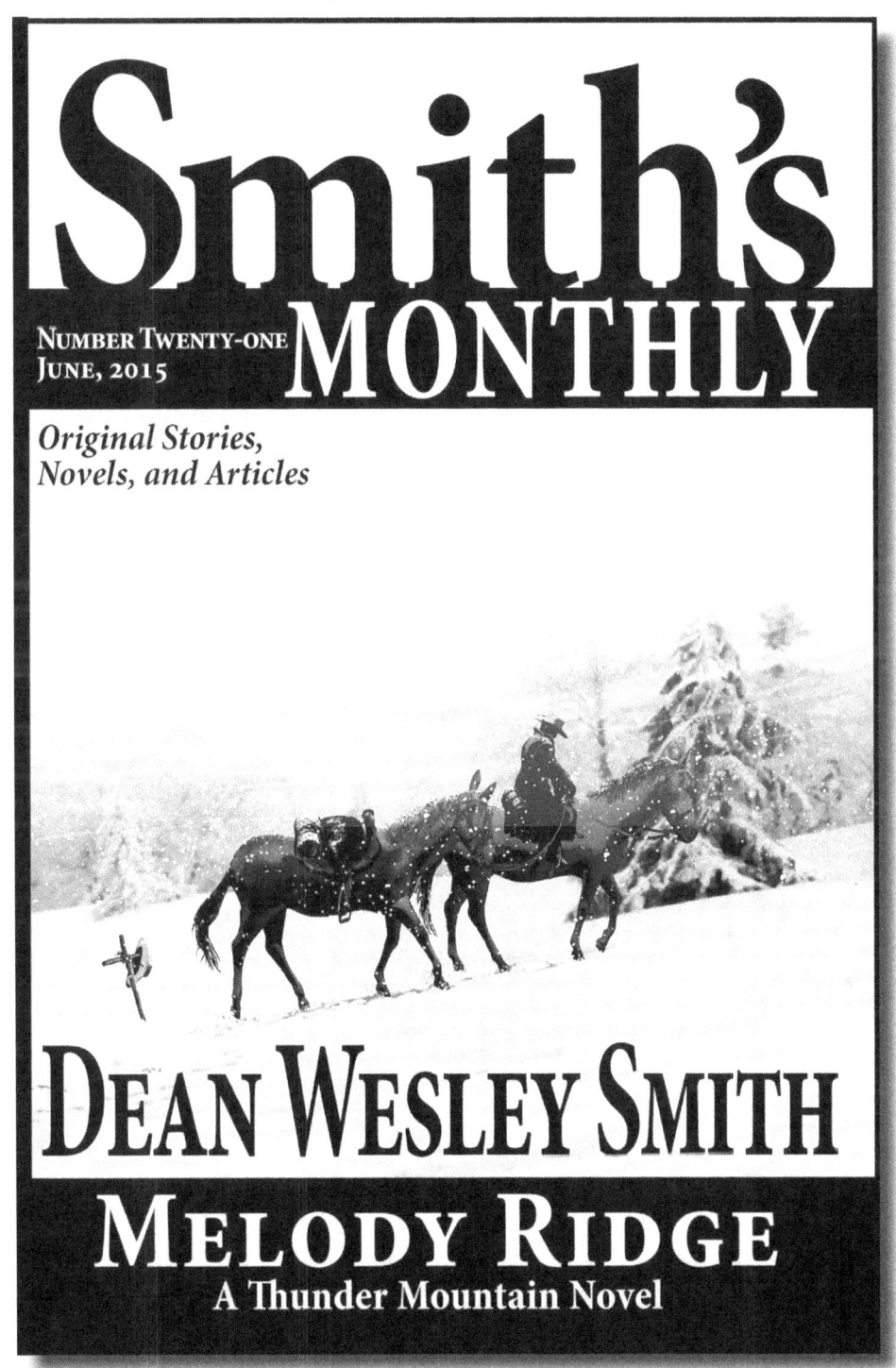

Smith's MONTHLY

NUMBER TWENTY-ONE
JUNE, 2015

*Original Stories,
Novels, and Articles*

DEAN WESLEY SMITH

MELODY RIDGE
A Thunder Mountain Novel

#1... October 2013

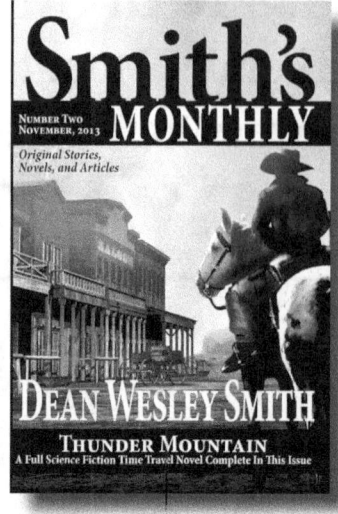

#2... November 2013

#3... December 2013

#4... January 2014

#5... February 2014

#6... March 2014

#7... April 2014

#8... May 2014

#9... June 2014

#10... July 2014

#11... August 2014

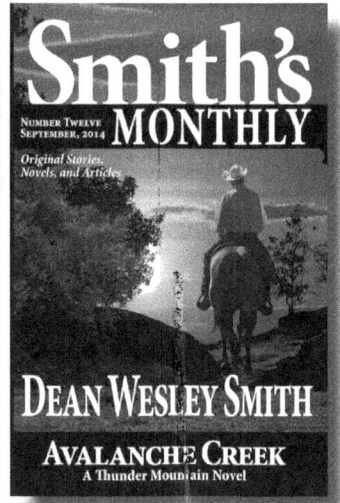

#12...September 2014

#13...October 2014

#14...November 2014

#15...December 2014

#16...January 2015

#17...February 2015

#18...March 2015

Thank You!!

Walter White Cat and I would like to thank
the following wonderful people who support my blog
and my work through Patreon.
Your support is very important to me.
Thanks!

Rob Cornell	Scott Gordon
Erick Lindman	Kathryn Rooney
Christopher Ridge	Sherman Cox
Miguel Angel Alonso Pulido	Fen
Nancy Hendrickson	Livia Quinn
Ryan M. Williams	Amri Ackers
Jacob Proffitt	Robin Brande
Ryan Whiteside	J.R. Murdock
Marian Goldeen	Kathleen McClure
John Connelly	Michael Kelberer
Gary Speer	Gunnar Gunderson
Megan Bryce	F.I. Goldhaber
Michelle Tatam	Mary Jo Rabe
Ann Tucker	John Kilgallon
Kari Wolfe	Dave Hendrickson

www.ingramcontent.com/pod-product-compliance
Lightning Source LLC
Chambersburg PA
CBHW081151170626
46813CB00009B/3153